P9-ARE-823

MY SISTER'S BETRAYAL

BLOOD SISTERS
BOOK TWO

ROBERTA KAGAN

Copyright © 2022 by Roberta Kagan

All rights reserved. No part of this publication may be reproduced, distributed, or transmitted in any form or by any means, including photocopying, recording, or other electronic or mechanical methods, without the prior written permission of the publisher, except in the case of brief quotations embodied in critical reviews and certain other noncommercial uses permitted by copyright law.

ISBN (eBook): 978-1-957207-26-1
ISBN (Paperback): 978-1-957207-27-8
ISBN (Hardcover): 978-1-957207-28-5
ISBN (Large Print): 978-1-957207-29-2

Title Production by The Bookwhisperer.ink

DISCLAIMER

This is a work of fiction. Names, characters, businesses, places, events, and incidents are either the products of the author's imagination or used in a fictitious manner. Any resemblance to actual persons, living or dead, or actual events is purely coincidental.

PROLOGUE

If we are to build a ruling class of perfect Aryans, a Reich that will last a thousand years, we must begin with our children...

Oliver Fredrich sat quietly in the waiting room for his interview. He'd already been sitting in that chair for over an hour. Three other young men in their late teens were seated beside him. They, like Oliver, wore their best clothes and were carefully groomed. That was because they had all come to be interviewed for the same position: chief counselor for the boys' division of the *Deutsche Jugend in der Slowakei* summer camp, German Youth in Slovakia. Oliver looked around him and assessed his competition. *All of us are German boys.* He could tell, or at least he thought he could. But as he scrutinized everything about them, he decided he was the most Aryan-looking of the bunch. He'd worn his only suit, a dark blue wool suit that didn't quite fit him since he'd grown so tall and muscular. Since he couldn't afford a new one, it would have to do. He donned it with a clean, freshly ironed white shirt and a navy-blue tie. Blue was his color. He knew that. The suit and tie showed off his deep blue eyes. He'd taken extra time to comb his light blonde hair back. He had wanted to make sure it was perfect, not a single hair out of place. This gave him the perfect clean German look he was certain his interviewer would be searching for. It was spring, and it was a hot day. There was no fan in the building, and he could feel himself sweating, the sweat trickling down his ribs and temples. He hoped the interviewer would not notice.

"Herr Fredrich," a young woman with a lovely figure and perfectly finger waved red hair called his name.

"Yes. I am Herr Fredrich, Oliver Fredrich," Oliver said as he stood up.

"Follow me, please," she said.

Oliver followed her down a long hall, where she turned right into an office.

"Heil Hitler." The man behind the desk stood up and saluted.

"Heil Hitler," Oliver returned the salute with enthusiasm.

"I see here your name is Oliver Fredrich," the man said as he looked over Oliver's resume. He was a middle-aged man, well-built, with a full head of graying hair. "Sit down," he commanded.

Oliver took a seat across from the interviewer, who looked him up and down and then smiled. "Well, well... aren't you a handsome devil," he said.

Oliver looked down modestly and smiled. "Thank you, sir."

"So, I have been looking over your credentials, and they look quite appealing. You certainly have what we're looking for. I see that you are quite the athlete. And you come from a good family, good German stock."

"Yes, thank you. I am proud of my German heritage. I was born in Germany but raised in Austria. We moved when I was seven, but I never forgot the beauty of our Fatherland."

"I'm sure you must realize the importance of the position you are applying for."

"I do, sir."

"As the counselor of the summer camp for the *Deutsche Jugend*, you will be instrumental in preparing our children for the future. It will be up to you to guide them and ensure they know they are the future of the fatherland. The future of Germany and a Reich that will last a thousand years. Do you think you have what it takes to assume such a huge responsibility?"

"Yes, sir, I know that I do."

"I must say that you do have the right look," the interviewer said as he stroked his chin. Then, under his breath, he said, "Blond, handsome, athletic. The young boys who are under his care will emulate him. They will want to be like him, and because he will be the perfect representative of an Aryan man, it will be good for the morale of the entire youth camp." Then the interviewer looked directly into Oliver's eyes, and in a firm, deep voice, he said, "I must ask this question."

"Yes, sir," Oliver said.

"And..." he hesitated for only a moment. "I am fairly sure that I already know the answer. However, I am required to ask."

"I understand."

"How do you feel about Jews, gypsies, *Untermensch*, that sort of thing?"

Oliver shrugged, then he causally spewed the same rhetoric that he had heard repeatedly at every Hitler youth meeting he had attended as he was growing up. "They have no place in the new Germany."

The interviewer nodded. "And," the interviewer's eyebrow shot up, "have you ever fraternized with a Jew? Your doctor or dentist, perhaps? Someone you knew as a child?"

I should have expected it. Of course, they would want to know this. Oliver thought. He'd never told anyone how he felt about Anna. And it was only because she was Jewish that he hadn't pursued her. For a moment, his mind drifted back to his first kiss and the girl he'd never forgotten. Even to this very day, even right now, sitting in front of this interviewer as he thought of Anna, his heart fluttered just a little. Anna Levinstein, with her bright smile, dark eyes, and warm, gentle voice. He'd never forgotten that day in the park.

All of his friends, the boys in the neighborhood, were out on the field playing football. The local girls who lived in the same area and attended the same school were sitting on the sidelines, watching. Oliver had been playing, too, until he noticed that Anna was setting up a food table. Once he saw her, he lost interest in football. Oliver couldn't concentrate on the game. He'd even mis-kicked the ball, causing one of his friends to get angry, but he didn't care. His eyes were glued to Anna. She wasn't one of the neighborhood girls. In fact, she didn't attend his school, and because of this, she shouldn't have been at the picnic. But as long as he had known Elica and Bernie, Anna was always with them. Everyone knew she was Jewish, and that she attended a Jewish school. Even then, Jews were not popular, and making friends with them was not a good idea. But no one dared say a bad word about Anna to Elica or Bernie. At least not then, because that was before Hitler's ideology became the norm in Germany, and everything changed. Once Hitler rose to power, it was not only socially acceptable to dislike Jews, but slowly the entire society turned against them. Laws were made that took all freedoms away from the Jews. They could not attend schools with or marry Aryans. Aryans could not work for Jews. Hitler's minister of propaganda, Dr. Goebbels, warned of the dangers of befriending and trusting Jews. He even published a newspaper article filled with reasons to distrust and fear the Jews. That was when all his friends and everyone in his neighborhood became openly critical of Elica and Bernie's friendship with Anna. As Hitler's power took root, things grew ugly, and Anna stopped coming around after a while. But that was later. On that lovely summer day, it seemed to Oliver that Anna was the only girl Oliver would ever love, and someday he would marry her. He wasn't thinking about her being Jewish. Perhaps he didn't realize that her being different from the other girls was part of what had attracted him in the first place.

Since he couldn't concentrate on football, Oliver excused himself. He walked away from the game, proclaiming he needed a drink of water. He watched Anna as he walked over to the table where she stood. And when she saw him, she looked up, and she smiled. His heart fluttered as the light in her eyes lit up his world.

"What can I do for you, Ollie?" she asked.

"Just a cup of water," he said.

"Of course." She handed him a cup and then filled it with water from a pitcher.

He drank the water in a single gulp and put the cup down. Oliver felt clumsy and awkward. He'd never been alone with Anna before, but he knew this was his opportunity to talk to her without his friends listening. He forced himself to be brave. "I like you, Anna," he got the words out. Then cleared his throat. "But you already know that, I suppose. I mean, I've told you before." He was rambling, but she didn't interrupt him. She didn't seem to mind. Her eyes were glued to his, and he was captivated. "Well, there's a dance next week at my church. Would you like to come as my date?"

She looked into his eyes. "I'd love to come," Anna said.

He had no idea where he got the courage, but he leaned over and kissed her. When their lips met, his entire body tingled, and he knew for sure that he was in love. But what was so interesting was that he had been awestruck the first time he saw her. They were just children, and already he'd been smitten. Oddly enough, it was at this very same park. He was with his friends, and she was with hers. *How old were we? Just children. It must have hurt her when, a week later, I told her that I was forbidden to bring her as my date. However, I still vividly remember how my heart skipped a beat every time I saw her.* It was very strange, but from the very first moment that he saw Anna, he was confident that she was the girl he would marry one day.

"Herr Fredrich!" the interviewer snapped. "Stop daydreaming and answer my question!"

"I'm sorry. I was only trying to remember if I had ever had anything to do with a Jew."

"And? So, you have so much you have to think about? I need an answer. What is your answer?"

"No, I have not had anything to do with a Jew. Nothing that I can recall, sir."

CHAPTER ONE

Summer 1940

Daniel Goldenberg came out of the bathroom with a towel wrapped around his waist. His dark hair was wet and shiny as he pushed it back from his face.

"You are so handsome," his young, blonde wife, Elica, sighed as she watched him.

Daniel smiled. "And you are so beautiful." He bent down and kissed her, then he let the towel drop.

"Michael Angelo's David has nothing on you," she giggled.

"Have you ever seen it?" he asked curiously.

"Only in books."

He pushed her gently until she fell back on the bed. Then he lay beside her and began to kiss her neck and moved lower to place passionate kisses on her breasts.

There was a loud wail that came from the room across the hall. "How does that child know when we are about to make love?" Daniel held Elica tightly, not wanting to let go, trying hard to will the baby back to sleep.

"I think sometimes he has some kind of magical hearing because he seems to hear us every time," Elica said, disappointed.

"Do you think he'll go back to sleep if we ignore him?" Daniel moaned.

Elica laughed. "No! I think your mother will come knocking on our door to let me know that it's time to breastfeed."

"Hmmm. Well, having a baby has done wonderful things to your breasts. I must admit that. However, little Theo is a selfish brute. He wants to keep them all for himself."

She shook her head and laughed again. "Theo is a baby. He is hungry. He doesn't even know that what he wants are my breasts. He only knows that he wants some milk."

"I'm jealous," Daniel teased.

"Don't be. I am going to feed him. Then I'll be back."

"Hurry, please?" Daniel smiled. "I'll die without you. I swear I will."

She giggled. "I doubt you are going to die. But I'll do my best. What time is your job interview?"

"Nine, and it's already seven thirty," he said.

"Well, perhaps we should wait until tonight when we have more time," Elica said.

Daniel moaned.

Elica stood up and blew him a kiss. He frowned in mock sadness. She smiled, slipped on her robe, and went into the adjoining room, where little Theo was fussing in his crib.

"Good morning, little man," she said in a soft whisper. "Did you sleep well?" Picking him up, she held his warm body against her own. He began to cry. "You're hungry. Of course, you are, and *mutti* is going to feed you right now."

Elica sat down in the rocking chair Daniel's parents had purchased for her to use when she fed the baby. Her breasts were already leaking milk. Carefully, she inserted her nipple into his mouth and gently rubbed his cheek. Almost immediately, he began to nurse. She gazed out the window at the sunrise and smiled. Life was good. Theo sucked greedily. He was a healthy, strong, chubby little boy who had Elica's coloring and the build of Elica's father. His hair was golden, and his eyes were bright blue. But unlike her father, she could see warmth and intelligence in her child's eyes. And this warmth and intelligence she believed Theo had inherited from Daniel, his own father.

Softly, she sang to Theo in German, rocking the chair slowly back and forth. He drank until he was full, then his eyes closed softly, and she marveled at his tiny eyelashes. She wanted to touch them, but she dared not. He'd fallen asleep, and she didn't want to wake him. Elica longed to be with Daniel. She craved his arms around her and his kisses, but she also savored these very special moments when Theo slept in her arms. Slowly, she continued to rock and watch him as he slept. Then she heard a loud knock on the door, followed by a commotion coming from the living room downstairs. She knew by the loud guttural demands that the Nazis were at the door like wolves.

She heard a loud noise, like the door had been kicked. Then she heard the front door downstairs fling open and hit the wall as it did.

Elica's heart was beating so fast that her chest hurt. Since the Anschluss of Austria, the Germans had begun rounding up the Jews. They would come into a Jewish home and arrest everyone living there. Daniel's parents had dismissed this. His father had assured the family that those arrested had probably done something against the law. He said he was confident that they would be safe because he was an owner of a large factory and had plenty of influential friends. But, in the end, none of that mattered. All that mattered was the fact that Daniel and his family were Jews, and that alone was a crime. They didn't need to do anything wrong. Being Jewish was enough.

Elica trembled as she heard the pounding of the jackboots on the stairs. She longed to go to Daniel. She wished she could collapse in his arms and let him be her strength. But she knew they were in danger, and no matter what happened next, she must hide her child. Quickly, but still holding tightly to Theo, she ran into the closet. The child was frightened. He sensed his mother's fear, and his eyes flew open. Elica rocked him as she closed the closet door. But his eyes were still open wide, and he was about to scream. To stifle him, she pressed him to her breast and put her hand over his mouth. Then she remembered that Daniel kept a bottle of kosher wine stored in the closet for Jewish holidays. The Nazis were hollering outside the room, and she could see that the unfamiliar sound of their voices was frightening Theo even more. He began to cry. She pressed him against her hard so that her body would muffle his cries. Then Elica opened the wine. Putting her finger into the bottle and got it very wet with wine. And then she put her finger into Theo's mouth. He sucked on her finger, and he stopped crying. *Thank you, dear God,* she thought. The wine seemed to calm him. She continued to do this until he fell asleep. Trembling, she held her sleeping son and listened as the Germans led Daniel and his parents away. Elica heard her father-in-law demanding to see someone in charge. Then she heard a gunshot. And her mother-in-law let out a scream. Instinctively, she rocked Theo. He continued to sleep.

She wished she could go to Daniel, but she dared not. She had to stay in hiding; she had to protect her son. If the Germans found out that Daniel had a child, even though she, the child's mother, was not Jewish, they might still take her baby. A half-Jewish child might still be taken or even killed on the spot for having Jewish blood. Elica could not take the risk. She wept as she heard the names the Germans were calling her husband. "Jewish swine. Dirty Jews." Her mother-in-law was weeping loudly.

"Shut up, whore," one of the Germans said.

Elica was trembling. She took a swig of the wine, trying to comfort herself. But she was certain that her father-in-law was lying dead just outside this room. Holding Theo tighter, tears ran down her face. She knew they were taking Daniel away. In a few minutes, he would be forced down the stairs and into the back of a truck filled with the other Jewish families the Germans had arrested in the neighborhood. Elica had seen this happen once before, just a few streets away from here. If only she could believe that her husband would be questioned and then return home soon. She knew he had done nothing wrong. But she also knew that when a family of Jews disappeared, they did not return.

It seemed like forever that she sat on the wooden floor of the closet, her legs tingling from lack of movement. Her arms were heavy from holding her precious son. It was not cold in the room, and yet she was freezing. But at least Theo was quiet. He slept peacefully in her arms. His breathing was heavy, and he was mercifully drunk from the wine she'd given him. She jumped when she heard the door slam downstairs. And then there was silence.

CHAPTER TWO

Elica had no idea how long she sat on the floor with the pants from Daniel's gray wool suit that was hanging in the closet waving against her face. But she was terrified to leave the safety of the closet. And even though there had not been a sound in the house for hours, she was still afraid that they might still be there. And, if they were gone, what would she find when she walked out of this closet? Was her father-in-law dead on the ground? Was Daniel dead too? *Dear God, let it not be possible, not Daniel.* She trembled because she knew she might never see her husband again.

Elica closed her eyes. Her arm had fallen asleep and was tingling like it was being pierced by small needles where the baby's head lay. She thought of her friend Dagna. They had not been on good terms since Elica and Daniel reunited. Dagna had been angry with her, but if it meant saving Daniel, she would do anything. She would beg Dagna if it meant that Dagna would help her.

Elica stayed in the closet until long after sunset, although she didn't realize it. She had no watch or window, so she had no idea of the time. When her son awoke hungry, she fed him. Then she gave him more wine to put him back to sleep. But she did not move. She finally emerged from the closet, trembling, after many hours of silence in the house.

Even though she'd heard the gunshot, she was still shocked to see her father-in-law lying on his back in the hallway. His eyes were wide open, and there was a pool of blood surrounding him. She stifled a scream. *I have to clean this up. I can't leave this here.*

Elica put Theo into his crib. He woke up and was fussy, but she had to take care of the body in the hall. Grabbing the bucket they used to wash the floor, she filled it with water and began wiping up the blood. But then her stomach turned, and she vomited. Her hands were stained red with blood. Elica began to cry. But she knew she had to finish. No one else was going to do it for her. And so she did. The body was so heavy that she could hardly pull her father-in-law down the stairs. In fact, she practically fell down the stairs trying. Elica was out of breath, but she pushed the body down, and it fell to the bottom of the stairs where it lay. In its path, it left a trail of blood. Not knowing what to do with it, she left it there. Then she began to clean the stairs. But her father-in-law's eyes seemed to be watching her, and she couldn't bear it.

I need help. I don't know what to do with him. He's dead, and there's blood everywhere. I can't do this alone. She did her best to push her father-in-law's body out of the path of the stairs. Then she went back up to Theo's bedroom. He had fallen back to sleep. *Dear God, I hope the wine didn't damage him in any way. He's so small and helpless. What have I done? What choice did I have?* She looked at her son and then collapsed on the floor, weeping. She lay there for a while, looking at the ceiling.

Crying doesn't help. There is no one here to see me cry. No one is here to help me. I must go tomorrow and speak to Dagna. She works at the police station. She will know where they've taken Daniel. I will beg her to help me. I will promise her anything she wants. I need her help. I know she's angry, but I think she will help me. Even so, I can't be sure. I can't trust her, so I won't bring Theo with me. I will leave him with Bernie. Bernie was a friend she knew she could always trust. *Dagna knows*

Daniel and I have a child, so I will tell Dagna that my son died. If she asks how it happened, I will tell her that he did not wake up one morning. That I found him dead in his crib. God forgive me. What a horrible thought. But I can't trust Dagna not to turn Theo in for being half-Jewish. So, I must make sure she believes he is dead.

Every morning Elica got up and told herself that she must go to the police station and talk to Dagna, but she couldn't bring herself to do so. She was paralyzed with fear. Two weeks passed. The dead body at the bottom of the stairs was giving off a powerful and terrible odor. Elica was not strong enough to take the body outside. She couldn't eat. She hardly slept. And she did not leave the house. Each day, she prayed that by some miracle, Daniel would return. But Daniel did not return. Finally, she knew she must go to the police station and talk to Dagna. She could not procrastinate any longer.

CHAPTER THREE

One afternoon Bernie returned home from work to find Elica sitting outside on the steps. She was holding Theo in her arms. When she saw Bernie, she stood up. Her lips trembled as she tried to smile.

"Elica? What are you doing here?" Bernie said as she walked up the sidewalk. She was unable to hold back the joy in her voice at seeing her old friend.

"I came to see you."

"How are you?" Bernie said.

"I'm fine." Elica was trembling, and she could hardly speak.

"It's so good to see you. I haven't seen you in months. What brings you here?"

"The truth is, I am not fine. I am not fine at all."

"What is it? Are you ill?" Bernie asked, concerned.

"It's not my health. But I need to speak to you."

"Is something wrong? With you? With the baby? With Daniel?"

"Yes, something is terribly wrong. But I can't talk here. I know there is no one around, but I can't take any chances." Elica felt the tears forming in her eyes. "Can we go inside where we can talk privately?"

"Yes, yes, of course," Bernie said. "Come in." She put her hand on Elica's arm, leading her to the door. "I'll make you a cup of tea, and we'll talk."

Bernie unlocked the door and opened it, then she motioned for Elica to enter. Once inside, Bernie locked the door and said, "Let's go into the kitchen."

Elica followed Bernie into the kitchen. "Sit down. Please make yourself comfortable. Do you want to put Theo on my bed?"

"No, it's best if I hold him. If I put him on the bed, he won't recognize his surroundings, and he'll cry."

"He looks heavy."

"Yes, he's getting so big. He's a toddler already. And I know I carry him around too much. I should let him walk more. But he's all I have." Elica sat down at the kitchen table.

Bernie looked at Elica. "What do you mean, he's all you have? What about Daniel? Did something happen?"

"Oh, Bernie," Elica said, and the tears began to fall.

Not knowing what to say, Bernie stood up and walked over to the pots piled neatly on the counter. "I'll put some water to boil for tea," she said.

Elica did not look up at Bernie, but Bernie knew she was crying. After Bernie filled the teakettle, she sat across from Elica and patted Elica's hand. "Now, please, you must tell me what's happening. What is wrong? Where is Daniel? Talk to me, Elica."

Elica sighed. "Bernie, I am frightened. I am so afraid for my son and for my husband. The Germans came to our house. They took my Daniel away, his mother too. They shot my father-in-law. He's lying dead in the middle of the living room. I tried to clean it up, but I wasn't strong enough to carry the body." She began to weep hard, gut-wrenching sobs. Sensing his mother's distress, Theo began to cry too.

"All right. Shhh, it will be all right," Bernie said, but she knew she could not justify that statement.

"I don't know where the Germans took them. I am so distraught."

"It's a good thing they didn't take you and Theo."

"They would have, I am sure, but Theo and I hid in the closet until I was sure they were gone. But I must find my husband. I must."

"When was this?"

"Two weeks ago."

"And your father-in-law's dead body has been in your house this whole time?"

Elica nodded. Her face was deep red. She began sobbing again. "I'm horrified. I can't eat. I can't sleep. I don't know what to do. All I know is I must find Daniel. I need him, Bernie."

"All right. All right. Calm down," Bernie said just as the teakettle started to whistle. The baby began to shriek. Elica tried to rock him, but he would not stop. Bernie turned off the stove and left the kettle without pouring the water. Then she placed her hand on Elica's hand, which held the baby, and said, "How can I help you? What can I do?"

"Well,"—Elica hesitated—"Dagna works at the police station. One of the mothers in my neighborhood told me that a few months ago. I don't know if they took Daniel there or not. But either way, I believe my only chance of finding my Daniel is through Dagna. I am sure she hates me for what I did. But we were friends for so many years, blood sisters. We had the pact to help each other, didn't we? I must go to her and ask, not ask but beg, for her forgiveness and help."

"Dagna," Bernie said. That was all she could manage to say. Dagna was never the kind of person who could be depended upon to forgive. She had always been cruel, and even though Bernie knew that Dagna had thought of Elica as her best friend, she also knew that Elica had betrayed Dagna.

"I hate to drag you into this, Bernie. But I came here to speak to you. To ask for your help because I can't bring my son to see Dagna. She knows that Theo is Daniel's child, and that makes him half-Jewish. I just can't trust her not to tell her German friends that my Theo is the son of a Jew. And if she does, they might take him away from me."

Elica began to rock Theo, and he started to quiet down.

"Yes, they probably would. And you're right. You can't trust Dagna. I'm sure she is angry with you for marrying Daniel."

"I know that she is. And besides that, she always hated the Jews. Remember how she treated Anna?"

"Of course, I remember."

"If it were up to me, I would never speak to her again. But I have to go to her. She could be the only chance I have of finding him. I must go and talk to her no matter what the consequences. I don't think she would try to have me arrested for marrying a Jew even though it's against the law, and she could do that."

"I don't think she would either. She always admired you. I'm sure she feels betrayed, but I don't think she would do something like that to you. Not after all the years she tried so hard to be your best friend."

"I am afraid of her because she does have connections, and she could hurt me. But I don't think she would."

Bernie nodded. "Yes, I agree with you. So how can I help? Do you want me to go to her for you?"

"No, she never liked you. Not really. She only wanted to be a blood sister because of me. She wanted to be a blood sister so she could be closer to me," Elica said.

"I always knew that."

"And, of course, she never liked Anna either. She was always so horrible to Anna," Elica said. "And Anna never deserved it." Then, in a sad voice, she added, "I was horrible to Anna too. I regret it every day. We were blood sisters. I can still remember that day when we cut ourselves and mixed our blood. We were so young. Do you remember that day?"

"Of course, I remember," Bernie said, then she smiled wistfully. "Blood sisters are forever."

Elica smiled too, but it was a sad smile. "Bernie, I need your help. I need you to watch my son while I go to see Dagna. I want to leave him with you."

"Of course, I will take him."

"But this is important. I want you to realize that there is a possibility that I may not return. I don't believe Dagna will hurt me, but I can't be sure. She might have me arrested. I am sure she is still very angry with me. She feels I betrayed her when I left the apartment we shared to marry Daniel. She struggled to pay the rent alone. I knew she would. I knew she couldn't afford to live in our flat without my salary. I didn't want to leave her that way, but I'll admit, I was selfish. I wanted Daniel. I wanted to marry him. And I wanted a home and a father for my son. To make matters worse for Dagna, she knew Daniel was Jewish. And we both know how she hated Jews."

"Yes, I remember that. She really had it in for Anna from the beginning. Even when we were children, she hated Jews."

"From the day she met Daniel, she had it in for him, too. So..." Elica hesitated for a moment. Then she sucked in a deep breath. "If I don't return, you must promise me you will take care of my child. Can you promise me that? Will you, Bernie?"

Bernie looked down at the ground. Then she looked back up into Elica's eyes. "Of course. I will love and raise him as if he were my own."

"I knew I could count on you," Elica said. She reached out and touched Bernie's cheek. Then tears began to run down her cheeks.

"But there is something I feel I must tell you," Bernie said.

"Please, what is it?" Elica asked.

CHAPTER FOUR

Bernie was trembling as she looked into Elica's deep blue eyes.

"What is it?" Elica asked. "Tell me, please."

"It's about Anna."

"What about Anna? I haven't seen her in such a long time. And I have so many regrets about how I treated her. I've tried to find her, but I can't. I went to her house, but it's been taken over by a German family. 'Aryanized,' I guess they call it. I didn't know where else to look. I hope she hasn't been arrested like Daniel. I am so afraid she has. And every time I think about it, I feel sick to my stomach. Do you know anything about what happened to her? Anything at all?"

"Elica," Bernie said, taking Elica's hand. "Elica, I have something to tell you. Something important. I know you will keep this secret because you have a secret, too."

"What are you talking about? What secret?"

"I mean that I have a secret to tell you about Anna. And I know you will not tell because you are keeping a secret about Theo."

"What is it? Bernie, I don't understand. You're talking in circles."

"I know, I know. Elica. Listen to me. Anna and her family are hiding in the attic," Bernie whispered.

Elica put her hand to her lips. She looked up. "Here in your house?" she asked, shocked.

"Yes. I hid them there when the Germans started arresting the Jews."

"Your mother knows?"

"Yes, she knows."

"She agreed to it?"

"Reluctantly, but yes. Anna's father paid her. She was glad to get the money. I didn't do it for the money, though. I did it for Anna. We're blood sisters."

"Oh, my lord," Elica said. "Is Anna all right?"

"Yes, she's all right. I mean, as right as she can be. She hasn't had any fresh air or seen sunshine in a long time."

"Oh, my," Elica said. "Oh, my. Can I see her?"

"That would be very dangerous. Too dangerous, I think."

"I know. I know it would. But please, can I see her? I have so much I want to tell her."

"You'd have to come to my house in the middle of the night and make sure that no one follows you. Can you do that?"

"I can and I will. I'll come tonight then. I'll bring Theo with me, and I'll leave him with you. Meanwhile, I'll have a chance to see Anna."

"You know I would do anything for you," Bernie said.

"I know. You've always been a good friend to both Anna and me."

CHAPTER FIVE

Late that night, Elica arrived at Bernie's home with Theo, a bag of folded cloth diapers, and a doll.

Bernie opened the door carrying a lit candle in her hand. "I didn't want to turn on the light," she said. "I didn't want to draw the attention of any of our neighbors."

"Good idea," Elica said.

"What's this doll for? It's not Theo's doll, is it?" Bernie asked, looking at the doll.

"Of course not. Boys don't play with dolls." Elica smiled. "It's mine. In fact, I can't believe you don't remember this doll?"

"No, I don't. I never cared for dolls. Should I remember it for some reason?" Bernie asked.

"Oh yes. This doll meant a lot to both Anna and me. We were just children. And I remember that I wanted it so badly. In fact, at that time in my life, I had never wanted anything as much. Then we all went to Anna's birthday party. And Anna got the doll as a present from her parents. I was so sick with jealousy," she sighed. "But then Anna did something remarkable. She gave the doll to me as a gift.

That was a very generous thing to do for a twelve-year-old. But that was Anna. She was always doing things like that."

"Actually, I do remember that."

"Yes, she was always that way, generous and kind. I didn't appreciate her when we were children. I was too jealous of her. But now..." She shook her head, and her eyes started to water. "Now I want to tell her how much she meant to me. And I want to give her this doll. She'll understand," Elica said.

Bernie looked down at the sleeping toddler in Elica's arms. "He's so beautiful," she said, then she sighed. "Do you remember that night when we were in the park, and we decided to become blood sisters?"

"Of course," Elica said.

"Sometimes I think about that night and how we didn't know at that time how much our lives would become intertwined. We had no idea how much we would go through together and how much the world would change."

"That's for sure. But I still feel the same way about you and Anna. However, Dagna has turned so mean. I guess she always was, but she was never mean to me," Elica said. "I am so afraid to go and talk to her tomorrow. I am dreading it."

"I don't trust her," Bernie said. "I wish you would not go to see her. Your safety means a lot to me."

"I have to trust her. I have no choice. She's the only person I know who has any connection to the Germans. She's working for them. She might be able to find out where they've taken Daniel. And she might just be my only hope of ever finding him again."

When Elica mentioned Daniel, she could see the hurt and longing in Bernie's eyes, and she felt sorry for her friend. But she also knew she could never give Bernie what she was looking for. Even so, Bernie or Anna were the only two people Elica would trust to watch Theo.

"I was thinking about Theo all day. If you don't return after two nights, I am going to take Theo to Italy. I have a friend there who works at an orphanage. She will watch over him. It's too dangerous with Anna hiding in the attic for Theo to be here, too. The neighbors might hear a baby crying and report it. They know I have no children. Who knows what they could do? But after you return, you and Daniel can go to Italy and get him, and at least you'll be out of Austria. Theo will be safe there until you are ready to pick him up."

"Italy?"

"Yes."

"That's so far away."

"But that's why I know he'll be safe. If the Nazis make any connection between you and me, at least Theo won't be involved. I'll take him if you're not back in a couple of days."

Elica contemplated Bernie's offer. "Yes, I think you're right. I think that would be best. Although I hate to be parted from him."

"My friend Viola will take care of him until we return."

Elica nodded, but she felt sick to think of parting with her son.

"Can I hold him?" Bernie asked.

"Of course. He's sleeping very soundly because I gave him some whiskey. I rubbed it on his gums," Elica said. "I know it's probably not good for him, but I was afraid he might cry when we were walking outside, and if the Germans saw us, they might question me as to why I was out so late at night carrying a child."

Theo slept soundly even as Bernie took him into her arms. "He's a big boy," Bernie said.

"Yes, he's almost two. I can't believe it."

"Don't worry about him." They stared into each other's eyes for a moment. Then Bernie said, "let's put the baby into this makeshift crib I've put together for him, and then we can go and see Anna."

"Come with me," Bernie said, and she led Elica into her bedroom. She'd taken a drawer out of her dresser and put it on the floor. It was lined with blankets. "He'll be alright in here." Bernie indicated the drawer. "I set this up for him this afternoon. He'll be safe here until we get back from the attic."

Elica nodded. Gently, she lay Theo on the makeshift bed and kissed him on the forehead. Then she took Bernie's hand, and by the light of a single candle, Bernie led Elica up the backstairs to the attic.

CHAPTER SIX

Anna was shocked and terrified when the door to the hidden attic room opened in the middle of the night. She'd been half asleep, but her eyes flew open wide. But then she saw Bernie, and she relaxed. Elica followed behind. It had been years since the last time Anna had seen Elica, and although she was glad to see her, she wondered why Bernie had brought her to the attic.

"Anna," Elica said.

Tears rolled down Anna's face. Elica put the doll down on the cot and hugged Anna tightly. Then she began to cry. For several minutes, the girls embraced while Anna's parents and her brother watched without saying a word.

Then Anna noticed the doll lying on the end of her cot.

"Daniel and his mother have been arrested," Elica said, her voice barely above a whisper. Tears flowed freely down her cheeks.

"I heard that you and Daniel got married."

"Yes, it's true."

"I am happy for you."

"It was wonderful. It's a long story. But once his parents saw Theo, they accepted our marriage. Before Daniel and I were married, things were very hard for us. I was living in an apartment with Dagna."

"I heard about that too," Anna said.

"It was rough. Every morning, I had to take Theo to the state childcare, so I could go to work. I lied and said he was a pure Aryan. They would never have allowed him in if they had known he was half Jewish."

"Everyone has had to do so much lying. My family and I are forever indebted to Bernie and her mother for taking us in."

"Yes, so much lying. I had to make up a story for the state childcare agency. I told them that I was the maid at Daniel's parents' home, but now I was no longer working for them because they were Jewish, and it was against the law. I explained that I had gotten a job at a factory, and I needed child care so I could work."

"And they accepted that?"

"They did. They wanted to know who Theo's father was; I told them he was a Christian, an Austrian, who was married. I explained that he left me when I got pregnant. They liked Theo; they liked his blonde hair." She smiled sadly. "But then Daniel came back to me. He said you sent him."

"I did. I went to speak to him, and I told him that he should be a husband and father to you and Theo. We talked for a while, and he could see that it was the right thing to do. He always loved you, Elica."

"I always loved him. But I feel so bad about you and him. I came between you two. And I can't believe that you sent him to me. You are so kind."

Anna smiled. "What Daniel and I had was nothing more than a teenage crush. We dated for a while, but the truth is, he belongs to you and Theo."

"After we got married, we were so happy together. We lived with his parents. They loved Theo. And everything was wonderful until two weeks ago, when the Germans broke into Daniel's parents' home and arrested Daniel and his mother. They shot and killed his father in the hallway."

"Dear God," Anna gasped. "Where were you?"

"I was hiding in the closet with Theo. Oh, Anna, it was horrible."

"I can imagine," Anna said. Being forced to live in an attic without adequate food and water had taken a toll on her. She was tired and angry. *Elica has always been selfish. It took me years to see it. But now it is so obvious that it's painful.* She had never been one to be critical of her friends. *Elica is so caught up in her own misery that she doesn't even acknowledge how difficult it must be for my family and me. I can't believe she never even asked how we were doing.*

"Do you remember this doll?" Elica asked.

"Of course," Anna said. "I got her for my birthday, and then I gave her to you. You wanted her so badly."

"Yes, and do you remember what you said?"

Anna shook her head. "I don't."

"You said you thought I should have the doll because it looked like me. Remember now? You said I should be her mommy because we looked alike."

Anna tried to smile. "I remember."

"Well, I brought her to you because I can't be here with you, but when you are lonely, you can look at her and think of me. I wish I could do something more for you. I didn't treat you well, Anna. I am sorry. I fell in love with Daniel, and he was your boyfriend. I should never have allowed that to happen. I knew it was wrong. But he is the love of my life." Elica began to cry.

"It's all right." Anna soothed her as she had always done. "It's all right."

"I am going to the police station in the morning. Dagna works there now. I want to see if she will help me to find Daniel."

"Please, Elica. You must be very careful not to tell her you saw me. Don't tell her where we are hiding. I know how sometimes you can start talking and forget yourself. But you must be careful. Dagna can't be trusted, Elica. I know you have always had a special bond with her, but I promise you she will turn my family and me in if she finds out where we are. And that would also put Bernie and her mother in danger. You don't want to do that, do you?"

"No, I promise you I won't tell her I saw you. If she asks about you, I'll say I don't know where you are."

"You must promise me. You must weigh every word you say. You can't be careless, or it could be very bad. Now, I know you don't think she would do anything terrible. But believe me, she would have me and my family arrested in a second if she could find us. So, please, please, please, you must promise me."

"I promise," Elica said.

CHAPTER SEVEN

B efore Elica left, she went back to Bernie's room to kiss Theo one last time. Bernie stood beside the bed and watched her.

"Please, be careful tomorrow," Bernie said.

They looked into each other's eyes. Then there was a moment of silence when all they heard was the sound of Theo's gentle breathing.

"Elica, remember the metal box we kept buried under the tree where we would meet when we were children?"

"I haven't thought about that box for years," Elica said. "But yes, I remember where we buried it."

"Since our lives are so uncertain, let's agree to leave any important information for each other in that box. In case something goes wrong and we can't get to each other."

"But nothing will happen. Nothing will go wrong," Elica said. There were tears in her eyes.

"No, nothing will go wrong," Bernie agreed, "but… just in case." Bernie felt her eyes burn with tears. She walked out of the room, leaving Elica alone with Theo to say goodbye.

CHAPTER EIGHT

Elica leaned over the crib and looked at her son. She wanted to record every single feature in her mind, the way his tiny eyelashes brushed his soft chubby cheek. The blond peach fuzz that covered his head. Ever so gently so she would not wake him, she touched his face. He didn't stir. Then she placed her hand against his, and his tiny fingers curled around hers even in his sleep.

"My little boy," she whispered, "I'm sure I am being silly to worry about this. Dagna would never hurt me. She's my blood sister." She sucked in a long breath. "But, if for some reason, God forbid, I don't return, I will always be with you. You are my little love, my heart. Bernie will take care of you. I know she will because she loves me, and because she does, she will love you too. I would give anything to see you grow into a man, to see you go on your first date, to see you all dressed up in your first suit. And how proud I would be when you get married.

Your father and I used to talk about how much we would love to have grandchildren. We would daydream about how we would watch your children so that you and your wife could travel. Maybe, just maybe, this dream might come true. Perhaps God will be good, and I will find your father and bring him home again tomorrow. Oh, how joyful that would be. We would be a family again."

Tears spilled down her cheeks and landed on the baby's little fist.

"But, just in case..." She leaned down and planted a soft kiss on his cool cheek, leaving it wet with her tears. "Just in case."

CHAPTER NINE

Elica lay in her bed that night and tried to sleep. But she couldn't rest. She knew Theo would be safe with Bernie, but she missed him. *I feel such an emptiness in the pit of my stomach. But at least he will be safe.* The house seemed so empty. So dark and empty. She thought of Daniel, and tears came to her eyes, but she quickly wiped them away with the bedsheet. She refused to believe he might be dead. But she knew that Dagna might refuse to tell her where Daniel was. After all, she did hate him. *What if she refuses to tell me? What can I do to make her tell me?* Elica was suddenly struck with fear.

Dagna has the upper hand. She can choose to give me the information or not. She climbed out of bed and took the whiskey out of the closet. Taking a sip from the bottle, she groaned. It tasted terrible, but it was warm going down her throat. *Dagna has the power to keep Daniel and me apart. What can I offer her to make her tell me everything she knows?* And then, an idea came to her. It was heartbreaking. But it would probably be effective. A chill ran through her as she wrapped her arms around her body and waited for morning.

CHAPTER TEN

As soon as there was a hint of daylight, Elica got out of bed and forced herself to eat a slice of day-old bread and a cup of ersatz coffee. Then she got dressed and made her hair look presentable. A quick glance in the mirror told her that her lack of sleep was taking a toll on her. There were thick bags under her blue eyes, which had lost all their sparkle. She looked into her pocketbook. She counted her money. She didn't have much left, but she knew that buying a few cookies at the bakery for Dagna would be a good investment. Especially since she knew how angry Dagna had been with her. And she had no doubt that Dagna still held a grudge.

They hadn't spoken since Elica had moved out of the apartment. Leaving Dagna with a large payment had been a terrible betrayal. But Elica had done it anyway because she had a way of always putting herself and her own needs first. Elica's leaving Dagna with a lease to pay forced Dagna to work two jobs. But Dagna didn't give up. And if Elica had to make a bet, she would say it was because Dagna was fueled by anger. Dagna worked all day, and at night she went to secretarial school. When she finished, she was hired at the police station. Elica felt guilty and knew that what she did was wrong. Yet she kept replaying it in her mind in an attempt to convince herself that what she had done was not selfish. It wasn't that she hadn't cared what happened to Dagna. It was just that she loved Daniel and was willing to do anything for him. Closing her eyes, she remembered how lost and frightened she'd been when she was pregnant, and her parents threw her out of the house.

Daniel was not speaking to me at the time. I was out on the street. If it had not been for Dagna, I would have been destitute. But Dagna had not known then that Daniel was the father of my unborn child. I couldn't tell her. At that time, no one but Bernie knew. Dagna is a devoted member of the Nazi party, and Daniel is a Jew. Dagna made no secret of how much she hated the Jewish people. She blamed them for all the problems in the world. I needed Dagna then; she might have refused to help me if she knew. And then, when Daniel came to see our son, he asked me to marry him. I was so in love with Daniel that nothing else mattered. I didn't think about Dagna. I was just so happy. But when Dagna found out that Daniel was Theo's father and that I had left her for him, she was furious. So, because of all of this, what I am about to do is very risky. But Dagna has always been in awe of me. From the time when we were very young, Dagna followed me around and admired me for years. And now I am hoping I can somehow use that admiration to make Dagna forgive me. After all, everything in my whole world depends on it.

CHAPTER ELEVEN

"I'm here to see Dagna Hofer. She's employed here," Elica said to the young man at the front desk at the police station.

"Dagna Hofer," he repeated. "Yes, I know her. Wait here."

Elica smiled at the man. He returned her smile, but not the way men had always returned her smile in the past. All the hardship Elica had endured had taken a toll on her and had chipped away at her beauty.

A few minutes later, Dagna walked out of the back room and headed towards Elica. "Well, well, well," Dagna said, her voice dripping with sarcasm. "Would you look at who has come to see me? If it isn't my old friend, Elica."

"I need to talk to you," Elica said in a small voice.

"About what?"

"Is there somewhere we can go and talk where we could be alone? Where we could have some privacy?" Elica said. Her words stuck in her throat.

"Hmmm. I suppose so," Dagna said. "Follow me."

Elica nodded. The arrogance in Dagna's voice and demeanor was so obvious that it made Elica tremble. But she still believed that she could win Dagna's forgiveness and regain the admiration Dagna had once had for her.

Dagna walked ahead of Elica, not looking back once to see if she was behind her. But Elica was right behind Dagna. Her knees were trembling, threatening to give out as she followed Dagna to the back of the building, where there was a long, dark staircase. This area was not well-lit like the rest of the building. It was obviously not open to the public. Dagna switched on the light. A single light bulb hung over a creaky wooden staircase with no banister. Elica trembled when she looked around her. *What kind of horrors have taken place here? Is Daniel here? Is he being tortured?* The walls were unpainted, gray concrete. Dagna did not turn around. She walked slowly down the stairs, the heels of her shoes clicking as she made her way to the basement. Once they were at the bottom of the stairs, Dagna flipped another light switch. Once again, a single bulb illuminated the dismal rooms. Elica looked around her. The floors and walls were the same gray concrete. Dagna did not speak. But she did turn around and look at Elica. Then she shook her head and began to walk forward. Elica followed as Dagna turned on another single bulb as they walked past two prison cells with rusty bars. An open door seemed to be waiting for the next prisoner. Elica saw red stains on the wall. Fear gripped her. *Is that blood? No, no, it must be paint.*

"Come in here," Dagna said, her voice echoing in the airless basement. Elica followed her into an office. Again, the only light was a single bulb that hung in the center of the room. "Sit down," Dagna commanded as she sat down and crossed her legs behind a metal desk.

Elica sat on an uncomfortable metal chair across from Dagna. She held her purse tightly in both hands and twisted the handle nervously. "I've come here to see you because we have known each other since we were children. We've always been best friends. Blood sisters, remember?" Elica said desperately.

"Of course, I remember. How could I forget? You and those friends of yours didn't want me in your club. But you let me in because I threatened to tell your mother that you were sharing blood with a Jew. Oh yes, I do remember." Dagna smiled, but it wasn't a sincere smile. It was a cold, frightening grimace that made Elica tremble. "Yes, Elica, I wanted to be your friend. More than anything in the world, I wanted to be like you because you were pretty and popular. I used to steal for you just to keep your friendship. In fact, I rented that room because you let that Jew boy get you pregnant. Of course, I would never have helped you if I had known that the Jew was the baby's father."

"Dagna... I'm sorry. I'm sorry about leaving you with that lease. I should never have done that."

"Now you say that. But let's face it, you weren't a very good friend to me, were you? How could you leave me in that apartment knowing that I could not pay the rent just so you could marry that Jew? I was your best friend. There was a time I would have done anything for you. Anything, Elica."

"I was wrong to leave you like that, but I had a baby with Daniel, and Theo needed his father. I am so sorry. So sorry."

"Hmmm. Yes, well, I'm sure you are sorry. Now. Now that your husband and his family can't help you. Only your old friend Dagna has the power to help you." Dagna let out a short laugh. "I want you to know that I struggled to pay the rent until I finished school and was able to get this job at the police station. I worked hard, Elica, but I was lucky enough to get hired here; otherwise, who knows what would have happened to me?"

"I am sorry."

"So, you're sorry. Apologies mean very little to me. Is that why you came here? You wanted to tell me you're sorry?"

"Yes, that and..."

"Of course, there is more. There's something you want, isn't there? That's the way you are, Elica. You never do anything that doesn't directly benefit you. You're selfish and, quite frankly, a lousy friend."

"Dagna, please. Please forgive me. I need your help. Daniel was arrested. I don't know where to find him. I need you to help me find him. I am begging you, please, please, Dagna." She was desperate. Tears began to spill down her cheeks.

"You're still so pretty even when you're crying," Dagna said.

"Please, Dagna, please help me."

"Arrested? Daniel was arrested. What did he do?" Dagna said sarcastically.

"He was arrested because he is Jewish."

"And you are Aryan?" Dagna said, shaking her head. "You should never have gotten involved with him in the first place. I've always told you that. But you were always a good-for-nothing little slut. Couldn't keep your legs closed. Not even to a Jew."

"Dagna, please," Elica begged. Dagna had never spoken to her this way before. She was suddenly frightened that she would not be able to win Dagna's forgiveness and that Dagna might not help her.

"Where is Theo? Your half Jew kid. I would never have helped you take care of him if I had known that Daniel was his father?"

"He died, Dagna."

"Oh? How?" Dagna seemed genuinely interested.

"He was sick. I put him to bed one night, and he never woke up in the morning."

"You're lucky. You're better off without him. He was nothing but a tie to that Jew husband of yours."

"Dagna, please. I have been through so much. I know you have too, and I said I am sorry. I promise that if you help me, I will never betray you again. I swear it. Please, Dagna, help me find Daniel."

Dagna stared into Elica's eyes. There was a long, uncomfortable silence. Then, in a voice that sounded like the hiss of a snake, Dagna said, "And now, after all you've done to me, you come here, and you want my help?"

"I'm begging for your help. I'll do anything. In fact,..." Elica felt her skin grow hot and itchy. *I don't want to do this, but it might be my only chance to convince Dagna to help me. God, forgive me. Bernie, forgive me. Anna... oh, Anna...* "I can give you some important information in exchange for my husband," Elica said.

"Oh?" Dagna raised her eyebrows. "What kind of information?"

God help me. I am so sorry. I am so sorry, Anna. "I know where you can find Anna and her family."

"Oh, do you? Now, this is very interesting. And in exchange for your Jewish friend, you want your Jew husband back. Is that right?"

"Yes, yes..."

Dagna laughed, a long-wicked laugh. "I've heard it said that people don't change. And it's true. Here you are ready to turn on someone else who you called a friend. Oh, Elica, you have no loyalty to anyone, do you?"

"Dagna, I am desperate. I don't want to do this. I don't want to hurt anyone. I just want my Daniel back. Please, help me."

"I might be able to arrange it," Dagna said. "So, why don't you tell me where I can find Anna?"

I shouldn't do this. I shouldn't, but what other choice do I have? If I tell her, Anna will be arrested, maybe even murdered. Probably murdered. Anna was my best friend. And now... She closed her eyes and imagined Anna lying dead in a pool of blood. Elica trembled. *They will go to Bernie's house and arrest Anna and her family. But Theo won't be there. Bernie promised that she was going to take Theo to Italy. At least he will be safe. But I don't know what will happen to Bernie when she gets back home. Even so, I can't worry about her. I need to help Daniel.*

"So, are you going to tell me?" Dagna leaned forward.

Elica felt a chill run through her entire body. She was suddenly afraid. There were a million things that could go wrong. She knew she could not trust Dagna. *What if Bernie hasn't left yet with Theo? What if they go to the house and find Theo? Dagna knows that Daniel is his father.* "I think I made a mistake coming here. I am going home."

"Oh no, you aren't. You aren't going anywhere, Elica. It seems that you don't understand the importance of the information you just revealed to me. You are under arrest and required by law to tell me everything that you know."

"I can't. I can't tell you. I thought this would all go much differently, but I should never have come to you. I should have realized you would not forgive me so easily."

"But you did come, and you did tell me. And now, you are not walking out of here until you tell me everything. You can do this the easy way and tell me what you know. Or I will see to it that you are forced to speak. How is it going to be, Elica? Will you suffer and try to keep silent, or will you turn on your Jew friend easily, without a fight, the same way you turned on me?"

Elica began to cry so hard that she could hardly breathe. But Dagna was unaffected. "So? Tell me where Anna is."

"No, no... I made a mistake."

"Ahhh, Elica, sweet, stupid Elica. You've made a lot of mistakes. And you are about to pay for them," Dagna said. Then she walked to the door of the room and yelled. "Guard, guard. Please come and help me with this prisoner."

CHAPTER TWELVE

The guard came. He squeezed Elica's breast before he practically picked her up, dislocating her shoulder. She let out a scream of pain. He ignored her. Instead, he took her arm and pulled her along beside him until he came to one of the cells. Then he threw her into the cell and slammed the door. Then he made sure it was locked. At first, Dagna returned every few hours, always asking the same question "Where is Anna?" But Elica refused to tell Dagna anything. "I made a mistake, Dagna. I won't tell you anything. I won't. I can't. I am sorry. But I can't do this. I can't."

"You stupid bitch. You still don't know which side to be on. Let me tell you something, Elica. You have chosen the wrong side. The Germans are the winners. Soon there won't be a single Jew left alive to befriend you. And you, an Aryan fool, will be a pariah. No decent Aryan person will want to be around you. The men who adored you will be repulsed by you and you'll be branded a Jew lover. Hell, you dumb fool, they might even just kill you. It could happen," Dagna said viciously. "Don't you realize I am your last chance to save yourself?"

"I can't, Dagna. I can't."

"Look at you. Your dress is filthy. Your hair is a mess, and you're lying on the floor of a jail cell in the basement of the police station. But, even now, you won't let me help you. So, I give up on you. You'll rot in here, Elica. That's all I have to say," Dagna said, and she turned and walked away. Elica felt sick as she listened to the heels of Dagna's shoes click against the concrete floor.

Hours passed. Maybe days? Elica lost track of time. She wept. She fell asleep. She awoke alone, terrified that she had been left there to die.

It was a long time before Elica saw another human being. But it was not Dagna who came this time. It was a huge, burly man. He unlocked the cell door and entered. Then he walked over to Elica and pushed her up against the wall. Then he put his face so close to hers that she could smell his rancid breath. She gagged. "Tell me where the Jews are," he said.

"I don't know."

"You do know. Now tell me."

"I can't. I'm sorry. I can't." Elica was crying, but the man only pushed her harder. Then he reached down and tore her blouse open. Elica gasped with fear. But he didn't stop. He ripped her bra off. Pain shot through her shoulder where it had been dislocated. Elica reached up and held her shoulder. The guard threw her onto the cement floor. He lifted her dress. "No. Please. No."

Dagna appeared inside the cell. She was watching as the guard forced himself on Elica.

Elica looked up, her eyes caught Dagna's eyes, and she said, "Please, Dagna, I beg you, please make him stop. Please make him let me go... I'll tell you what you want to know."

"Stop," Dagna said.

The guard ignored her. He didn't stop for several minutes until he had finished.

Then he stood up and zipped his pants. Elica sat up and vomited.

Then she pulled her skirt down to cover her body. She felt his nastiness dripping down her thighs, and she gagged again.

"Tell me what I want to know, or I swear, Elica, I'll bring another man viler than this one, and another man after him, and another until you tell me," Dagna said.

"Anna and her family are hiding in the attic in Bernie's house."

"Jew lover," Dagna said. Then she spat on Elica, "You're nothing but a Jew lover. Look at what you went through just to protect Anna, a Jew. You married a Jew. You should be ashamed of yourself, Elica." Then she turned to the guard. "Brand her," Dagna said. "The world should know exactly what she is by looking at her face."

Elica's eyes grew wide. She trembled. "I told you what you wanted to know, Dagna. Now please, please just let me go."

"I will, but not yet. First, I have to scar you so that everyone knows what you are." Dagna smiled.

Elica felt her blood run cold.

The guard took a small knife out of his pocket. Elica tried to get up from the ground and get away from him. But he was strong, very strong. He knocked her back down and held her there with one hand. Then, with his other hand, he carved a Star of David into her lovely face. She screamed with pain and horror. She begged Dagna to stop him. But Dagna just stood there, looking into Elica's eyes. She was watching, and she was smiling. Blood flowed down Elica's face and into her torn blouse.

"Just look at you now," Dagna said. "Now you will wear the sign of a Jew. That's because you're a Jew lover. You always wanted to be one. I can still remember how envious you were of Anna. Well, now your fate is almost as bad as if you had been born into a Jew family. How does it feel?" Dagna taunted, "You were always such a beauty. And I was always so jealous of you. I wanted to be like you. But now, you are ugly. You will never captivate men the way you once did. And I am no longer jealous of you. Because now, I am prettier. If we walked down the street, men would stare at me, but they would shudder when they looked at you. Your face is ugly now. It's ugly!" She let out a laugh. "And I am just as pretty as you are. Poor Elica, you will never be a great beauty again. And, by the way, just to let you know, your Jew husband... is dead. He died the same day he was arrested. Pity, isn't it?" Dagna shook her head and laughed.

CHAPTER THIRTEEN

A few days after Elica left to go and see Dagna, Bernie grew worried. She was very nervous as she went up the stairs to see Anna. Bernie made her way up into the attic to bring food and water to Anna and her family. She laid a loaf of bread and a carafe of water on the table, then she turned to Anna. "Can I speak to you?" she said.

"Of course. What is it?" Anna asked.

"I have brought you as much food and water as I could get my hands on. But I am leaving today for Italy. I can't take the constant worrying anymore. There's been no word from Elica, and every time I hear the siren of the Gestapo, I'm sure they are coming for Theo. I know I sound crazy, but I can't keep him here anymore. I must get him to safety. So, I decided I would take Theo to stay with a friend of mine in Italy. I spoke to my mother, and she said she will bring you more food and water in a couple of days."

"Did Elica go to see Dagna?"

"She told me she was going to see Dagna to try to find Daniel."

"Yes, I know. Do you think Dagna would have turned on her?"

"Well, it's very possible. After Elica and Daniel married, Dagna and Elica were no longer friends. I don't know what Dagna might do. She's a terrible person and not very forgiving."

"She is a terrible person. At least she was when I knew her," Anna said. "Even so, I don't think she would turn on Elica. You must remember how much Dagna admired Elica when we were younger. She wanted Elica's friendship so badly."

"Well, yes, that is true. And it was because Elica was the prettiest girl at school. Everyone wanted to be like her. I think Dagna thought that if she was friends with Elica, other people would look at her as if she was as pretty and popular as Elica was."

"That's kind of crazy."

"Yes, but it's true. Dagna wanted everyone to see that Elica was her best friend. She went out of her way to make sure people could see that they were inseparable."

"Yes, but now Dagna is a member of that National Socialist party."

"But don't forget that Dagna has always been very vindictive. I didn't want Elica to go. But I knew she would not rest until she did everything she could to find her husband. I am afraid for Elica, but there is nothing I can do to help her. I have her son with me. The child is half-Jewish. Of course, Dagna knows the boy is half-Jewish. If Elica slips up and tells Dagna where her son is, we will all be in trouble. So, the best thing for me to do is get him out of here right away. I need to get him to my friend in Italy, where he'll be safe. Once Elica returns, she can go to him there. I have a little bit of money saved, but I also have a ring that my grandmother gave me. I'll sell it. That will make sure Elica has the money to go."

"So, are you coming back, or will you stay in Italy too?"

"I've been giving it a lot of thought. If it weren't for you and your family, I would take the child and leave Austria for good. But I can't leave you behind. So, as soon as I drop Theo off, I'll return home."

"I hate to be such a burden," Anna said.

"You are not a burden. You are a good friend." Bernie sucked in a deep breath. "I do have something that I must talk to you about."

47

"Tell me."

"Do you remember that I mentioned to you that I had met someone when I traveled to Italy right after we returned from our summer in Berlin? A girl who I was attracted to in the same way I was once attracted to Elica."

"I do remember."

"The girl is the same one I am going to see in Italy. She is the one I am going to leave Theo with. We have been communicating by mail for a couple of years now. And... well... let me just say that for the first time in my life, I feel as if my feelings are returned."

"So, that's good. She feels the same way about you that you feel about her?"

"Yes. She's told me in letters."

"But how do you think she will feel about you leaving Theo with her?"

"I don't know. But she was studying to be a nun at a church that has an orphanage. It would be the perfect place to hide Theo. He looks so much like Elica with his blond hair and blue eyes. No one will know that his father was Jewish."

"Did you say she is going to be a nun?"

"She was before we met. Then we both realized how we felt about each other. It's not your average relationship. There are a lot of perils involved. I am not happy that I am like this. But she makes me happy. Does that make sense to you?"

"Yes." Anna nodded. "And you deserve to be happy."

"I only know that she loves me, and I love her. But I promise you that I will return to Austria and take care of you and your family until this is over. And I do believe it will end. It has to end. And once I know you and your family are safe, I will go back to Italy and spend the rest of my life with her. If, God forbid, Elica does not return, I will raise her child as my own. What else can I do?"

"So, you are leaving today?"

"Yes, I must. I don't want to wait too long just in case the Germans come looking for Theo."

Anna let out a little sigh.

Then Bernie took both of Anna's hands and continued. "I know you are dependent on me. I would never take that lightly. So, please don't worry. I won't abandon you. I will return to Austria. I promise. Everything will be all right. You'll see. I'll leave Theo with Viola. By the way, Viola is her name. She's Italian. But she speaks perfect German." Bernie smiled. "Anyway, I am sure she will take care of Theo until I am able to return to her."

"A two-year-old child is a lot of work. Are you really sure she will be willing to do this?"

"I am not sure. I haven't asked her. But I believe she will. She's truly wonderful. She's compassionate. She loves children. And she is kind."

Anna sighed. A bead of sweat trickled down her cheek. It was hot in the attic. "How long do you think you'll be gone?"

"A week, maybe. I'll get back as quickly as I can."

Anna nodded.

"Please trust me. I can see you're afraid that I won't come back. But I will. I just can't keep Theo here. It's too dangerous. You know how Elica is; she could have started talking to Dagna and forgotten herself. She sometimes talks without thinking. And I can't trust that Elica didn't make the mistake of trusting Dagna and telling her all about Theo. So, it's best that I get him out of here as soon as I can. You understand, don't you?"

"Of course I do," Anna said, but then she turned sheet white, and a pit developed in her stomach. She could hardly get the words out. "You... you don't think that Elica would tell Dagna where I am, do you?"

"No, she's not that dumb," Bernie laughed, but more nervously than she wanted to appear. "She might talk about her son and accidentally tell Dagna too much. But she would never do that to you."

"Yes, you're right," Anna said, but her voice cracked.

"I know you're afraid. I am too. But I have no other choice. I think it's best to leave right away."

"I agree with you. This is the best thing to do," Anna said.

Bernie reached over and hugged Anna. "It will be all right. You'll see."

"Please be careful," Anna said.

"Of course, you know I will. And I'll be back before you know it. But until then, you can count on my mother."

CHAPTER FOURTEEN

Bernie sat down at the small desk in her room. She tapped her pencil on the desk, closed her eyes, and pondered the gravity of her impending action. She must make papers for her and Theo, which had to be perfect because if they were caught with false documents, they would be arrested. And the horrors that would follow were unthinkable. She'd made papers once before, for Anna, when the girls were going to work as nannies in Berlin. It hadn't seemed serious then. She put her head in her hand as she remembered that time.

Three years earlier, there was the calm before the storm when life was simpler, or at least so it seemed. Before the Germans entered Austria and drastically changed the lives of the blood sisters forever, Bernie, Anna, Elica, and Dagna went to Berlin for the summer on a work program. Hitler was already in power, but they had not yet seen the extent of damage that he would do. And after all, it was only one summer. One short summer in Germany, they spent working as nannies to earn extra money and, more importantly, to experience an adventure.

When we first decided to go to Berlin, Anna was not able to join us because she was Jewish, and it was against the law in Germany for Jews to work for non-Jews. But I was willful in those days and refused to accept those terms. I remember staying up all night until I came up with a plan. It would have been far easier to go to Berlin without Anna. Anna didn't need the money, but money was not the only reason we wanted to go. We wanted to get away, to have a summer away from our families. Bernie's plan took a great deal of effort, but she was stubborn. She'd always been stubborn and didn't like the idea that Anna could not join them because she was Jewish. Bernie believed it was wrong. Despite having to attend school in the morning, she stayed up for several nights, teaching herself how to forge papers that appeared genuine. It took what seemed like months, but once she felt that she'd mastered the art, she carefully forged papers for Anna, which gave Anna a Christian name and hid her Jewish bloodline. But Bernie was a perfectionist. And as she studied her work, she hoped the papers were perfect. She showed them to Anna, and they both agreed that Anna would take the risk of using the false papers to travel to Germany. *How foolish and reckless we were in those days before we realized that the Nazis were heartless madmen.*

Anna applied for one of the jobs as a nanny, and she was easily hired. Bernie had arrived in Berlin before Anna. *I remember how I held my breath waiting for Anna in Berlin, praying that the papers would pass any inspections. And they did.* When Bernie saw Anna disembark from the train at the station in Berlin, she let out a sigh of relief. She and Anna were certain that this was going to be a wonderful summer for all the girls. And it had started out to be just that. But Dagna hated Anna. And Elica was losing her fondness for Anna. Dagna and Elica told Bernie that when they looked at Anna's pretty clothes and lovely shoes, they asked themselves why Anna had so much and they had so little. And this jealousy began as a seed and grew into an oak tree by the middle of the summer. If Dagna had kept her mouth shut, it would have been the perfect summer. No one would ever have learned the truth about Anna. However, Dagna's hatred was starting to consume her, and because of this, she told Anna's employers that Anna was Jewish. If Anna's employers had chosen to report her, this might have proved to be fatal for Anna. Instead of bringing the situation to the attention of the authorities, Anna's employers just insisted that Anna leave their employment and return to Austria. They might have gotten into trouble if it were found out that they had hired a Jew, and besides, they were concerned about what their friends would have said. It was far better to just discharge Anna and quietly send her home.

At that time, Bernie thought she was done falsifying papers. However, now, she would have to use the skill she'd mastered that summer. She had to forge papers again. Only this time, the consequences seemed so much more dangerous. She sat at the small desk in her room, tapping her pencil and wondering how she had been so casual about all of this three years ago. *I hadn't seen how cruel the Germans could be. Hitler hadn't yet shown us his true nature. At that time, I thought that if Anna got caught by an inspector on the train, the worst that would happen was that she would be sent back home. What a fool I was. What a risk we took. Thank God, nothing horrible happened.*

Again, Bernie tapped her pencil on the desk. She put her head in her hands. It felt heavy with the burden of deep thought.

I will change our names. I will become a young German mother, and Theo will be my son. We will be traveling to see a cousin who lives in Italy. At least that country is allied with Germany. I will tell anyone who asks that my husband, the child's father, is a German soldier. This lie should appeal to the guards who will be checking our papers at the border. After all, Germany loves their women to be mothers, and the wife of a soldier in Hitler's army should be shown respect and treated kindly. Once I arrive in Italy, I will explain everything to Viola. I will ask Viola if she could temporarily keep Theo at the orphanage until it is safe for him to return. He could easily blend in with all the other children in the orphanage.

Bernie created the fraudulent papers with greater care than she had done three years ago when she had not considered it a matter of life and death. After she'd finished, she scrutinized her work. *I hope these get us through.* She thought, then she got up and began to pack the few things that Elica had given her for Theo.

As Bernie packed to leave, she looked down at the papers she made and thought: *If this works, and all goes well, I'll make papers for Anna and her family when I return. I offered to try two years ago, but Anna's father was afraid to take the risk and refused. I can't blame him. But, if I can make these papers pass, he might be willing to try now.*

Bernie had to argue with her mother when she brought Anna and her family to hide in their attic. She had not approved of Bernie helping Anna's family. But Bernie knew how to entice her mother. She gave her the money that Anna's parents had given her. And seeing the large sum of money, her mother finally agreed. But now Bernie's mother was livid that Bernie had agreed to watch this half-Jewish child for her friend Elica. There had been no financial payment for this, and Bernie's mother told her that she could see no reason to break such a law without compensation. "Aiding Jews is dangerous," her mother warned. "It can be punishable by death in some cases. It's bad enough that you have that family up in our attic. But now, you have a half-Jewish child in your care. Bernie, sometimes I think you want to bring trouble to yourself."

"I don't. You're wrong. I wish that this was not necessary. But what could I do? The Nazis took Elica's husband. She had to go and see if she could help him. And she couldn't take the child with her. She had no idea what was going to happen."

"So, she gave the burden to you."

"I took him. And now I am going to take him to Italy, where I believe he will be safe until his mother returns."

Bernie's mother shook her head. "I might as well tell you right now. I just lost my job. I was going to let you know, but you sprung this on me too fast."

"Oh, no."

"Yes, and you want me to keep feeding those Jews when we barely have enough money to feed ourselves?"

"I'll get a second job," Bernie said, "as soon as I return."

"If you return," her mother scoffed.

"I will be back, and then I will get another job."

"Maybe you'll get those Jews out of here too?"

"You were happy to take their money."

"Yes, but they have already cost us so much more than they gave us."

"You know that's not true. You drink up all the money we have. It's not them who cost us dearly. It's you."

"Shut your mouth. You're disrespectful and ungrateful. Go, take the child. Get yourself into even more trouble. I don't care. Just keep me out of it. And when you get back, get these Jews out of our house. Do you understand?"

"I do understand. I promise you I will do something when I get back. But until then, you must promise me that you will bring them food and water. Mother, you can't leave them up there to starve. If you do, they will die, and four dead bodies will stink up the house. You'll have to bring them down one by one and bury them. Can you do that?"

"You bitch. You leave me no choice. I have to feed them, or they will be discovered."

"Thank you, mother. Thank you."

"Listen to me. When you get back, you must get them out of here. Do you understand me? You must."

"I will do what I can to find them another safe place as soon as I return. But for now, you must feed them and bring them water."

"Yes, you made that clear," her mother hissed.

CHAPTER FIFTEEN

Bernie helped Theo get dressed. She gazed at his golden hair, bathed in the sunlight pouring through the window like liquid gold. *Poor child. I have to do the best I can for him. He trusts me. He is still so young and so vulnerable.* Bernie took a deep breath. *I will get him to Viola. He'll be alright there. I am sure of it.*

Bernie thought of her mother. She worried that her mother might forget to bring food or water up to the attic. Her mother was a heavy drinker, and now that she'd lost her job, Bernie was certain she would lie in bed and drink. Everyone in town knew her mother was promiscuous, that she had several lovers who helped her pay for her rent and the alcohol she loved so much. And because of this, Bernie was ashamed of her mother when she was growing up. But even worse, Bernie had never felt that her mother loved her. She'd always felt like she was no more than a burden to her mother. Her father died when Bernie was very young, and she never really knew him. But for as long as Bernie could remember, her mother would say things like, "If I didn't have you, I would be free to go on with my life. You are the reason I am stuck. You're the reason I drink too much. I have nothing else. If I wasn't burdened with a child, I could find a decent man to marry me and take care of me. But I could never find happiness once you came along and saddled me with a million overwhelming responsibilities. So, I drank. Having children is a curse, I tell you. Giving birth to you has ruined my figure, and after you were born, you ruined my life."

These words were branded in Bernie's mind. Many nights when she was a young child, she had cried herself to sleep, wishing her fate had been different. Where Elica had always wished she'd been born into a wealthy family, Bernie didn't care about material things. Instead, she had spent her entire life longing for love. But unlike her friends, she could not find it in the arms of a man. It wasn't that she hated men. She didn't. They made for decent friends, and she often enjoyed playing sports with the boys in the neighborhood. However, her heart had always searched for another female when it came to love. At the beginning of her life, that female had been Elica, her best friend. Although she'd kept her love quiet, she never admitted her feelings to Elica because she knew Elica did not feel the same way. This was a terrible burden for a young girl, knowing she was different and wishing she wasn't. For as long as Bernie could remember, she knew she was a lesbian. And for many years, the sound of the word 'lesbian' made her cringe. In her early teenage years, Bernie tried to deny her sexual differences. She went out on a few dates with a couple of boys she knew from school. One was a friend who she got along well with. They went to a movie and shared a soda. They had a good conversation, but at the end of the night, when he went to kiss her, she turned her lips away, and his kiss landed awkwardly on her cheek. He never asked her out again.

The other boy she went out with was more aggressive. He took her for a soda, followed by a walk in the park. It was early evening. Once the sun set, he insisted they stop and talk under a tree. But there was very little conversation between them. He put his arm around her, pulled her close, and kissed her. She allowed him to kiss her, hoping she would feel something inside of her stir. But, the truth was, she felt nothing. It seemed like he spent hours just kissing her.

The stubble on his chin burned her face, and she wished she could just go home. When he put his hand on her small breast, she again allowed it, hoping she would feel something. But she felt nothing, nothing at all. Well, that was not entirely true. She felt annoyed, and finally, she said, "We should go. I have to be home. My mother is expecting me." Of course, this was a lie. Bernie knew her mother was out and wouldn't be home until late at night.

"All right," he said. "Maybe we can go out again next week?"

"We'll see," Bernie said. But she made excuses when he came to see her until he stopped asking. She never went out with a boy again.

During her early years, Bernie's fantasies were always of Elica. She often daydreamed that she and Elica were married and lived together. These dreams caused her great shame, and she never told anyone about them. She kept them buried in her heart until, after years of knowing Anna and realizing she could trust her, she admitted to Anna that she was different. And for the first time, she used the word lesbian to describe herself. When she said the word, it physically hurt in the pit of her stomach. "Lesbian." She told Anna that it was a curse, but she had no choice but to accept herself because there was no possible way for her to change. Accepting herself didn't make Bernie happy. It only gave her more reason to feel alienated from the rest of the world. And although she stood by her blood sisters and vowed to help them whenever she could, when they went out with boys, she felt strange, left out, and alone. That was until she went to Italy. Until she met Viola.

Italy did not disappoint. It was a country filled with natural beauty. Bernie was stunned by the magnificence of it. The food was delicious, and the people were warm and kind. She hadn't planned to meet anyone that afternoon as she sipped a cup of strong coffee in a very crowded café. She studied the pastries in the display case and was trying to decide which one she wanted when a pretty dark-haired girl sitting at a table just a few feet away from her said, "I had that one. It was wonderful."

"Excuse me?" Bernie said, "I didn't catch that."

"That one." The pretty girl pointed to a pastry with whipped cream and berries.

"Oh." Bernie was surprised that the girl was talking to her about the pastries. "Was it good?"

Just then, a man walked over to them. He introduced himself as the restaurant owner. Then, in an almost pleading voice, he asked them if they would mind sharing a table because the café was so crowded, and he needed to be able to seat more people.

Viola shrugged and said, "Why not?" Then she turned to Bernie. "As long as it is all right with you?"

"Sure." Bernie walked over to sit at Viola's table. She was uncomfortable. She didn't know what to say, so she smiled. Viola returned her smile.

They were only a couple of years apart in age. Viola was nineteen, and Bernie was a few years younger. At first, the conversation was clumsy and awkward. Bernie ordered the pastry that Viola suggested, even though it wouldn't have been her first choice. She didn't care for heavy cream or overly sweet pastries. But she was in Italy, and the deserts were different from they'd been in Austria or Germany. Even so, she began to eat the rich, creamy pastry and found she was enjoying it.

They each ordered a second cup of coffee.

"I'm Viola," the girl said.

"I'm Bernie."

"You're not from around here."

"No, I'm from Austria, Vienna, to be exact. I'm here on holiday," Bernie said.

"I've never been to Austria. In fact, I've never left Italy."

"I think if I were born here, I would never want to leave," Bernie said. Then she smiled. "You were right. This pastry is delicious, and it's very rich. Would you like some? I couldn't possibly finish it."

"Are you sure?"

"Absolutely."

Viola smiled and picked up her fork. She took a forkful of the pastry and put it into her mouth. Then, closing her eyes, she purred. "Oh, that is so good."

"Have some more," Bernie said.

Bernie felt an unexplainably strong connection to this girl, who she hardly knew. They sat in that café and talked for almost an hour before Bernie asked Viola about her family.

Viola told Bernie how her parents split up when she was young. "My father left my mother with me. But she didn't stay. She was not the same after he left. I'll be honest and tell you something I've never told anyone; my mother went crazy. She kept trying to kill herself and failing. I was so young and terrified by the thought that I could wake up one morning and find her dead.

"Then, one morning, I woke up, and she was gone. Would you believe I was relieved that she was not dead? In fact, I thought she went to the market and would be right back. But she never returned. A week passed, and I was in our apartment all by myself. I had no money, very little food, and no idea where my mother had gone. I kept hoping she would return. But the day turned to night and then back to day again. I was so frightened. I was only nine, and being alone in the house in the dark terrified me."

"It sounds terrible," Bernie said as she reached over and touched Viola's hand. Viola squeezed Bernie's hand, and Bernie felt an electric current run from Viola into her.

"At nine years old, I didn't know how to take care of myself. The food my mother left in the cupboard ran out quickly. Then, to make things even worse, a week later, the landlord came to collect the rent. I couldn't pay him; I didn't have any money. He left, but he must have told one of our neighbors because a few hours later, one of the ladies who lived in our building came to get me. She gave me a sandwich, then took me to the priest at her church. When he saw me, he must have been shocked. I was a dirty little ragamuffin. After all, I hadn't bathed in weeks. But he was kind and gentle, and he told me that I would be all right. Then he brought me to an orphanage a few streets away, where the nuns took me in. That was where I grew up, in that orphanage," she sighed. "It was far from heaven. We had to listen to the nuns and obey them. But I am not complaining. It was a warm, safe place, and I never went to bed hungry again. We always had food to eat. So, because I know how much it means to a child to have a place to live, I decided that I am going to become a nun and work with the children at the orphanage."

"Are you still living at the orphanage now?"

"Yes, but now I am working there as a teacher."

"And do you really want to be a nun?" Bernie asked incredulously. "I would think it would be a very hard life."

"I have given it a lot of thought, and I think it's what is best for me."

"Have you ever thought about getting married and having children of your own?"

Viola shook her head. "I don't want that. No."

"You don't want children?" Bernie was surprised at herself. She knew she was prying deeply into this young woman's personal life. But Viola had opened the window to her life just a crack, and Bernie wanted to come in.

Viola didn't seem to mind. She seemed to want to tell Bernie all about herself, and Bernie wanted to listen.

"I do like children. I love them, in fact. That's why I don't want any."

"But that doesn't make any sense, really," Bernie said. Although, strangely, it did make sense to her because she felt the same way. She could not see herself married to a man with a child, even though she loved children, too.

"It does make sense. At least to me, it does," Viola said. "There are so many unwanted children at the orphanage who need my love. I can do so much good there. Far more than I could do raising a family of my own. Besides, after what my father did to my mother and me, I couldn't imagine ever getting married."

Bernie nodded and smiled. "I suppose it makes sense."

"For me, yes, it makes great sense," Viola said. Then she added, "How long are you staying here in Italy?"

"I'll be here another week and a half."

"Are you alone?"

"Yes, I am."

"Well, like I said, I was born here. I know this country very well. Would you like me to show you around?"

"I would. That would be wonderful." Bernie loved the idea.

"Good, then let's do it."

CHAPTER SIXTEEN

Bernie spent two weeks touring the most beautiful country she had ever seen. It was magical, just as she had imagined it would be. But she had not imagined that she would meet someone like Viola. And then, like a dream come true, on the night before she was planning to leave to return home to Austria, Viola confessed that she was falling in love with Bernie.

While they were sitting in the small, inexpensive room Bernie had rented, eating sandwiches, and drinking wine, Viola said, "I will miss you when you leave."

"I will miss you, too. It has been the most wonderful two weeks of my life. This trip was everything I had hoped it would be and more," Bernie admitted.

"I don't want to ruin it," Viola said. "So... I should probably keep my mouth shut. But..."

There was a long, silent pause. "No, if there is something you want to say, please say it. You couldn't ruin our time together," Bernie said. "What is it you want to say?"

"It's just that, well, this is a rather odd thing to say."

"Go on... please..."

"I think I love you," Viola said in a small voice. "I have never said that to anyone before."

Bernie felt the tears well up in her eyes. She'd never felt so accepted. And until this moment, she believed she was destined to spend her life alone. But now, she'd met another woman who wanted her love, and she felt more fulfilled than she'd ever felt.

Viola stopped for a moment. "Don't cry," she said.

Bernie touched Viola's cheek.

Then Viola went on, "I have always had this, well, this feeling inside that I was different. I mean, the other girls I knew liked boys. They were crazy about them, in fact. But not me. I never felt that. I guess it was because of my father." She looked away. "Maybe I shouldn't have told you. I should have kept my mouth shut. Have I ruined our lovely time together?" Viola stood up. "I guess I should go back to the orphanage tonight."

"No, please don't leave." Bernie stood up. "You haven't ruined anything. I feel the same way you do. I've never been like the other girls, either."

Their eyes met. Bernie was trembling as she leaned forward and placed a gentle kiss on Viola's lips. Viola did not turn away. She took Bernie's hand and held it in her own. Then she kissed the palm and rubbed it against her face. Bernie smiled, leaned over, and kissed Viola again. This time, she was more confident. The sweetness of that kiss, the warm and wonderful feeling that she was finally accepted for who she was, stayed with Bernie over the next two years. Each day she thought about the kiss, and warmth spread over her when she did. And even though the world was falling apart around her, and the Nazi invasion of her homeland brought horrific change, she had a sweet memory that gave her strength. She and Viola wrote to each other weekly. Bernie cherished each letter she received. There was much they dared not share in letters because much of the mail was being censored. But just holding the same piece of paper Viola had held was enough to make Bernie happy.

During that time, when the girls were connected by the mail, Viola told Bernie that she had decided she was not right for the nunnery. Even though neither of them discussed why Viola had made this decision, they both knew the reason. It was because they loved each other. Through their letters, they made plans for Bernie to return to Italy. Bernie was packed and ready to go, but then something terrible happened. The Nazis marched into Austria. They were welcomed by large groups of joyous Austrians who stood in the streets cheering. Bernie had bad feelings about the Nazis from the day they arrived. And somehow, she knew she could not leave her friend Anna. Anna would need her. And if it had not been for Anna, Bernie would have already gone to live in Italy. She could not tell Viola in her letters what was keeping her in Austria, but she promised she would come as soon as possible. Viola said she understood and that once Bernie was on the way, she would find a small flat, and they would move in together. But when the Nazis began rounding up her Jewish neighbors and ripping them away from their homes, Bernie watched in horror. No one knew where these Jewish people were being sent. And no one dared ask any questions. As Bernie predicted, Anna was now in grave danger. So when Anna came to ask Bernie for help, Bernie could not refuse. "You're right. You must hide immediately. There is no time to think this over," Bernie said.

"I'll speak to my father when he gets home from work tonight. I'll tell him that you've agreed to help us," Anna said.

"You should come to my house tonight, after dark. Bring whatever you can without bringing a suitcase. Layer your clothing. And bring whatever food you have."

"All right. I'll talk to him."

Anna spoke to her father and mother. The family was desperate. "We'll pay her and her mother," Anna's father said.

"Must we go tonight?" her mother asked.

"Yes Lilian, I am afraid we must. The Nazis could come to our neighborhood tomorrow, and then it would be too late. Anna's friend has been kind enough to offer us this refuge. We must take it."

"But Austria is our home, Michael. I can't just leave everything behind. Look around you. Even though our home has been taken from us and been reduced to living in this small apartment. This place is filled with all of my things, and all of them have such memories. My mother's menorah, my bubbies Shabbat candle holders. Your mother's dishes. All of this we are going to leave behind?"

"I'm afraid so. These are just material things. As long as we have each other and we are alive, we have everything. It would be far worse if the Nazis came and took it all and sent us somewhere."

"But where could they possibly send us, and why?"

"I don't know why Lilian, and I don't know where. What I do know is that Jews are being taken away by the Germans every day. It's best for us to go to Bernie's house."

Anna sat on the sofa beside her brother and listened. They would have no say in the final decision.

"All right, Michael. But I would like to tell my sister where I will be."

"Lilian, you don't understand. You can't tell anyone. We must leave after sundown tonight. And you must not speak a word about this. Do you understand?"

"But my sister."

"I'm sorry. You must do as I say."

Anna's mother nodded. She sunk down onto the sofa, and she was crying softly. Her husband sat down beside her. He took her into his arms and rocked her.

That night, the family put on as many clothes as they could, one layer over another. Then, when the sun set and darkness came, they walked in the shadows and hid from the light until they arrived at Bernie's house. Bernie opened the door, and they entered quickly. Then she showed them to the attic room, which became their home.

Viola wrote to Bernie the following week, asking her when she would be coming to Italy. Bernie wrote back immediately. She longed to explain why she could not leave and come to Italy, but all she said was, "You must trust me. I will come to Italy as soon as I am able." Bernie dared not tell Viola in a letter that she was hiding a Jewish family. Bernie waited nervously for Viola's answer. And then, like a miracle, a letter from Viola arrived, and she turned out to be the wonderful person Bernie knew she was. "I understand," Viola's next letter said. "It doesn't matter how long it takes you to get back to Italy. I will wait for you. I trust your judgment." Bernie's heart swelled with love, and their letters continued.

A shriek from Theo, who was playing on the floor, brought Bernie back to the present moment. She glanced down at the helpless two-year-old little boy who had lost the ball he was playing with. It had rolled under a cabinet.

"Oh dear, Theo. Let me help you," Bernie said. "I'll get that ball for you." Bernie got down on the floor and reached under the cabinet until she'd retrieved the ball. Theo smiled. *He is so sweet, and he is my responsibility. I owe Elica that much. Poor Elica, God only knows where she is and if she is alright. She's entrusted her child to me, and I must do what is best for him.* Theo caught Bernie looking at him, and he giggled. She smiled at him, and he bounced the ball hard on the floor. He was dressed in a blue outfit she had bought for him only a few days ago at a secondhand store. As she watched him playing, a nursery rhyme ran through her mind.

> *Little Boy Blue,*
> *Come blow your horn;*
> *The sheep's in the meadow,*
> *The cow's in the corn.*

> *Where is that boy*
> *Who looks after the sheep?*
> *He's under a haystack,*
> *Fast asleep.*

Will you wake him?
Oh no, not I,
For if I do,
He'll surely cry.

Tears ran down Bernie's cheek. *This little boy should be with his parents. But for all I know, Elica and Daniel are both dead.* She felt a chill run through her. *And if the Germans find Theo, he will probably suffer the same fate. Not only Theo but Anna, her family, my mother, and me.*

Bernie thought about her mother. She hoped her mother would keep her promise to bring food and water upstairs to the attic each night. *She is so irresponsible.* But Bernie had made a deal with her. She'd promised her mother that if she brought food and water to Anna and her family while Bernie was gone when she returned, she would give her some money. Bernie's mother knew Bernie always seemed to have some money. That was because she saved every penny she could. And because her mother knew Bernie had money, she'd agreed, but reluctantly. *I know I can't trust my mother. I never could, but I have no choice. I must believe she will do what she promises. I must get Theo out of here, just in case. Every hour that we are here is dangerous. It is time I get this child out of this house for everyone's safety, especially his own.*

Bernie studied the papers she'd created for Theo and herself. "Adelaide Bohnen," she said. It was the name she had given herself. It sounded so foreign to her when she spoke it aloud in the empty room. *When they ask for my name, I say Adelaide Bohnen. And this is my son, Dustan.*

Everything was done, and Bernie was ready to leave. She was packed. Theo was packed. She'd made all the arrangements for Anna and her family. The falsified papers were complete, and they looked authentic. The back of her neck itched, and she knew she was probably breaking out into a rash from nerves. *I have no choice. There is no other choice; I must do this. I must be brave and do this. If I can just get this child to the orphanage, he will be safe. He'll blend in with all the other children. I am sure of it. Then everyone will be safe.*

Theo let out a shriek of laughter as he threw the ball across the floor. The sound made Bernie shudder. Then Theo looked up at her and pounded his little fists on the ground. Bernie knew he wanted her to play with him and would start crying any minute if she didn't get up and get his ball. But there was no time for play. She just couldn't indulge him right now. They had to leave, yet she was still glued to her chair, paralyzed with fear. He pounded his fists harder on the ground and let out a shriek. *He's* angry. *What a temper this little one has.* She stood up and got his ball. As she had guessed, he wanted to play. But she was up and moving now. If she sat back down, she would feel that emotional paralysis again. So, she placed his ball into the bag she had packed for him with diapers and bottles for the trip. His little face was red, and his lower lip was jutting out. She picked him up and rocked him in her arms for a moment. He pushed away from her. "Do you want to walk?"

"Walk," he said.

They left the house and went to the park. Theo loved the park. He pointed to the swing, his favorite. "Push me?" he said, but Bernie had to refuse him. She had an important task to complete before she could leave Vienna. She retrieved the letter containing the information on where to find Theo, intended for Elica, from her dress pocket. She held it close to her heart.

"Park," Theo said, "Swing."

Bernie managed to give the child a smile. But her lips were trembling. She looked around to make sure she and Theo were alone. To assure herself that no one had followed her. Then she went to the secret place where she knew the box would be buried. Theo stood beside her and watched as she took a stick and used it to dig up the box. It was there. Right where they left it. Memories of her childhood flooded Bernie's consciousness, and she began to cry. This was the tin box that the blood sisters had used as a message box since they were eight years old. They left each other secret messages inside and shared their deepest feelings. But Bernie was not a child anymore. She thought of Elica. If Elica survived, would she know to look in this box to find information about where Bernie had taken Theo? *I have no other choice; I cannot tell anyone else where I am taking Theo. Anna knows. If she survives, she will tell Elica. But who knows if any of us will survive?*

Bernie opened the box. Inside, she found so many memories. There was the pocketknife that her uncle gave her for Christmas one year. Her mother had wanted to sell it. She ran her fingers over the cool steel. She found two melted lipsticks that Dagna had stolen for Elica. They had hidden them here because Elica was not permitted to wear lipstick at the time. So, she would come to the park and put it on. Bernie had to let out a short laugh when she remembered Elica trying to keep the lipstick on her lips but ending up getting all over her face. Still looking through the box's contents, Bernie found two letters about two different boys that Elica had written. There were letters that Dagna had written too. They both confessed their secret crushes. Bernie found Anna's red hair ribbon; it was still tied in a bow. She'd given it to Elica because Elica wanted it so badly. But Elica could not take it home for fear that her mother might recognize it and accuse her of stealing it. Bernie opened another pocketknife that Elica had brought from home. There was blood still staining the blade from that day when the girls had cut themselves to become blood sisters. Bernie thought about that day. *It changed all our lives. And these small, unimportant possessions told the story of four girls who shared a deep friendship.* Bernie began to weep openly. She hung her head and allowed herself to let the sorrow and fear come out of her in tears and wailing. *I should bury this box.* She thought, but she couldn't stop looking through the box. Then she came upon a letter to Anna from Elica telling Anna that she wished she was her sister and that she wished she lived in Anna's big house. Also, that she wished that her mother were not Anna's maid. Bernie remembered how sad Anna had felt when she read that. *I can't look in this box anymore. Going through our past is making me sad and weak. And if I am going to save Theo, I have to stay strong.* Bernie placed the letter back in the tin box. Then she put the box back in the ground and covered it with the rich black earth. She patted the ground until it felt solid.

"Swing," Theo said, looking at her, his eyebrows raised in question.

"All right, all right," she conceded. "One time. But then we must go."

Theo giggled as Bernie put him on the swing. Her hands were shaking, but she pushed him softly. How he loved to swing. A breeze blew his golden hair as he giggled. She hated to stop. He was enjoying it so much, but they needed to leave. "We have to go now."

"No, swing... again."

"Maybe later." Bernie took Theo out of the swing. He kicked his fat little legs and started to cry, but she kissed his cheek and said, "Don't cry. We'll swing again later." She knew that soon they would be far away from the park, and he would not be going on the swing anytime soon. She had never lied to him before. And she felt guilty as she took his hand and headed for the train station. It was hot, and Theo got tired. "Up," he said.

She picked him up and carried him for a while. He was heavy and big for his age. But at least he was quiet.

Bernie had been saving money for as long as she could remember. She planned to use that money when she returned to Italy after the war was over. But now she realized that this trip would take a lot of her savings. Sighing, she walked up to the ticket seller and bought her tickets for the train. Then she sat down on a wooden bench and waited. Theo sat beside her.

"I want story," he demanded.

I don't know how Elica does it. Children need constant attention. They don't care if you're nervous or sad or even sick. They demand attention. I am already drained. Yet if I want to keep Theo quiet, I must read to him.

"All right," she said, "sit down beside me and be a good boy, and

I'll read you a story." She reached into her bag and pulled out one of the books she'd packed for Theo.

"No. Other one," he said.

"Yes, all right."

Bernie found Theo's other book and began to read. He fell asleep on the bench with his head in her lap.

CHAPTER SEVENTEEN

Theo was a spirited little soul. He was awakened by the train whistle and having been awakened like that in an unfamiliar place made him angry. He was wet and clammy because he'd been sweating from the heat. Bernie wiped his face with a soft cloth diaper. She wondered if he was so edgy because he had not seen his mother for so many days. She picked him up and held him in her arms. Then she gave him his bottle. Contented, he began to suck on the nipple when an old woman sitting on a bench across from them asked Bernie. "How old is your son?"

Bernie tried to smile. *This is the first test. Be calm.* "Dustan is almost three."

"He's too old for that bottle. It's going to ruin his teeth. I suggest you take him off it as soon as possible."

"I will, thank you," Bernie said, trying to put an end to the conversation. But the woman continued.

"My son was so attached to his bottle that when I threw it down the stairs to prove to him that it was gone, he threw himself down after it."

"Oh!" Bernie gasped. "Was he alright?"

"He was fine. He cut his lip was all. Children are more resilient than we think."

"Well, that's good," Bernie said, wishing the old woman would stop talking.

"He was always a difficult boy that one was. Always giving me a fight for everything I tried to do," she laughed. "Now he's got children of his own. I am glad to see it. They fight him the same way he once fought me."

"Yes," Bernie tried to muster a smile.

"So, where are you two going?"

"To see my friend in Italy," Bernie said.

"Where is your husband?"

This old woman was asking too many questions. "He was a soldier, but he died. I am alone."

"Oh, dear. From what? What happened to him? Was it the war?"

Bernie felt the sweat beading on her forehead. "The flu," Bernie said. "He got sick and died from the flu."

"You poor dear child," the woman said. "It's hard for a woman all alone."

"Yes, that's true."

"No wonder you haven't taken him off the bottle yet. Is he toilet-trained? I remember when mine were small, I couldn't take them anywhere until they were toilet trained."

"No, not yet," Bernie said.

"You just have to be consistent. Reward him when he does what he's supposed to do."

"Yes, thank you for the advice. I will do that," Bernie managed to say. *Old women feel it's their duty to give advice to women with children. But right now, I have no interest in what this woman has to say. And I really wish she would just leave me alone.*

The passengers began to board the train. Bernie stood up, took Theo's hand, and got in line. The old woman was right behind her. She followed as Bernie took a seat at the back of the train. Then the old woman sat across from Bernie.

How does one tell someone that they wish to be alone? Bernie thought. But she didn't say anything. Instead, she just smiled a half-smile at the old woman.

Bernie was quiet. She wished she could just watch the countryside pass by outside the train window, but the old woman was not to be silenced. She continued with stories of her children when they were small. Bernie plastered a smile onto her face and nodded, but she wasn't listening. She was worried about Anna and her family, worried about Elica and what had become of her, and worried about whether bringing Theo to the orphanage would somehow put Viola in danger.

Finally, the train came to a stop, and the old woman gathered her things. "Well, this is where I get off," she said. "It's been so pleasant visiting with you."

"Yes," Bernie said, relieved to see her leaving. But before the passengers were permitted to leave the train, two German officers entered.

"Papers!" they cried out in German. "Have your papers ready."

The old woman began to search frantically through the contents of her handbag. She looked flustered. She dropped the handbag, and her things flew all over the floor. Some rolled under the seat. But she was old and was not limber enough to gather them. "Please, can you help me?" she asked Bernie.

"Sure," Bernie said and got down on her knees. Theo watched Bernie and giggled as she gathered several papers, a hairbrush, lipstick, and a mirror.

"Papers?" the young German officer said. He was young and handsome.

Bernie stood up, unaffected by the way he was eyeing her. She opened her own handbag and took out the papers she'd made for herself and Theo. Her eyes met the eyes of the German. He was handsome, but something about him sent a chill through her, and she was frightened. But the man barely looked at her papers. Instead, he glanced over at her breasts. Then he smiled. Trembling, Bernie returned his smile.

Then one of the other officers who had boarded the train to check for papers walked over to the old woman. He demanded to see her papers. Bernie was still holding the things that the woman had dropped. Things that she'd pulled out from under the seat. She handed them to the woman, who looked at the items desperately.

"Where is your identification?" the German asked. His voice told Bernie he was annoyed.

"I don't know," the woman stammered. "They must still be under the seat. They must have fallen out of my purse when I dropped it."

The German officer bent down and looked beneath the seat. "I don't see any papers."

"Let me take a look," the other officer said, and he bent down to glance under the seat. "I don't see them either."

"Do you know this woman?" the handsome young officer asked Bernie.

"I... I..." Bernie stammered.

"I'm her grandmother," the old woman said.

Bernie turned a frightened gaze at the old woman, then she looked at the officer. He handed Bernie her papers. "I asked her, not you," the man said to the old woman. Then he looked Bernie square in the eye and asked, "Do you know her?"

I can't protect her. I have to protect Theo and myself. She is not just some old woman. It seems to me that she is in some kind of trouble. Why doesn't she have papers?

"Well? Do you know her? Is she your grandmother? Or a friend, perhaps?"

"I don't know her," Bernie said. She was trembling. "We met here on the train a few hours ago."

"Why are you lying, old woman? What is it you think you can hide? You can't hide anything from me. So, my advice to you is not to even try." Then he laughed, "Don't tell me you're a Jew, are you?"

"I am not. I swear it. I am not."

"I see. So, tell me, old woman, why do you have no papers?" The nice-looking officer's face was distorted, and he no longer looked handsome. He looked mean and stern and very dangerous.

"I am not lying. I am her grandmother," the old woman said feebly. "I am."

"Arrest her," the other officer said.

Bernie bit her lip. She felt sorry that she hadn't lied for the old woman. *But I couldn't. If I did, I would have drawn attention to myself and Theo, and therefore, I would have put Theo at risk. I have to stay quiet and try to remain unnoticed.*

The Nazi guard, once handsome, now appeared ugly and terrifying as he roughly seized the old woman by the arm and began dragging her away. But before he did, he turned to Bernie, smiled cordially, and softly said, "Sorry to bother you."

After the Nazis left the train, Bernie breathed a sigh of relief even though she still felt guilty. *Who was that woman? What was she hiding? Did she spill her purse on purpose? Was she a spy, or maybe she was Jewish? Either way, I couldn't afford to try to help her. Too many other people depend upon me right now. But at least all the attention she drew to her distracted the Germans. And because they were so concerned with her papers, they didn't look too hard at mine.*

The train rolled out of the station, and Bernie let out a sigh. *For now, we are safe.* She thought. The motion of the train put Theo to sleep. He lay with his head in her lap as the day turned to night outside the window.

CHAPTER EIGHTEEN

Bernie tried to sleep, but she couldn't. Every time she closed her eyes, she thought of that old woman. *What is going to become of her? Maybe I should have taken the risk. Maybe I should have tried to help.* It was so difficult to shake the guilt she was feeling. She had always tried to help others. In fact, she'd gone out of her way many times, but this time, she hadn't. And it was so out of character for her that she felt distanced from herself. It was almost as if she didn't know herself. It was a shame that it was so dark outside as the train made its way through the alps. Bernie knew that view would be spectacular. And she would have loved to share it with Theo. But it was too dark to see anything. And besides, he was still asleep in her arms. Finally, Bernie nodded off. She slept deeply, the sleep of pure exhaustion. And it seemed like she'd only slept for a few moments when she opened her eyes and realized that she had been asleep for hours. The train had stopped. People were leaving. *This is it. This is where we get off.* Bernie realized. She stood up and gathered her things. Then she gently awakened Theo. He smiled at her, and when he smiled, he looked so much like Elica that Bernie almost started to cry. *I have no time to get sentimental right now. I have to be careful. We are not out of danger. I must make sure that Theo and I look as if we are just a mother and son making a casual trip to Italy to see a friend.*

"Papers." A German officer looked Bernie up and down as she got off the train.

She smiled, but she felt her lips trembling.

"Your papers," he said. "I need to see your papers."

Bernie nodded as she put Theo on his feet. "Don't move. Stand right there," she told Theo.

"What a cute little boy. So blonde. So, Aryan. He doesn't look at all like you. Are you his mother?" the German asked.

"Yes," Bernie lied, trying her best to hold her hand steady as she took the falsified papers from her handbag. *Please, God, let him not look at these too closely.* "He looks just like his father, who is in the German army," she managed to say.

The German tapped the table. "Come on. I don't have all day. Papers, right here. Put them right here." His eyes looked at her darkly. There was just a hint of a smile on his face.

He knows. She thought. *He knows the truth.*

CHAPTER NINETEEN

Oliver looked around the room of the cabin. The boys who attended the *Deutsche Jugend* camp had guilty looks on their faces. The girls from the *Bund Deutscher Mädel* who had set up camp only a half mile away were red-faced and embarrassed. They covered their naked breasts as they looked away from Oliver, unable to meet his gaze.

"I'm sorry, Herr Counselor," one of the boys said, "*bitte*, please, don't call my parents. My father will kill me."

"I see." Oliver pretended to be very angry. "All of you have been very bad. You know better than to do this sort of thing. Who invited the girls to come here? Who was it?"

The boys looked down sheepishly, not wanting to tell on each other. But this is an important step. *They must learn that it is their duty to inform the authorities if they see anyone, even a family member, breaking the rules. They were taught that it was their duty to report Jews and even family members to the Gestapo if they discovered any violation of the law. They had spent their entire lives learning this. It is only through strict discipline that we can build the new Germany.*

"Who is responsible?" Oliver repeated. "Either one of you tells me, or I will call all your parents. Which of you boys had the bright idea of bringing these girls here and do the things you've done?"

There was a moment of silence. Then Werner Schmidt blurted out, "It was him. It was Hans Berns. It was his idea. The rest of us just went along."

Then, like a pack of wild dogs, the other boys chimed in, "Yes, it was Hans. He's the one who is responsible."

"No, it wasn't me. We all decided to do it."

"That's not true, Hans. It was you."

"All right. Now, I want the girls to put on their clothes and return to their campsite. The rest of you boys will do one hundred pushups. And Hans, you should pack your things. I am going to call your parents. You are going home tomorrow afternoon."

"No, please, Herr Counselor. Please give me one more chance. Please, I beg you."

"There are no second chances here. You must be disciplined. A good Aryan man has discipline. You don't deserve to be here. You are going home."

Oliver stormed out of the cabin and walked back to his office. He sat down at his desk and lit a cigarette. Hitler firmly told us that we are not to smoke, yet most of us do. He took a long drag, and as the hot smoke filled his lungs, he thought of Anna. His manhood grew hard as he remembered how he'd felt when he kissed her. He was ashamed. *She's a Jew. I should not be having thoughts like his about a Jew. I hope no one ever finds out that I am a hypocrite.*

CHAPTER TWENTY

I t was late afternoon when Anna opened her eyes. The sun was bright and golden. Soon, it would set. She was sitting on her father's lap in the back seat of an automobile that seemed to be traveling quickly. "What happened?" she asked her father in a whisper.

"You fainted."

"Where are we?"

But before her father had a chance to answer, she saw the face of the driver in the rearview mirror. He wore a Nazi uniform, and on the seat beside him was a hat with the death head symbol. Anna had no doubt that he was a Nazi. She stared at the back of his head. And then he turned around, and although it was only a moment. She gasped. *His face was unmistakable. Yet it couldn't be... Could it?*

"Ulf? Am I dreaming?" Anna said. "Ulf, is that you?"

"It's me," he answered.

"You arrested us? What happened?" She paused a moment. The memory of a giant nazi officer came into her vision. "Where is your partner, the other Nazi who was with you when you found us?" Anna asked.

"He's dead," Anna's father said. "This man who you are calling Ulf shot him. What's going on here, Anna?"

Anna turned to her father and said, "I don't know." Then she asked Ulf, "How did you find me?"

"Your friend, Elica," Ulf said. "She told me where to find you. Do you know who I mean?"

"Yes, I know who you mean," Anna said.

"She came to the police station looking for Dagna to help her find her Jewish husband. I remembered Dagna from that day when she told my mother that you were Jewish. That day, my parents fired you and then sent you home."

"I remember," Anna said.

"So, I asked Dagna if she knew where you were, and she told me to ask Elica. I did. I asked her if she had any information about you. At first, she was reluctant to tell me anything. You see, Anna, I have been searching for you since this arrest of Jews began, but I couldn't find you. Then in November, there was this terrible night when many of my friends were secretly sent to the Jewish neighborhood in Berlin. We were sent there to make mischief. But it turned out to be a lot worse than I expected. It was a free for all. Windows were broken, and people were hurt. Some people were killed. I was horrified, but I dared not say anything. If I did, I would be branded as a traitor. A Jew lover. However, I realized how wrong I was about Hitler and the Nazi party that night. I saw terrible, horrible things that are still branded on my mind. You see, when I knew you, I was enthralled with Hitler. I believed that he would bring Germany back to its rightful place in the world. But that was not what I saw that night. What I saw that night was brutal. I was sick of it. In fact, I even took time off from work to recover. But I never told anyone that I was disheartened by Hitler. But as things got worse for the Jews, I knew I had to find you and help you if I could. So, I went to your house in Vienna."

"Our house?" A wave of emotions came over her.

"I traveled there because I had to speak to you, but you and your family were gone. When I knocked on the door, a German family was living there. I tried to speak to your neighbors. I asked everyone I could find if they knew where you had gone. But no one in your neighborhood would give me any information. Perhaps no one knew. So, to try to find you, I took a job working at the police station here in Vienna. I hoped that being in the area where you lived might help me to find you somehow. And I was right. Dagna worked with me. I asked her several times if she knew what had happened to you, but I had to be careful. I couldn't be branded as a traitor, or I would end up in serious trouble. She said she had no idea where you were. And I dared not ask again. However, when her friend Elica came looking for her Jewish husband, I heard Elica and Dagna talking about you. I was elated, but I kept my mouth shut. When I heard Elica tell Dagna that you were in hiding at Bernie's house, I thought I had better make sure that I was the officer who went to arrest you. Even if I had to kill my partner to save you. I did that because I knew that if anyone else had come for you, there was a possibility that you and your family might be killed or sent off to a prison camp."

Anna was trembling. "Oh, Ulf. I am so glad you came for us."

"I was afraid it was just a matter of time before they came for you. And it would have been. It was only a few days later that I happened to see Bernie's address written on a paper that was lying on the desk of my superior. I read it quickly, then stuffed it in my pocket."

Anna could hardly catch her breath.

"I waited for my superior officer to return from his lunch hour. Then I told him that my partner, Helmut, and I would be happy to make the arrest. This was the part I was most worried about. If he had denied us and sent someone else, I knew you would be in terrible danger."

"But he allowed you to do it?"

"Yes. And I was so grateful because if he had sent anyone else, I would have been powerless to help you."

She let out a long-ragged breath.

"Anyway," he went on, "I let Helmut handle things when we were in the attic. You gave me quite a scare when you fainted."

"I didn't even see you. I was so terrified that I was fixated on your partner."

"I know. I wanted it that way. I didn't want you to see me and accidentally say my name. At least not until we got out of that house. But, once Helmut had loaded you and your family into the car, and we were on our way back to the police station, I told my partner, Helmut, that I had to pee. And I couldn't wait until we got back to the station. So, he pulled over in a very rural wooded area. We both got out to stretch our legs. He said he might as well go and pee too, but he would wait until I was done. That way, he could keep an eye on you and your family. So, he stood by the car, watching. I went into the woods. When I came out, he nodded. Then he said he would be right back. As he walked into the woods, I pulled out my gun and shot him in the back. I didn't want to. I didn't hate him. But I didn't care for him either. He had a mean streak, and he hated Jews. I knew he would not understand that I didn't feel the same way he did about Jews. Especially about you, Anna." He was quiet for a minute. Then he continued, "I walked over to him to make sure he was dead. Then I got behind the wheel and turned the car around. I drove the car with you and your family inside as fast as I could. I knew it was best to get as far away from the police station and Helmut's dead body as possible."

"Where are we going?" Anna asked, her voice shaking. She was nervous.

"I don't know, actually. I have never done anything like this before. I think that I will let you and your family out in the forest. Then I will make arrangements to meet with you and your father once a week when I bring food and whatever supplies I can gather."

"And what will you do when the police find out that your partner is dead?"

"I have some ideas that I have been mulling over in my mind about that."

Anna looked at her father. He looked worried, but he didn't say a word. She cleared her throat. "I'm afraid," she said.

"I know. So am I. But what could I do? When I heard about you and your family, I had to do what was right. The way I treated you in Berlin was despicable. I hope you can forgive me."

"I forgive you. Of course, I do," Anna said.

"My brothers never did. They were furious with mother and me for sending you away. They loved you. They said you were the best nanny they ever had."

"I adored them. How are Gynther and Klaus?" she asked in a small voice.

"They're fine."

"I'm glad they're all right," Anna said.

"There's just too much hatred in this world, Anna. I can see where it has taken Germany, and I am not happy about it. Hitler is trying to conquer the world, and he doesn't care who he steps on to do it."

"That's true," she said. "But if my family and I are caught, you will be in trouble, too, won't you?"

"Only if you give my name. And I don't think you would do that to me."

"No, of course not," her father said. "You have put yourself in danger to help us. We appreciate everything you have done."

"It took a lot of thinking things through. But as time passed, I knew that I could not stand by and watch this treatment of the Jewish people. Especially after knowing Anna."

"You must have been afraid," Anselm said.

"Yes, I was. But once I set things into motion, there was no stopping. I had to do it, and well, here I am," Ulf said.

"You were very brave," Anna's father said.

"Was I brave or foolish? It's hard to say. But either way, it doesn't matter. I knew I had to save Anna, and if I had to kill a man to do it, then I would kill him. A man must do what he believes is right for the woman he loves, or he won't be able to live with himself."

"That's not true of all men," Anna's father said. "Only the good ones."

Changing the subject, Ulf said. "I am driving in a crazy roundabout direction. That is because I am trying to avoid as many of the check stations on the way as I can. And that's because I don't know how I would explain all of you. I just hope I wrote down all the locations of the stations correctly."

Anna cleared her throat. "If we must go through a check station, you could tell them that you just arrested us, and we are on our way to a prison."

"I would do that, but they might not believe me, especially if they have already found the body of my coworker. There was no time to hide it."

"So, you just left a dead body there in the woods?"

"Yes, I had to."

"When you return to your post at the police station, you must tell them that your partner was trying to let us escape. You must say that you shot him after he let us go, and he was running away with us. Tell your superiors that you did not want to let us go, but could not catch up with us."

"That's a damn good idea."

"Yes, then you can stay at your job at the police station and help others if you so choose. And if you tell your superiors this story with conviction, you will be above reproach. You will be their hero because you will have killed the Jew lover."

"That's brilliant, Anna," he said.

"Let's just hope it works," she said, sighing.

For a while, they drove, and no one spoke. Every so often, Anna would catch her mother looking at her with questions in her eyes. But she didn't ask Anna anything, and Anna didn't volunteer any answers. As they entered the mountains, a lovely fresh breeze danced through the automobile's open windows. The ground was covered in green. Having not seen the outside world in so long, Anna was bewitched by the beauty around her. Tears of joy welled in her eyes. *Even if we get caught, God forbid, it will have been worth it to be out here and see all of this beauty.*

Night fell, and they still had not reached their destination. Ulf rubbed his eyes, then said, "We will have to stop. I am very tired. I can't keep driving. I need to rest."

Ulf pulled the automobile off the main road and out of sight. Then he turned to Anna's father and said, "I need you to do something."

"What is it?"

"I need you to beat me up. Seriously, beat me up. I need to look like I am in very bad shape."

"I can't do that," her father said.

"You must. It's your turn to save my life. If you don't do this, I can't use Anna's plan and return to my job."

"Why would you want to?"

"Because if I don't, they will hunt me down with dogs, and they will find me, and when they do, they will find Anna too. You must do as I ask."

Ulf got out of the car, followed by Anna and her family.

"I've never been a violent man," Anna's father said.

"Just do it."

Anna's father punched Ulf's arm.

"No, you must hit me in the face where it shows. I need a black eye. A broken nose. Come on. Just do it."

Anna's father struck Ulf as hard as he could in the face. Ulf's lip began bleeding.

"Again," Ulf said. "In the eye this time."

Anna let out a gasp as her father punched Ulf in the eye.

"Again."

And so it went on until Ulf's face was bruised and bleeding.

"Good," Ulf finally said. "I'm ready to return. When they see me, they will believe that I fought with Helmut before he let all of you go."

The sun set slowly as the sky turned shades of orange, pink, and purple. And once the darkness blanketed the mountains, it was cooler than it had been during the day. Ulf lay down on the front seat of the automobile and promptly fell asleep. Anna and her family slept huddled in the back seat, all except for Anna's father, who could not close his eyes for a moment.

The sun had not yet fully risen when Anna's father nudged Ulf to awaken him. "It's still dark, but perhaps you should start driving back to Vienna."

"Yes," Ulf said, forcing himself to awaken. He'd learned to wake up at the crack of dawn when he was still a foot soldier in the army. But that was before his father had paid a substantial amount of money to have him promoted to a less dangerous job.

Anna heard her father talking to Ulf, and she stirred awake. But she kept her eyes closed and pretended to be asleep as she listened.

"Right here is as good a place as any," Ulf said. "We will meet here once a month, you and I? I will bring supplies if I can. If I don't come, it means I am unable to get any food. Or worse, I've been caught. Let's meet on the second Tuesday of each month."

"This is very kind of you," Anna's father said.

"I care deeply for Anna. I will try to come to our meetings. But I can't promise anything. I don't know what will happen to me once I return. But I will be here on the second Tuesday of next month if I am alive and I can get food."

"Maybe it would be better for you if you just stayed here with us," Anna's father said.

"I can't. At least not yet. It might be a mistake to go back, but I feel that I must. If I disappear, they will know that I killed Helmut and let you go. They will hunt me, and they will find me. And not only that, what will they do to my family? To my little brothers. No, it's best if I return. For now, all I can do is wish you luck and pray that you aren't caught."

"Good luck to you too, Ulf, and thank you," Anna's father said.

"I want to say goodbye to Anna."

"Of course."

Ulf walked over to the car. He climbed into the front seat and leaned over to reach out to Anna. Gently, he shook her shoulder. She opened her eyes. "I am leaving," he said softly. "I will be back in a month from now with as many supplies as I can get my hands on." He was whispering because Anna's mother and brother were still asleep in the back seat.

"Let's get out of the car," Ulf said.

Anna nodded, and they both got out and closed the car doors softly to avoid waking the others. Then they stood side by side under a weeping willow tree.

"Thank you for everything. Thank you from the bottom of my heart. This was so brave of you," she said, then she added, "and very risky too."

"Yes, but you see, Anna, when I told you how I felt about you that summer when you were in Berlin, I wasn't lying. I feel so close to you. So, attached. This time that we've been apart, I missed you every day. I tried to go out with other women, but it never felt right. This might sound crazy, but from the first time I saw you, I knew you and I were meant to be together."

"And... then you found out I was Jewish." Anna looked away from him.

"Yes, and I was upset, at least at first. That was because you lied to me. But I was also caught up with Hitler and his idea of making Germany a world power. He hated Jews, and because of that, your being Jewish didn't fit into my dreams for us. Even so, I never thought that Hitler would kill Jewish people. I thought he might not treat them as equals, but kill? I never thought he would do that. And once he did, I no longer felt the same about him. I don't know if this is making sense to you or not."

"It is."

"I wanted to marry you. But how could I? It was against the law.

And besides, I wanted to be a part of the new Germany. I was angry. Then... once you left and went home, I missed you. And then... I joined the army. That's when I saw how Hitler treated his troops and got an idea of what kind of man he really was. I could see he was not helping to make our fatherland a better place. He is an egotistical, power-hungry bastard who is only interested in his own glory. I knew I'd made a mistake. I personally never hated Jews. In fact, you were the first Jewish person I ever knew. And... I loved you. I still do."

"What a mess we're in!" Tears filled her eyes.

"Yes, we are. But... you're here, and you're safe. And as long as I live, I will never let you out of my sight again. You are mine, Anna. And... someday when this is over, Anna, I am going to marry you."

He kissed her. Then he asked her to wake the rest of her family and tell them they must get out of the car because he had to head back to Vienna.

CHAPTER TWENTY-ONE

After Ulf left, Anna's father walked over to her. He could not look directly into her eyes, but he said, "*Nu*, so something happened when you were in Berlin. Something you never told us about."

Anna nodded.

"You love this German?"

"I don't know. I mean, like him," Anna said, clearing her throat. "He thinks he loves me. It's almost scary how much he loves me."

Her father nodded. "Did anything happen between you two? You know what I mean."

"Oh no, papa. Nothing like that."

He nodded. "Good. Well, we are very fortunate that he came to the attic and found us before the Gestapo did."

"You were listening to what he told me?"

"I couldn't help it. I saw him shoot the other Nazi, and I had to know what was going on. Our lives depend on it, Anna."

CHAPTER TWENTY-TWO

Ulf went home and freshened up quickly. He washed his face and hands, combed his hair, and then returned to work at the police station, where he waited outside his superior's office. An hour passed, then another. There was a fan in the building, but it was too far away from the waiting area, and the hot, stifling air made him feel clammy. Finally, his superior officer's secretary told him he could go in.

"Heil Hitler."

"Heil Hitler," his superior said. Then he looked into Ulf's eyes. Ulf felt a chill run down his spine. "What is going on here? You were sent to make an arrest, and then you were to bring the Jews back here. It was a simple mission. But you were gone for two days? Where are the Jews? Where is Helmut?" His face was red, and his fists were clenched. Just looking at him, Ulf felt himself losing his confidence. His superior officer was staring right into his eyes. He dared not look away lest his superior officer detect that he was lying. "You certainly look terrible. Your face is a mess. Black and blue, dried blood. What happened, Wolfgang?"

"The Jews are gone, and Helmut is dead. I trusted Helmut, but he tricked me. I never suspected it, but he was a traitor to our fatherland. He helped the Jews to escape. When I tried to stop him, he beat me up. I had to shoot him."

"Go on. How did it happen?"

"Well, we found the Jews in the attic, just like the girl told us we would. The arrest was easy. But as we were driving back to the station, Helmut said he had to urinate and couldn't wait until we returned. We passed the forest, and he insisted that we stop so he could relieve himself. He got out of the car and headed behind a tree. When he returned, his gun was pointed at me. He told me not to move as he let the Jews out of the back seat. Then he told them to run. I asked him why he was letting them go. He said it was not my business. I told him it certainly was, and that was when he smashed his fist into my face. Helmut said that the Jews paid him and planned to do this again the next time we made an arrest. He said that either I was with him or against him. I told him that he was making a mistake. He hit me hard with his pistol, and I fell down. I was losing consciousness as I watched him walk in the same direction as the Jews he'd allowed to escape. I pulled my gun and shot him in the back. Then I passed out. The next thing I knew, I woke up in the forest with Helmut's dead body. I got in the car and drove home, where I cleaned up as much as I could. Then I came in to work to tell you what happened."

"Are you all right?"

"I'll be fine. I just need some rest. But Helmut's dead, and the family of Jews is gone."

"Which way did they go?"

"Towards Switzerland, I think," Ulf lied. He'd left Anna and her family close to the border between Vienna and Slovakia. Now he was sending the Germans in the opposite direction.

"We'll send out a search party with the dogs. We'll find them. Meanwhile, why don't you go home? Take the day off. Get some rest. I'm very surprised at Helmut. I never suspected that of him."

"Yes, sir. So am I. I would never have expected it of him either."

CHAPTER TWENTY-THREE

Helmut's body was found, and Ulf received a promotion that put him in charge of a small group of people who worked at the police station. Although Dagna was not under his charge, he saw her each day. She worked in a small, unimportant clerical position. But she smiled at him whenever he passed and always said hello. She made him uneasy. But he wondered if that was because she was watching him, and he thought she somehow suspected him or if it was all just his imagination.

When the month passed and the time arrived for Ulf to bring supplies to Anna and her family, he felt nervous and uncomfortable. He was proud of himself because he managed to help them escape. Ulf loved the idea of being a hero, a rebel who was strong enough to go against Hitler and his forces. But those were romantic ideas he liked to entertain in his mind. The reality was much more dangerous, and he knew that if he were caught, he would most certainly face death. When he left work that afternoon, he told Pippi, his secretary, that he would not be in the following day. "I must go to Berlin to see my stepmother. She's ill," he said.

She nodded. "Don't worry about anything. I'll take care of everything."

Ulf knew that Pippi had a crush on him, and he was flattered. She was a pretty young girl with silky blonde braids. *Any other man would be interested*. He thought. But he was attracted to the forbidden.

Ulf went home and waited until evening to leave his apartment. As he drove towards the place where he'd arranged to meet Anna and her family, he constantly watched in the rear-view mirror to see if he was being followed. But he saw no evidence of it.

Over the past month, Ulf had purchased extra potatoes, cabbages, and preserves. Things he knew wouldn't go bad quickly. As well as a few blankets, which he knew Anna and her family would need once the winter set in.

CHAPTER TWENTY-FOUR

U lf arrived in the forest after a long drive. He hadn't slept all night because he had left right after work the day before. When Anna saw him, she ran to him, threw her arms around his neck, and hugged him, but before he could kiss her, her father walked over to them.

"It's good to see you. Thank you for coming," Anna's father said.

"I brought food and blankets."

"Good, good, thank you."

Anna's father helped Ulf unload the car. Then Ulf asked Anna to take a walk with him. She agreed.

"Don't go far," her father said. "There are wild animals in the woods."

"Yes, father," Anna said.

They walked in silence for a few moments. Then Anna said, "Thank you for bringing us all those things."

"You're welcome." He smiled.

"I mean it. Thank you." She smiled.

He leaned down and kissed her. She melted into his arms. But then he lowered her to the ground and began to lift her skirt. His breathing was rapid. *I've been waiting for this.* He thought as he reached up under her dress.

"Don't please, don't," she said, pushing him away and standing up quickly.

"What's the matter with you?" He could hear the frustration in his own voice, but he couldn't control it. He was angry. *I drove all night. I purchased all that stuff to bring to her family. And now this Jew bitch pushes me away?* Suddenly he realized that when he was angry at her, he thought of her as nothing but a Jew, a woman who was beneath him. A woman who should bow to his every wish. *I am an Aryan. I have the power to do anything I please with her. Who the hell does she think she is?*

"I'm sorry, Ulf. I'm just not ready for that. Please understand."

He stood up and shook off his uniform. He wanted to slap her across her pretty little face. But he didn't. He just stood there looking at her, his anger and frustration building. Then he turned and walked to his car and drove away.

CHAPTER TWENTY-FIVE

Bernie tried to look casual as the German at the desk glanced down at the papers she'd handed him. He seemed to be taking a long time. And she felt the sweat beading up on her brow. But then, like a miracle, Theo began to scream. "Pee pee," he said.

The guard stared at the child, whose annoying high-pitched voice made the hair on his neck stand up. "Shut him up."

"I would, officer, but I can't. He's only two years old, and I am working on toilet training him. If I don't get him to a toilet soon, he will urinate all over himself and the floor right here, too."

"He doesn't wear a diaper?"

"I just took away his diapers. I must get him to a toilet."

"Yes, of course," the young officer said. He was no longer interested in Bernie's papers. He just wanted her and her child to go away before there was a mess on the ground. "Here." He handed Bernie the papers. "Take him away."

Bernie grabbed the papers and stuffed them into her bag. Then she lifted Theo and began to walk away quickly.

"Pee pee," Theo screamed.

"All right. All right. We'll get you to a toilet."

After they found a bathroom and Theo was taken care of. Bernie sat down and took a long, deep breath. Then she gave Theo a hug. "You don't know it, but you were a hero today. That was the first time I was actually glad that you had a little tantrum," she said, smiling.

"I went pee pee in the toilet," he said, smiling, proud of himself. "Pee pee in the toilet!"

"You certainly did." *And you let out a blood-curdling scream at just the right moment.* She thought. "All right, now we must catch a bus that will take us into the mountains. I am not sure where we are going or exactly how to get there. But I have an address, and I guess we'll just have to figure it out together."

CHAPTER TWENTY-SIX

The bus driver told Bernie which way to walk when he let her and Theo off three miles away from the orphanage. It was a hot, dusty afternoon, and it was getting late. Theo could not walk down the stairs to get off the bus. He stood at the top and tried to make his short leg reach the first step. He tried several times. The bus driver didn't seem to mind. But Bernie wanted to arrive at their destination before dark, so she lifted Theo and carried him down the three stairs of the bus. Then she put him down on the ground and reached up to get their suitcase. The heat made Theo irritable. "Come on, little man. You are going to have to help me. This is no time to get fussy. I need you to walk for as long as you can," Bernie whispered to the child, knowing he did not understand what she was saying.

The ground was filled with stones, and there were deep drops in the mountains. She held tight to Theo's hand but was almost relieved when he began to cry and demand to be carried. Yes, it would be more difficult to carry him and their suitcase, but at least she wouldn't be worried about him falling into one of the deep gorges in the mountains. Bernie had always been strong, and right now, she thanked God for the strength of her body. She could never do this if she was not physically fit. The sun burned through her shirt and penetrated into the tender skin of her back. Bernie carried Theo in one arm and their suitcase in the other. And she walked until she was so hot and out of breath that she had to stop for a moment.

"Eat," Theo said. "Hungry. Eat."

"Yes," she said, but she knew she could not take the time to eat or drink. Bernie had to get to their destination before dark. This terrain was dangerous during the day, but it would be treacherous by night. She stopped for a moment and reached into her handbag. She pulled out half of a cheese sandwich and a container of water. Quickly, she put Theo down on his feet and held the precious water while he drank. Then she put the sandwich in his hand.

"Don't drop this. I don't have another one," she told him. Then, picking him back up, she continued on her way. Telling a two-year-old not to drop something was a waste of time, and within a few minutes, he dropped the sandwich. Bernie lost patience. "I told you to hold on to that," she yelled at him. Theo began to cry, and the magnitude of all she was facing suddenly struck Bernie hard like a kick in the stomach. She could not go on. She plopped down on the ground and began to weep. Seeing her weep frightened Theo, and he stopped crying. He reached over and touched her face.

"No, cry," he said.

She gave him a little squeeze, then she managed a smile. "We're going to be all right," she said, picking up the sandwich and shaking the sand off it. Then she took a bite. Theo reached for the sandwich, and she gave him a bite. "I don't suppose a little sand will kill us," she said, smiling and wiping her tears on the sleeve of her blouse. She took a swig of water and gave Theo another one. Then she stood up. She stretched her limbs and tried to stretch her back. Bernie lifted the little boy into her arms, grabbed the suitcase, and said. "It won't be much longer."

The sun was beginning to set when she saw the orphanage in the distance. Although Bernie was exhausted, she ran. Dropping the suitcase once and having to stop and pick it up.

She knocked on the heavy wooden door and waited. A nun in full black habit answered, "yes, may I help you, young lady?"

"I am a friend of Viola Parisi. I need to see her, please."

The nun assessed the situation. She looked at Bernie, her shirt stained with sweat, and the child with his dirty face and hands, and assumed that Bernie was a young mother in need of help. "Come in," the nun said.

Bernie entered a large room. She put Theo down on his feet but held on to his hand so he could not walk around and explore the area.

"Wait here. I'll get her for you."

"Thank you, sister."

Theo pulled his hand away and sat down on the cool floor. Bernie didn't tell him to stand up. In fact, she wished she were only two years old and that it would be appropriate for her to sit on the floor too.

A few minutes later, Viola walked into the room. When she saw Bernie, her face lit up. Bernie felt her heart flutter. They embraced. "Bernie!" Viola said.

"Yes, it's me!"

The nun nodded. Then she left the room.

"Yours?" Viola glanced down at Theo. She looked a little surprised at seeing a child with Bernie.

"No, of course not. This is Theo. He's the son of a good friend of mine. Can we go somewhere that we can talk? I'll tell you everything."

"Yes, of course."

Viola led Bernie to her room. It was small, clean, and sparsely furnished. Bernie sat down on a chair in the corner. Theo sat on the floor, and Viola sat on her bed. "You look exhausted," Viola said.

"I am. Have you ever carried a toddler for three miles in the mountains in the heat?"

"I can't say that I have," Viola said. "Let me get you some water, and I'll see what I can do about getting some food, too. You both must be famished. Stay here. I'll be right back."

"Thank you," Bernie said.

"No need to thank me. I am so glad to see you," Viola said as she walked out of the room.

Viola was gone for fifteen minutes, but when she returned, she had bread and water, which she gave Bernie. Theo reached for the bread. "Easy little man," Bernie said. "I know you're hungry, but eat slowly."

Theo didn't listen. He gobbled up some of the bread and drank the water so quickly that he choked. Bernie picked him up, and he began coughing.

"Is he alright?" Viola asked.

"He's fine," Bernie said. Then she looked into Theo's eyes and said, "Now, will you please listen to me?" Then she thought about how much Theo had been through and how small and helpless he was. She took his small chubby hand in hers and gently massaged it. "Now, please, Theo, I know you're very hungry, but eat slowly."

The little boy nodded, and this time he did as he was told. Between the food filling his belly and the events of the long day, when he was done eating, he lay on his side and fell asleep. Bernie and Viola could hear his breathing grow calm.

"I can't believe you're really here." Viola's eyes were shining. "I hoped and prayed that you would return. But the truth is, I didn't know if we would ever see each other again with the war and all. I know we were always making plans, but they didn't really seem possible. As time passed, it seemed to me that you were becoming more of a dream than a reality. But every morning, I ran to see if I received a letter from you." She let out a soft laugh. "Oh Bernie, I was always waiting for your letters. You can't imagine what they meant to me. But now, here I am, standing right next to you. You're really here. And I'm so happy you came."

"Viola. I am happy too. I—" Bernie hesitated for a minute. Then she said, "I waited for your letters too. They have been my lifeline. Things are bad in Austria. My Jewish friend and her family are in trouble. I am helping them, and every day is a risk."

"Helping them?"

"Can I speak candidly? Are we safe?"

"Yes. No one can hear us."

"Yes, I am hiding them in the attic in my home."

"Dear God, Bernie. Are you mad?"

"Probably. But I can't help it. I couldn't let the Nazis take my friend and her family away. Jews are disappearing left and right. No one knows where they are going. But they never come back."

"Oh, Bernie," Viola said. She put her arms around Bernie and hugged her. "I'm so glad you're here and you're safe. You are staying, aren't you?"

"I can't. Anna and her family are still in the attic of my home. If I don't return, I can't be sure that my mother will bring them food and water. They are dependent on me. Without my help, they will die."

Viola put her face in her hands and took a long, deep breath. When she moved her hands, her cheeks were wet with tears.

"Please, don't cry. You don't know how good it feels to see you again." Bernie reached out and took Viola's hand in hers. "My friend," she said then in a voice that was barely a whisper. Then she blushed with embarrassment, but she added, "My love."

"My love," Viola answered in a soft voice. "Please tell me what's going on with this little boy. Who is this child? And how can I help you?"

Bernie sucked in a deep breath. Then she sighed. "Do you remember me telling you about my blood sisters? The girls who were my childhood friends?"

"Of course. You said you had two close friends and a third who you didn't care for. You told me how you were good friends, and when you were eight or so, you made a pact whereby you cut your-selves and mixed your blood. Right?"

"Yes, you do remember."

"Of course. I remember everything you ever told me, Bernie. Now, please, you're being evasive. Tell me what's going on."

"Elica is one of my blood sisters. She is the baby's mother. But it's not that simple. The baby's father is Jewish," she whispered. "Before Hitler invaded Austria, Elica fell in love with a Jewish man. She got pregnant. They broke up for a while. But after Theo was born, he went to see her, and they decided to get married. The marriage of a Jewish person to a non-Jewish person is forbidden under German law. The Germans have gone mad with their hatred of the Jews. They have begun arresting Jewish people for no other reason than that they are Jews. That's why Anna and her family are hiding in my attic, and I have brought Theo here to you. He is half Jewish, and that makes it unsafe for him to be in Austria."

"Have both of his parents been arrested?"

"I am pretty certain that they have. His father was arrested. Then Elica went to the police station to find out what had happened to her husband. That was when she left Theo with me. I waited, but she didn't come back. I didn't want to take the chance that the Germans would come looking for Theo, so I brought him here. When... if... Elica returns; she will come to this orphanage to get her son."

"Oh my," Viola said.

"Yes, I brought him here to the orphanage, hoping you could take him in. Hide him; keep him safe, at least for now. He's a good boy, Viola. A little spirited and demanding, but he's just a child."

Viola nodded. "I understand. I will speak to the Mother Superior. I'll tell her everything. I don't know what she will say. I mean, after all, taking a child in that is half Jewish could put all the children at risk," Viola said.

"I know. But tell her to please consider it. He is so small and so alone in the world."

"I will. She is very kind. I'll see what she says. How long are you staying here in Italy?"

"Just until I am sure Theo is safe with you. If not, until I can find him another place to say."

"I had no idea about your friend in the attic or this child. You never mentioned any of this in your letters," Viola said.

"How could I? How could I trust that no one would censor them?"

"You couldn't, I suppose," Viola sighed. "Oh, how I wish you were staying here with me forever. I've missed you. I've missed our special bond."

Bernie's face turned red. "Me too. But I will be back. I can promise you that. As soon as this terrible war is over, I will come back."

"I have decided that I cannot be a nun. I know that what we have between us would be considered unnatural by the church. A sin." Viola looked down at her shoes. Then she raised her head, and her eyes were shining. She looked directly at Bernie. "But what we feel for each other is not something dirty or unnatural. It's love, and I believe that love comes from God. Even our kind of love. You and I are different from most people in the world. But we have found each other and, well... I want to be with you."

"I want that more than anything. Before I met you, I thought I was destined to live a lonely life. I never thought there would be anyone in this world for me. I knew that I would never marry and have children like other women. Oh, I tried. I went out with boys. I wanted to be like everyone else. But I couldn't do it," Bernie said.

"Neither could I. I tried too. I thought my attraction to other women was a curse, and I couldn't understand why I had been cursed with it. But then you came into my life, and I knew what real love felt like. And now... well... you are a blessing to me. It is so much more than a physical attraction."

"Yes, I would agree. Our physical attraction is not as important as our emotional one," Bernie said, wiping the tears from Viola's cheek.

"Stay here and wait for me. I am going to go and talk to the Mother Superior about Theo staying with us. I have to tell her the truth about everything."

"I wouldn't expect you to do anything else," Bernie said. "I'll wait here for her decision."

"I'll be back as soon as I can." Viola walked out of the room.

CHAPTER TWENTY-SEVEN

The promotion gave Ulf more power. He found that he enjoyed the way it made him feel. But because his job had become more important, it was also more difficult to get the time off from work that he needed to go and see Anna. He made outrageous excuses and began to worry that his boss might catch on. Besides that, the drive was long and tedious. And he had to be careful when he stored and hid the food he would bring. However, the worst part of all of it was that his visits with Anna were less than satisfying because her parents and brother were always there. He could not try to bed her while they were only a few feet away. But the more he was unable to satisfy his desire for her, the more intense it became. She was warm and appreciative, but he didn't think she was grateful enough. She had rejected his advances the last time they were together, but he had invested too much time and effort to give up now. *I will have her one way or another.*

CHAPTER TWENTY-EIGHT

Anna saw Ulf's face as he drove up to the clearing. His face lit up when he saw Anna and her father hiding in the trees. He parked his automobile between two trees and got out. Still wearing his uniform, he walked over to Anna.

"How are you doing?" he asked her seriously.

"All right," she said. "It's been a little difficult learning to live outside, but we are grateful to be alive. Thank you for all you have done for us, Ulf."

He nodded. Then he went back to the automobile and took the supplies out of the back seat. He handed them to Anna's father. "I've brought some food, water, and more blankets," Ulf said.

"We have been trying to find a stream. We need to have a source of water," Herr Levinstein said.

"Have you seen anyone? Does anyone know you're here?"

"No. We've been careful and lucky."

"That's good. I brought food, as much as I could get."

"I am so grateful to you. My family is too."

"Shall we take a walk?" he asked. "I brought you a special

present." He was still frustrated but found a way to hide his feelings. His voice was sweet and inviting.

They walked for a few moments without speaking. Then, when they were far enough away from her family, Ulf took a small box out of his pocket. He handed the box to Anna. "This is for you," he said

"Oh, Ulf." She took the box and sat down on a tree stump. He sat across from her.

"Open it."

She looked up at him and smiled. Then she opened the box and saw a pearl necklace. "It's beautiful," she said.

He smiled. "I'm glad you like it," he said warmly. *If she knew that I got that necklace from one of my friends who took it from a Jew that was shot at one of the ravines, she would be appalled.*

He leaned over and kissed her softly.

"Ulf, I must ask you..." Anna said, closing her eyes tightly. Then looked directly at him. "Do you know what happened to the people who owned the house where we were hiding? I am worried about my friend Bernie. Was she arrested?"

"The Gestapo raided the house. Your friend wasn't there. Only an older woman. I am assuming it was her mother," Ulf said.

"Was her mother arrested?"

"Yes."

"Oh," Anna said, her hands flying up to cover her mouth.

"Apparently, her daughter, your friend Bernie, was out of town."

"I hope she finds out what happened and stays far away from home."

"Do you know when she plans to return?"

"I don't know."

"I'll see if the Gestapo have any information about her. But I doubt it. If they did, they would have already arrested her."

"You're in the Gestapo?" Anna asked, her eyes wide with disbelief.

He nodded ruefully. "I am." Then he added, "Don't think I feel good about it. But, yes, I am."

"So, you have been arresting Jews?" she asked.

"Anna, why are you asking so many questions?" Ulf smashed his fist down on a tree stump. It began to bleed, but he ignored the blood. When he looked at her, his face appeared to be completely changed. His face was flushed, his brow was knitted, and his eyes were narrow and angry.

"I'm sorry to pry. But I don't understand. I just can't imagine you doing these things."

"The world has grown ugly. We are caught in the middle of it. I want to run away, but how can I? If I run, you and your family will starve, won't you? Or is your father an expert hunter or fisherman?" he asked sarcastically, spitting the words out like a snake hissing.

"Must you be mean to me? I was only asking."

He looked away. His shoulders dropped. He hung his head and put his hands on his temples. "I'm sorry. I suppose I have become mean. I've been forced to do ugly things to stay alive. Every day, I must prove my loyalty to the Reich. If they should ever suspect that I am their enemy, they would torture and kill me. Make no mistake of this. It's true."

"But why would they test your loyalty? Have you ever given them a reason?"

"Never. But they trust no one. They check everyone's family tree to make sure that there is no Jewish blood and no gypsies. And God helps anyone who has someone disabled, mentally or physically, in their background. Bloodlines are very important to the Nazis."

"How do they test you? Do they ask you questions?"

"Please, Anna." Again, his face grew tight and red. Then, in a deep warning tone, he said, "Don't ask me what they make me do to prove my loyalty. Don't ever ask me. That makes me go insane with rage."

"Oh, but you do have courage. If you didn't, you wouldn't have come for me. You wouldn't have shot your partner. All of that took great courage." There was a long silence. Then, in a soft voice, Anna croaked out, "Thank you for the food. Thank you for the beautiful necklace." Anna looked away. She was shaking. She knew better than to ask for details of what he'd done that he was so ashamed of. He looked like a madman, and she was afraid of him. If she pushed this any further, he might shake her, hit her, or even kill her. His eyes told her that he was out of control.

A warm wind rustled the leaves and brushed softly through Anna's loose dark hair. A flock of birds chirped in the distance. The sun was hot on their shoulders. Neither Anna nor Ulf spoke for several minutes. Then Ulf said, "I brought as much food and water as I could get my hands on."

She looked into his eyes. She was glad he hadn't told her the things he'd done. However, she knew he would eventually, and she was afraid that she would look at him differently once he did. But now, as he gazed at her, she could see his eyes were soft, and he seemed to be almost pleading for forgiveness. "Thank you for every-thing," she said softly, and she meant it. She was grateful to him for everything he'd done for her and her family. But she could not look past his uniform and the memories she had of the things he'd said when he found out that she was Jewish.

"Anna..." he said.

"Yes?"

"I... I..." He took her into his arms and kissed her. Anna felt sick to her stomach. He kissed her again, more passionately this time, and pulled her to him. His hand caressed her breast. She felt the bile rise in her throat. *Has he killed women? Children? He's a murderer?*

If she didn't push him away from her, if he kissed her again, she was certain she would vomit. His breath was hot on her neck. She could smell the faint odor of sauerkraut. "Ulf," she said, finally pushing him away.

"What?" he asked. "What did I do wrong? What did I fail to give you? Why do you humiliate me?"

She shook her head, unable to speak.

"What is it? Do you want to know what I did? Is that it? Do you want to know? Well, if you do, then I'll tell you."

"No, please," she said. "It's all right. You don't need to tell me anything more."

"I killed Jews. Hundreds. I shot them. Threw their bodies into a mass grave," he snorted. "Now you know. Are you satisfied? This is what is expected of me. I was only following orders."

Anna was shaking.

"I'm sure that you remember that summer when we first met. And I am sure you remember me saying all those terrible things about Jews. But I don't really hate Jews. I don't care about them one way or another. But I have orders, Anna. I must do what is asked of me. You have to understand this. It has nothing to do with us. Nothing to do with how I feel about you."

Anna was trembling. *What has he done?*

"After all, I mean, why would I hate them? I hardly knew any Jews except you and a few I'd met at the University."

He's insane. Anna thought. But then she couldn't help herself. She lost control of her voice and blurted out, "But you murdered Jewish people. You did. You are a murderer." She began to cry.

His face turned scarlet. His features seemed to change right before her eyes. His eyes narrowed and turned cold. A deep furrow appeared between them. "How dare you judge me? You are nothing but a Jew. You are powerless against me. Do you know this? Do you realize what you are doing?" he growled.

She suddenly remembered who he was and the power he held over her. Fear crept into her heart. "I'm sorry, Ulf," she said.

"You had no right," he said. Then he stood up and began pacing. "No right. I did what I had to do. Yes, that's right. I did what I had to do. What was expected of me? Sometimes, when I try to sleep, I close my eyes, and I see piles of dead bodies lying in a ravine. Piles of them, I tell you. Women, children... babies. Shot dead. Dead. Some we buried alive. I do what must be done. You understand, don't you?" He was raging. His face was red. His fists were clenched. And she was frightened.

"Please, forget that I brought this up. I will never bring it up again."

"See to it that you don't. See to it that you never ask me anything, or I swear I will kill all of you. I can do that, you know. No one would care," he said. "I rescued you, and now I have the power to choose to let you live or to kill you. There would be no consequences. None at all."

Anna felt the sweat beading under her arms and on her face. Looking at him, she could see that he was visibly shaking. *How do I calm him down? What do I do? He looks like he's losing his mind. Whatever he did, it damaged him, and now he's unstable.*

They walked to his car.

"Don't hate me, Anna. I did what I had to do," Ulf said. He grabbed her and held her in his arms. "Forgive me," he said, holding her tightly. He was weeping. She had to get out of his grasp. She pushed away from him, but he hugged her tightly. Finally, she pushed hard enough to make him release her. He glared at her as he got into his car and turned it on. But he didn't pull away. He stared straight at her. Then he drew his gun and held it pointed at her. She gasped. He began to laugh.

Anna wanted to run, but she couldn't. She felt like she was glued to the ground. Her heart began to race as she looked into his eyes. But then he dropped his gaze and the gun. He put his head in his hands and looked like he was weeping. He glanced up at her one more time. Then he drove away.

Anna was trembling all over. Despite the warm weather, she felt chilled. She stood up and vomited.

"What happened?" her father asked as he walked over to her. "You threw up? He left? What happened?"

"Yes, he left. And I threw up because I was terrified of him. He pointed his gun at me. I am so afraid of him. Terrified of him. I've made him angry. Very angry. I don't think he feels the same way about me, and I am afraid of what he might do."

"Oh, Anna, this is so much more than a teenage puppy love argument. This young man holds our lives in his hands. You must never make him angry." He cleared his throat, took her into his arms, and held her. "*Shhaaa*," her father said, but Anna was weeping.

"Papa, he pointed his gun at me before he drove away. I think he has been involved in the murder of many Jews. Oh, papa, I am afraid of him. He seems confused and on the precipice of going insane."

Her father held her for a few minutes until she quieted down. "Perhaps we should take the food he gave us and leave this area. Quickly. He could change his mind about helping us and come back and shoot us. I think we should go right now while we still can. What do you think, Anna? Do you think we can still trust him? I mean, the food he's brought will really help us. But then again..."

She shrugged her shoulders. "I don't know," she said. "I didn't mean to make him so angry. Oh, papa, I am scared."

He nodded. "Yes, so am I." Then he said, "We can't risk it. We have to go. We'll find food somehow. But we can't trust him now."

"But you're right. We can barely survive without the food he brings," Anna was crying softly. "And this is all my fault."

"Stop blaming yourself and the self-pity. I overheard you two talking," Anna's mother said as she walked over to them. "None of that matters now. What's done is done, and whatever happened between you and that Nazi *sheigetz* is water under the bridge. It was nice to have his help, but if we don't have it anymore, then we don't. That's all there is to it. We must protect ourselves. We can't trust him after he went crazy and pointed his gun at Anna. We can't trust anyone. I say we take the food and blankets he brought and get out of here. The best thing for us to do is just to keep moving. If we stay here, we are easy for him to find. And if he's angry at Anna, who knows what he'll do?"

"Nu? You're right," Anna's father said.

"But Anselm? It will be hard on him to walk through the mountains," Anna said.

Poor Anselm had almost died when he was born. He had always been sickly. His parents had named him Anselm, which means *old* in

Yiddish. They gave him this name out of superstition. It was meant to confuse the angel of death. The superstition went that when the parents of a sickly child named that child Anselm the angel of death, would think the child was not a young person at all, but someone old. And since the angel of death preferred to take a youngster, he would lose interest in the child with the name Anselm and search for someone younger and healthier to take.

Anna thought it was a silly superstition; she knew it was nothing more than a *bubbe-meise*, an old wife's tale, and yet, it gave her parents comfort. And she knew how much they needed something to grasp onto through Anselm's continuous battles with the disease in his blood that everyone knew would eventually overtake him.

"I know it will be hard on him, the poor soul. But it doesn't matter, Anna. We must do it. If we stay here, we are putting our trust in that Nazi. And after the two of you just had a fight, and he pulled his gun, well, anything could happen. If he is angry at you, he might regret rescuing us and decide to turn us in or shoot us. We are completely at his mercy. It was kind of him to help us, but now who knows what he'll do? I say we must go. And we must go right now," her mother said in her firm, matter-of-fact tone.

"Yes, you're probably right," Anna said. "But he did risk so much to help me, to help us. He even shot that other Nazi."

"Yes, and that was wonderful of him. But we just can't rely on him. Anna, what if he has changed his mind? What if he can't live with the guilt of having murdered that other man? What then? We just can't take that kind of risk."

"But we don't even know where we are," Anna said.

"It doesn't matter. He knows he can find us here."

"You're right, Lilian," Anna's father said. "Let's go."

Anna and her mother packed up the food and blankets, and the family began to walk. Anna and her father led the way. Anselm and her mother walked slower.

CHAPTER TWENTY-NINE

Viola returned to her room, where Bernie waited nervously. "The mother superior said that the child can stay here," Viola said. "He will blend in with the other orphans. He'll be safe here."

"Good. That's good news. Thank you," Bernie said.

"I wish you didn't have to return to Austria."

"I know. But like I told you, Anna and her family are dependent on me. So, I must go back."

"Do you think you will ever come back here to Italy?"

"You know I will. I promised you I would, and I will," Bernie said. "If I am alive, I will return."

"I will be here to help take care of him as a teacher, but not a nun," Viola said.

"That's because of me. I feel bad," Bernie said.

"It's because of us. It's what I have chosen. So please don't feel bad. Of course, no one knows about us, and I can never tell anyone. I realize that if we ever get together, we will face a lot of challenges in our lives. We must always live in secret. People don't understand our love, so they don't approve of it. If they find out, they will make things difficult."

"Are you sorry that we found each other?"

"Never. I am never sorry. And no matter what we face, I will never regret loving you."

CHAPTER THIRTY

Theo was introduced to the other children while Bernie and Viola stood by and watched. At first, he was nervous and kept looking back to make sure Bernie was still there. But an older girl of about seven or eight years came over and began to mother him. Theo took to her right away, and within a half hour, they were playing. But that night, when it was time to go to bed, Theo began to cry for his mother. He was placed in a small bed in a large room filled with other boys. Bernie stayed with him until he fell asleep. Then she went back to Viola's room.

"Theo cried a lot," she said. "I felt so guilty leaving him there. But what can I do?"

"You're doing the best thing for everyone involved," Viola said. "You have no choice but to leave him here. I'll go and see him as often as I can. He'll be all right. He'll adjust. And hopefully, his mother will be able to come and get him soon."

"Yes, I hope she's all right."

Bernie spent the night with Viola, and she would love to stay in Italy forever. But she knew she couldn't depend on her mother to provide for Anna's family. And although her mother had received a nice sum of money from Anna's father, Bernie knew if she were not there, her mother would never share her rations or do errands for the underground to have a little extra food to give the Levinsteins like Bernie did.

The following morning, when Bernie awoke, Viola was already awake. She turned over and looked at Viola. "I must leave today."

"At least have some breakfast," Viola said.

"Yes, I will," Bernie said.

They went downstairs to the kitchen, where they ate dry toast and sipped on weak ersatz coffee.

"Can't you spend at least one more day?"

"I'm sorry. I wish I could, but I've already been gone too long. I can't trust my mother to take care of the Jewish family I am hiding."

"You're the one who should have been a nun," Viola said with a touch of sarcasm.

"Are you angry with me?"

"No," Viola smiled. "I would expect nothing less from you."

"I went down to check on Theo before you got up," Viola said.

"How is he doing?"

"He's fine. He was playing with that little girl he made friends with yesterday. He hardly noticed me when I came in."

"I'm glad he has a friend."

"Yes, me too. The Mother Superior says we should rename him. She thinks we should give him an Italian name, so he doesn't stand out so much."

"Yes, it's probably a good idea," Bernie said.

"I mean, with that blonde hair and blue eyes, he does stand out."

"I know. He looks just like his mother. I've known her since I was a child," Bernie said.

"Was she the girl you told me about when we first met, the one you had a crush on?"

"Actually, yes, she was."

"Do you still have a crush on her?"

"No, I don't feel that way about her anymore. But I'll always care

121

about her. She is an old and very dear friend. And, since she left her child with me, I feel responsible for him. Do you promise to watch him and take care of him until I can come back or send Elica to get him?"

"You know I will." Then Viola handed Bernie a small bag. "I packed you some food for the trip. It's not much, but I know you'll be hungry, and it was all I could get."

"Thank you. I know I will be hungry too," Bernie said, taking the bag. Then she planted a soft, innocent kiss on Viola's cheek. "And Viola, thank you for making me happy," Bernie said as she lifted her suitcase and made her way to the door. Before she walked out, she stood at the door for a moment. There were tears in her eyes as she turned and looked into Viola's eyes. Then she smiled and waved. Viola waved back. "I'll see you soon," Bernie said.

Viola nodded. "Yes, very soon, I hope."

"Me too."

CHAPTER THIRTY-ONE

Bernie walked to the train feeling sad and unsettled. She wished she were the type of person who could put her own needs first. If only she could put Anna and her family out of her mind, or Elica and her problems, too. *If I could just think of my own happiness, I would turn around and stay here. But I can't. I have never been one to put myself before the people I care about. So, I must return and help those I love. But I am so sad. It feels like it might be years before I can get back here. And that is devastating to me. I want to turn and run back to the church, to Viola. Yet, my feet still go forward. One step in front of the previous one. And soon, I'll be home in Vienna and far away from the person who makes me the happiest. I am a fool. But this is who I am.*

Bernie ate the food Viola packed for her, then she fell asleep on the train.

The following morning, Bernie arrived in Austria. She walked slowly through town, towards her home, stopping at the local bakery to purchase a roll to eat. She had known the Hofbauers, who owned the bakery, her entire life. In fact, she'd helped Frau Hofbauer many times by watching her three young grandchildren. And when

Herr Hofbauer was ill, she brought food to their home to make things easier for Frau Hofbauer.

"Good afternoon Frau Hofbauer," Bernie said, smiling when she walked into the bakery. It was a little after twelve. The morning crowd had cleared out. The *hausfraus* had come and gone, and the working people were at their respective jobs. The bakery was now empty. The shelves were almost empty, too.

"Bernie, how are you?" Frau Hofbauer tried to sound casual, but Bernie could see in her eyes that something was wrong. Frau Hofbauer was nervous. "What can I get for you?"

"Just a roll. I've been traveling all night. I just got off the train. I'm on my way home."

The chubby woman put two rolls in a bag and handed it to Bernie. "I gave you an extra one just in case you were hungry. A little gift from me."

"Thank you, Frau Hofbauer. That was very kind of you," Bernie said, then she paid her and turned to leave. Frau Hofbauer cleared her throat. For a moment, she seemed to be tongue-tied. Then she said, "Bernie, before you leave, come here. Come close."

Bernie walked up to the counter again. Frau Hofbauer put some cookies into a bag. "Just in case anyone is watching us from outside, take this." She handed the bag to Bernie. Then she said, "Get out of town. Hurry up and get out of here. The Gestapo went to your house. They are looking for you. They've arrested your mother, and also, they arrested a family of Jews who she was hiding in your attic. They are searching for you. One of them came into the bakery a few days ago asking questions. They wanted to know if I knew you and if I had any idea where you were. Get out of Vienna right away. I am taking a risk telling you this, but you have always been such a good girl. Such a kind girl. I have to help you if I can. Go now, go right back to the train station. Get the first ticket you can. Go wherever it takes you. Just get out of here. Hurry." Then the old woman thought for a moment. She opened the box where she kept her money. "Here, take this too. She stuffed a bunch of crumbled Reichsmarks into Bernie's hand. Maybe you'll need it. Now go."

Bernie looked at Frau Hofbauer with surprise. She hadn't been expecting this. She stood frozen, unable to move for a moment. Then Frau Hofbauer said, "Please go, Bernie. Please, I am an old woman. My husband is old and sick. We don't want no trouble."

Bernie was brought back to reality by that statement. She nodded at Frau Hofbauer. "Thank you," she said, still holding the bills.

"Go."

Bernie left the bakery and began to head towards the train station. She was trembling. The news had shaken her. She began to walk quickly. She was afraid. For the first time since this had all begun, she was terribly afraid for her own safety. *I'd like to drop this suitcase and run, just run as fast as I can back to the train station. Did the Gestapo see me in the bakery? Is anyone following me? God forbid, did I endanger Frau Hofbauer? The Gestapo could be there right now, questioning her. The poor old woman would be terrified. All because of me. And what about my mother? What have I done to her? And Anna and her family? Are they alive or dead? And Elica too? My mother has been arrested. She is a mess, and the Germans will see it. If they hurt her, I will never forgive myself. I feel so guilty. But I don't dare go by the house to see if she has returned. What have I done? What have I done? Did I make a mistake going to Italy? Was it my leaving Austria that alerted the Gestapo somehow? Or was it something else?*

She wanted to go home to her house to be sure that Frau Hofbauer had not been mistaken. But she knew in her heart that what the old woman had told her was all true. After all, Frau Hofbauer knew about Anna's family in the attic. That alone was all the indication she needed. I have to get on a train headed out of here. She thought as she walked up to the window to buy a ticket. "When is the next train to Italy?"

"Tonight."

"Tonight?"

"Yes, at seven pm."

"Where is the next train going?"

"A train is leaving for Paris in twenty minutes."

Paris is out of my way. But at least I will be far away from Austria. Once I am in Paris, I can buy another ticket back to Italy. "What time exactly does that train leave?"

"That will be twelve fifty."

"I'll take a ticket on the train to Paris," Bernie said. She had been saving money for quite some time, but she was worried because she was spending so much. The money Frau Hofbauer gave her would come in handy. Her hands were shaking as she counted out the bills to pay the ticket agent.

The ticket agent didn't seem to notice. He took her money and handed her some change and her ticket. Bernie counted her change carefully. A thick woman with a pink dress and large pink hat who was waiting in line behind her began tapping her foot impatiently. Bernie glanced back at her, and then she walked away.

Searching for a place to sit where she would be alone, Bernie finally decided on a bench in the corner. She sat down and put her suitcase on the ground beside her. *I wish I could close my eyes and just disappear from here, and when I opened them, I would find myself back in Italy with Viola.* She looked up at the large, round, black-rimmed clock on the wall. It was twelve thirty-five. Fifteen minutes to wait. These were dangerous minutes. At any time, the Gestapo could come and take her away. Her mouth was dry. Looking into the bag with the rolls she had bought, Bernie realized that she'd lost her appetite. She tucked the bag into her purse and tried to think of something else, anything else. But her mind was fixated on the clock. She couldn't take her eyes off it; every second seemed like a lifetime. Sweat beaded under her bra and made her feel itchy. *If only I had a book or a newspaper. Something to read, anything to take my mind off this. Poor Anna. She must have been so scared when they came. And my mother... dear God, my poor mother. I know she has not been the best mother, but she didn't deserve this. Who could have turned us in, and why? Was it for the reward? It had to be for the reward.* Suddenly she felt a chill run through her as if someone had poured ice water into her veins. *Who knew Anna's family was hiding in my attic? And who would have wanted the reward money badly enough to turn them in?* Bernie felt sick to her stomach. *Could it have been my mother? But if it was, she would not have been arrested. Unless, of course, that was just a front. I have to admit to myself that she would sell her soul for money to buy alcohol. Is this what she did? And then maybe somehow it might have backfired on her. I just don't know. It would not have been Elica. She would never have put Theo in danger. But then again, she knew that Theo and I were on our way to Italy. Still, she wouldn't turn Anna in. She loves Anna too. We are blood sisters. But who else knew? Who else could have done this? At least Theo is safe. Oh, Dear God, how did this all go so wrong?*

A man in a dark coat walked into the station. Bernie looked over at him and shivered. *Is he Gestapo?* He walked up to the ticket booth. From where she sat, Bernie could see him talking to the man behind the booth. He didn't take any money out of his pocket. *Maybe he is looking for me?* Her knees were shaking as she quickly walked to the lady's washroom. She went inside and stood against the wall. A woman with a small child looked at Bernie suspiciously. As she began to wash the child's hands, Bernie slipped into a stall so as not to appear so nervous and out of place. She stood inside the stall and waited until it was quiet in the bathroom. Then she quickly looked out the door of the stall. The woman and child were gone. *Does that woman know anything about me? Maybe my face has been in the newspaper with a reward for my capture. That woman could have recognized me. I feel so suspicious of everyone. It feels like I am going mad. I am so afraid. Every person I see feels like a threat. But maybe I will be safest if I stay here in this bathroom until the train arrives. I wish I had a watch so I could be sure of the time. Although there will be a whistle when the train arrives. When I hear the whistle, I'll go out and board as quickly as I can.*

It seemed like a lifetime that Bernie remained in the bathroom stall. Several women came and went, but no one seemed to be searching for her. Finally, she jumped when she heard the loud train whistle. It was time to leave the safety of the bathroom stall and board the train. *The Gestapo might be out there looking for me.* She thought. But she summoned all her courage and left the bathroom. Bernie took the ticket out of her pocketbook and held it in her hand as she climbed on board. She found a seat in the back of the train car and slid in quietly, hoping not to be noticed. Then she waited anxiously for the train to move.

CHAPTER THIRTY-TWO

The train jumped to life. But it started to move slowly at first, then gained speed as it gained momentum. The rocking movement was comforting, and Bernie began to relax. She thought of Viola and how happy she would be to see her again. But fear nudged its ugly head into her thoughts. *What if the Nazis were following me? I hope I am not bringing danger to Viola and the orphanage. Perhaps I should stay in Paris for a while until this settles down. Yes, maybe that's what I should do. I'll try to find work and...*

The gentle rhythm of the train as it passed through farms and open land rocked Bernie to sleep. And the next thing she knew, the train had stopped. She was in France. But two Gestapo agents stood in front of her. One, a tall and lean fellow with a pointed nose and thick glasses, said, "Papers?"

Bernie quickly stirred awake.

"Papers!" he yelled in her face. "Where are your papers, Fräulein?"

"Oh. Yes. Of course. My papers. I'm sorry, just give me a moment. I was asleep." She was breathless, having been awakened from a deep sleep, and now she was confronted by her greatest fear. She took her papers out of her handbag.

The Nazi studied them for a moment. Then he looked over at his partner. Their eyes met. For a moment, no one said a word. Bernie shivered. *Can they tell that my papers are false? Do they know who I am? Were they looking for me? Is that possible? Is it possible that they know that I am running away from them?*

One of the agents nodded. He handed Bernie her papers, and then they both walked away. Bernie tried to catch her breath. She felt sick to her stomach as her heart raced. But then she looked up and saw a young girl sitting across from her. She must have gotten on the train at the last stop. I can't believe I slept through all of this. The girl saw Bernie looking at her and asked, "Are you all right?"

"I am. Thank you. It's just that I was sleeping so deeply. And then to be awakened by someone screaming in my face was a little shocking," Bernie admitted. Then she smiled, hoping her excuse for being so shaken up sounded plausible.

The girl didn't seem at all suspicious. She just nodded and gave Bernie a smile. "I'm Alice."

Alice was a pretty blonde in her late teens or early twenties. She wore no makeup. Strands of her light blonde hair were coming loose from her braid. Her dark blue cotton skirt and blouse were worn and stained. Looking at her, Bernie couldn't help but think that Alice would be very pretty if she cleaned herself up.

"I'm B--Adelaide."

"It's nice to meet you, Adelaide."

"The same."

"I'm on my way to Paris. Where are you headed?" Alice asked.

"The same. I'm going to Paris," Bernie lied. She didn't know Alice and saw no reason to tell her about the convent.

"I have some friends in France. I can't wait to see them," Alice said. "I've been saving money to take this trip for years."

"Yes, travel can be expensive," Bernie said. She purposely ended her sentence without a question in hopes that Alice would get the message that she didn't really feel like talking. But it didn't work. Alice seemed lonely, like she needed to talk to someone.

"Where do you call home?" Alice asked.

"Austria. Vienna, Austria."

There were several moments of silence. Then Alice said, "I lied to you. I hope you can forgive me. I am not going to see friends. I'm running away."

"What?" Bernie asked. She felt the tiny hairs on her neck stand up. *Why is she telling me this? I don't want to know any of her personal problems. This is none of my business, and I don't want to make it my business. If she's in trouble with the Gestapo...*

"I'm sorry, I lied to you."

Bernie nodded. "It's all right, really," she said, then she turned away from Alice and looked out the window, hoping to discourage Alice from telling her anything more. *The more I know, the more involved I become, and I don't need to be involved in whatever this girl is doing. She is clearly unstable. She wouldn't tell a stranger about her personal business if she wasn't.*

"I'm running away from my husband. He's a terrible man. He beats me. I've had all I can take." Alice showed Bernie a large purple bruise on her upper arm. "I have never told my parents or my friends. But I can tell you because you hardly know me, and once I get off this train, you won't know me at all. So, I can finally tell someone the terrible secret I have kept for a while. It feels good to let it out."

Bernie nodded again. "I see. Well, that's certainly a bad situation. And it's a good thing you got away." *I don't know why she won't leave me alone. I don't want to get involved.* Then she looked closely at the bruise. It was massive, purple and red. It looked like it still hurt. *Still, no woman should have to put up with that from anyone.*

"He's been hitting me since we got married a few months ago. I just couldn't take it anymore. What would you have done?"

"Me?"

"Yes, you?"

"I don't know." Bernie inhaled deeply. "I guess I would have left him, too."

"Are you married?"

"No." Bernie didn't want to answer any questions. She didn't want to explain her lifestyle, and right now, she would have given anything to shut this girl up. She had her own problems, and she really didn't feel like taking on someone else's.

"My mother didn't know that he was hitting me. She knew I was unhappy, though, and you know what she said? She said that I should stay with him. And I tried. I really did. But I can't put up with it anymore. What would happen if I got pregnant? How could I protect our child when I couldn't even protect myself?"

Again, Bernie nodded. Then she waited a few minutes and said, "Alice, I'm sorry. I'm very tired. I'm going to try and sleep some more. Perhaps you might want to try and get some rest."

"Yes, that's probably a good idea," Alice said. She took a ratty gray sweater out of her handbag and rolled it into a ball, making a pillow for herself. She put the sweater under her head and fell asleep.

CHAPTER THIRTY-THREE

Bernie didn't know how long she had slept, but it was dark outside when she was awakened by another inspection. "Have your papers ready," a uniformed guard said to Bernie and Alice.

Alice was frantic as she fumbled with her handbag. "I can't find my papers," she said nervously.

A tall, muscular man in uniform walked over to Alice. "Papers," he said.

"I can't find my papers." Alice's voice was filled with panic. "I can't find my money either. I think I was robbed while I was asleep."

The guard stood over Alice. He reached out and grabbed her breast. "Perhaps we could go into the bathroom. You just never know. If you're a good girl, I might just overlook the fact that you don't have papers."

Bernie gasped softly. The guard gave her a look that told her she'd better shut her mouth and mind her business.

"No, please, not that. Not that," Alice said.

The guard squeezed Alice's breast.

"That hurts. Please stop."

Bernie didn't want to get involved. She tried to ignore the situation. After all, she had her own problems, and right now, she began searching in her own handbag, and to her dismay, she couldn't find her papers either. *Is it possible we were both robbed and slept right through it? What am I going to do now? Why would someone take my papers?* She was rifling through her purse, searching desperately. But when the Nazi thrust his hand up Alice's skirt, and Alice screamed, Bernie gasped. She wished she had the courage to stand up to this man. But she was not the courageous girl she'd been in her youth. Bernie had been through too much to stand up to anyone.

Still, the look on her face was one of disgust. It angered the Nazi, who looked at her and shook his head.

"Oh my, wouldn't you like to be a man with your short ugly haircut and lack of lipstick? And just look at that matronly dress. It makes you look ten years older than you are." The Nazi said mockingly to Bernie. "If you were a man, you could defend her virtue. But as it so happens, you are nothing but a misfit of a woman. So, turn that ugly face of yours away. I don't want to look at you."

"Please leave her alone," Bernie begged.

"You have some nerve trying to tell me what to do. Who in the hell do you think you are?" The guard said. He punched Bernie in the face. Her lip started bleeding.

"And, besides, where are your papers, misfit?"

Bernie knew she should have kept her mouth shut. Now she was in trouble. "I think they were stolen. I think that someone might have stolen our money and our papers while we slept."

"Do you? How convenient for you. Your papers were stolen." A wicked smile came over his face. "We'll just have to see about that. Let's go."

CHAPTER THIRTY-FOUR

Bernie was tossed into the back of a police car. Her heart was beating hard. A dull pain was raiding down her left arm. *This is it. I am going to die.* She thought. *I am so stupid. I should have kept my mouth shut.* She thought of Viola. *At least I saw her one last time.* Bernie felt like crying, but she knew it would do her no good. *Men like these have no hearts; they don't have the capacity for sympathy.* Then the car stopped. Bernie was dragged out and forced at gunpoint to follow into the basement of the Gestapo headquarters.

"Were you hoping that girl would sleep with you, a misfit?" The Gestapo agent asked.

Bernie didn't answer.

He punched her in the jaw, sending her sprawling across the room. The pain was so severe that she thought her jaw might be broken.

"You disgust me. Do you know what a mess you are? You are a freak. That's what you are. But you know that, don't you? You've lived with that knowledge all your pathetic life." He kicked her in the stomach as she lay on the floor. The pain was so fierce that she felt tears come to her eyes, but even worse, she couldn't breathe. *Don't cry. Don't let him see you cry.* Bernie rolled into a fetal position, her arms wrapped around her stomach.

"Didn't anyone ever tell you that you would do better if you learned to mind your own business? Especially a misfit like you. You should keep your mouth shut. You should never have poked your nose into a conversation between that girl on the train and me."

Bernie didn't say anything. She knew he was right. *I should have stayed out of it. But how could I? I couldn't let a man treat a woman that way and do nothing. Now, I will pay the price.*

He kicked her again, this time in the back. She let out a scream. But at least she was able to breathe again.

And then he beat her with his fists until she was unconscious.

When she awoke, she was in a dirty cell. A guard was prying at her with a long rifle. "Get up. Follow me."

Blood was crusted across her face and had dried on the front of her blouse.

"Get up now," he said as he led her at gunpoint back to the room where the questioning had taken place.

I'd rather die than face another beating like this. Bernie thought.

"You unnatural piece of shit. You're a homosexual through and through. An embarrassment to Aryan women. Well, since you like women so much, I have a special treat for you. I've decided that I am going to teach you a lesson. And that's because I hate women like you. I have a special kind of hatred for them." He spat at her and then continued, "So, I am going to send you somewhere where you will learn a valuable lesson. Do you know what that is?"

Bernie didn't answer. She glared at him as she lay on the floor.

He smiled that wicked smile again. "You are going to learn that women are not perfect. They are even more vicious than any man could ever be. What do you think of that, you homosexual?" He said, then he kicked Bernie in the stomach. She doubled over in pain, and once again, she couldn't catch her breath. "I'd like to kill you here and now. I would enjoy it. I tell you, I would. But since I know you will suffer in ways you could never imagine at Ravensbrück, I asked permission from my superior to send you there. He agreed with me that it is the best place for a misfit. So, you will be going there. But not before I show you what you are missing." He unzipped his pants. Bernie felt the bile rising in her throat. He pulled her skirt up to her waist and tore off her underwear. She kicked his leg and he slapped her so hard that her head spun. Then he mounted her. She was too weak to fight anymore. His hands grasped at her breasts. It felt like he might tear them off her body. Closing her eyes tightly, she wished she could disappear. It felt like she was being torn in two. She vomited. But he ignored her. He grunted, breathing heavily. Pounding into her until, finally, he was done. Then he rolled off of her, stood up, and zipped his pants. Then, in a loud voice, he called out, "Guard, take this good-for-nothing piece of dirt back to her cell."

CHAPTER THIRTY-FIVE

The guard was right. Ravensbrück was hell. The female guards were as vicious as men, if not worse.

Bernie was strong. She'd always been strong and healthy. But even so, Ravensbrück was taking its toll on her. Each day, she was losing a bit of her will to live. The barracks where she was forced to sleep were overcrowded beyond anything she could have imagined. The women were crushed together, and there was never enough food. Disease ran rampant, and there was nowhere to hide from women who coughed in her face while she tried to sleep at night. Bernie could not have imagined that humans could have built such a torture chamber for others. When she arrived, she expected to see mostly Jewish prisoners, and there were plenty, but not as many as she had anticipated. There were all sorts of women who were confined in Ravensbrück. These were women who were considered enemies of the Reich. They were prostitutes, lesbians, and women who had broken the law by marrying Jewish men. There were political prisoners, women who had resisted the Reich. Some of the women were handicapped, and others were clearly mentally ill. The first thing Bernie did when she arrived, whenever she had a free moment, was to search for Elica. But there wasn't much free time, and when there was, Bernie was so exhausted that she wanted to sleep. She thought that perhaps she might find Elica at Ravensbrück because Elica had married Daniel. So when she could find the energy, she tried to walk through the long blocks of barracks where she asked everyone she met if they knew Elica, but no one did. It was hard to communicate because the women were from many different countries and spoke so many different languages.

Ravensbrück was unforgiving. The weaker the prisoner, the more terrible the guards treated her. It was a sad and dreadful place. Most of the guards were cruel, merciless, and even sadistic. Some of the prisoners that Bernie met had wounds from experiments done on them by a sadistic woman doctor who enjoyed torturing other women. But the one guard who frightened Bernie the most was a beautiful young guard who was as vicious as she was beautiful. Her heart was as dark as her hair was light, and she was as ugly inside as she was stunning on the outside. Her name was Irma Grese, and Bernie had never met anyone like her. She was warned about Irma before she met her. "She's heartless," one of the women told her. But Bernie didn't believe it until she saw a beautiful young woman with hair the color of spun gold beat another woman to death with her bare hands.

And then there were the children, young children, babies, and toddlers imprisoned in this horrific place. Children who had somehow made it through the selection process when they first arrived. However, they were still alive, but they would be murdered soon enough. When Bernie saw them—dirty, emaciated little skeletons barely walking or crawling, she felt that she was living in hell. The lack of food arrested their development, so it was difficult to determine their age. However, the older ones did their best to comfort and quiet the young ones. These innocent children learned fast that even if they were terrified, starving, or sick, they must not cry or search for their mothers because, if they did, even worse tragedy would befall them. Bernie saw them each day as she walked to and from her job on the roads. Her thoughts always turned to Theo, and she was grateful that she had been able to drop him off at the orphanage before she was arrested and sent here. Because if he had been with her, he would be amongst these tiny waifs. If she couldn't raise and protect him as her final gift to Elica, at least she had saved him from being exposed to a place devoid of humanity and compassion.

At night Bernie slept on a long hard wooden cot with women sandwiched on both sides of her. When she first arrived, she'd found it difficult to sleep. The women were dirty, and the smell of their unwashed bodies, combined with the odors that rose from the buckets filled with human waste, made her gag. Besides that, she could not move. She was unable to turn once she'd laid down, and at first, she felt paralyzed by the other women who were lying so close to her. But after a few weeks of living in Ravensbrück and enduring hard labor and rising early before dawn, she was so tired that when she lay down, she was asleep almost instantly. Everyone in Ravensbrück had a job. And Bernie's was not one of the better ones. She was sent to join a crew of women whose job was to build roads. A paving roller was attached to her back, and she had to pull it like a workhorse. It was heavy and taxing work, and she began to have terrible back aches and shoulder pain. Bernie hated everything about this place, but most of all, she despised the lack of privacy. There were no private lavatories. Everyone had to do their business in full view of everyone else.

After a day of hard manual labor, Bernie was given very little to eat, a bowl of watery soup, and a small hunk of stale bread. She devoured it because she was always hungry. And Bernie found that hunger was a strong motivator. She had never thought she could be a thief. She had always prided herself on being honest. But now, she was stealing bits of bread whenever an opportunity arose. It was not as difficult to forgive herself for stealing from the kitchen, but once she stole a hunk of bread from under the bed of another inmate. This made her strongly dislike the woman she was becoming.

Early one afternoon, as fall was turning to winter and a bitter wind penetrated the thin striped uniform Bernie was forced to wear, a new girl was brought to the work at the road work site. She was small in stature and already very thin. Her badge was a yellow triangle, indicating that her crime was that she was Jewish. Adele, one of the prisoners who had been a prostitute in Frankfurt, looked at the new girl and whispered to Bernie, "I give her less than a week. She's too frail to make it."

Bernie didn't say a word, but this tore at her heart because she knew it was true. The girl did her best to keep up, and she did not complain. But she was too weak to handle the job, and the others who worked with her were constantly nagging at her to pull her weight. This girl's lack of strength made their jobs more difficult. Bernie glanced over at her, and she could see by the girl's red face that she was pulling the roller as hard as she could.

The following day, Bernie purposely stood beside the new girl. She knew that her work was going to be harder because the new girl couldn't keep up, but she didn't care. "Hello," Bernie said in German, "I'm Bernie."

The girl smiled and answered in Yiddish, "I'm Moriah."

"You're speaking Yiddish. Are you German?"

"No, I'm from Poland. Are you German?"

"Austrian," Bernie said. Then she looked at the girl, who was at least a head shorter than herself, and added. "I know this is very hard work. I am going to help you as much as I can."

"God bless you," Moriah whispered.

CHAPTER THIRTY-SIX

There was no work on Sunday for most of the prisoners. However, the kitchen must continue to run, so the prisoners who worked in the kitchen took turns taking Sundays off.

The women in Ravensbrück waited for Sunday like a child waits for Christmas morning. On Sunday, they were permitted to relax, sleep late, and talk. Every Saturday night, the camp was filled with excitement and expectation for the coming day. But by late Sunday afternoon, a heavy dark cloud of depression fell upon the inmates. Soon Sunday would be over, and they would have to begin another week's torture while waiting for the following Sunday.

One cold Sunday morning, Bernie got up late. Then she searched through the blocks for Moriah. She had almost given up. However, when she turned the corner to head back to her barrack, she saw Moriah sitting alone on the ground outside. Bernie walked over to her.

"Hello. You must be freezing."

"Bernie." A smile came across Moriah's face. "I am freezing. The ground is terribly cold."

"May I sit down with you?"

"Of course."

Bernie plopped down beside Moriah. Then she said, "You're right. The ground is damn cold. Why are you sitting out here and not inside?"

"I wanted to be alone. We are stuffed together with other people on top of us all the time. I just wanted to rest and be by myself."

"Shall I go?" Bernie asked.

"No, you can stay. I'm glad you came. You're the only person who is nice to me. I guess I am a problem for everyone. I can't do my work properly. I'm just not strong enough for this work. And, besides that, I am Jewish. There are other women in here who hate Jews. Imagine they are prisoners just like me, yet they hate the Jews. They are as bad as the Nazis. They suffer the same as Jews, but still want to believe they are better somehow." She shook her head. "You know, it's a sin to say this, but sometimes I wish I was not born Jewish."

"I can understand that," Bernie said. "One of my very close friends from childhood was a Jewish girl, and things were difficult for her."

"I grew up believing that the Jews were God's chosen people. But, if that is true, why are we so hated by everyone?"

"I don't know. I wish I could tell you. But I don't hate you. I could never hate you," Bernie said.

Bernie and Moriah sat silently for several minutes. Bernie picked up a stone and rubbed its smooth surface with her thumb. Then Moriah asked, "Why did you come out here to sit with me?"

Bernie looked at Moriah. "I thought you might need a friend."

"And you don't care that I am Jewish. You must realize that your friendship with me will make the others stay away from you?"

"I don't care what they do. It doesn't matter to me. It never has," Bernie said boldly. Bernie's badge was red, which meant she was considered a political prisoner. She wasn't sure why she'd been given that badge, but she wore it.

"Well, you are the only woman I have met so far who is willing to befriend a Jew. Of course, that is, except for other Jews."

"Really?"

"Yes, really. I have met a few of the other Jewish girls and befriended them. But the non-Jewish women don't want anything to do with me. They call me dirty jew, pig jew, and every other insult they can think of." Moriah looked down at the ground, then back up at Bernie, and continued, "I don't judge them for being prostitutes, thieves, or even murderers. But they instantly judge me for being a Jew." She shook her head. "Wouldn't you think that after the way the Nazis have treated them, they would have some compassion? But they don't."

"I agree with you. I have never hated Jewish people. As I said, I had a very good friend who was Jewish. But that was before I was arrested. I don't know what has become of her." Bernie sighed as she thought of Anna and her family.

Moriah shrugged. "Nothing good if she's Jewish, I would assume. However, maybe she was able to hide. I've heard that a lot of Jews are hiding. The Nazis came to the village where I lived and took all of us. I was separated from the rest of the group and sent here because one of the doctors wanted me for an experiment. Then, at the last minute, she changed her mind about me for some reason. She decided that she didn't want me, so I was sent to work on the roads with you."

"I can't say that you were lucky. I don't know which is worse. I've heard that these crazy doctors are sterilizing women and doing even worse things. From what I hear, they are torturing women in the name of science."

"What could be worse than sterilization? Every woman wants a child. Doesn't she? I mean, I do. I want one someday if this ever ends."

"I've heard that they are amputating healthy limbs for no good reason at all. Healthy limbs, can you just imagine that?"

"No. But that could have been me." Moriah shuddered and crossed her arms over her body.

"But I've also learned that lots of rumors go around this camp, and unless you hear something directly from the victim, you can't be sure that it's true. So, maybe it's a lie."

"It's true," Moriah said bitterly. "I've seen it with my own eyes. Some of the other Polish girls who were brought here with me have been permanently damaged by that same doctor. Her name is Oberheuser, and she is a very sick woman. I hate her. I wish I could kill her with my bare hands." Moriah's face turned crimson. "Like I was telling you. She is a miserable woman. A sadist. She has this group of prisoners who are called 'the rabbits' because she uses them for testing the way rabbits are sometimes used for testing in labs. But Oberheuser isn't really testing anything. She does all kinds of sadistic things to these poor women under the guise of medical experiments. The truth is, these so-called experiments are nothing more than pure torture. Sadistic torture. Oberheuser did something to one of my friend's legs. Her name was Hannah. She was a pretty Jewish girl. A dancer. It must have been terrible for her because, after the procedure, she knew she would never dance again. But it was even worse than that. She got a terrible infection where Oberheuser cut her. She was a perfectly healthy young woman before Oberheuser got her hands on her. But that infection was terrible, and Hannah suffered, oh how she suffered. I saw it all. I wanted to help her, but there was nothing I could do. I was helpless. Finally, she died. She was only twenty-two years old. And I am sad to say she wasn't the only girl who suffered like this. I know of at least two other women who died because of Oberheuser's vile experiments. And that woman calls herself a doctor. She's amputated the legs and arms of healthy women without anesthesia. And she does this for no reason other than to see the women in pain. It makes me sick."

"That makes me sick to my stomach, too," Bernie admitted.

"Yes, doesn't it?" Moriah agreed. "And then there is the sterilization. So far, they have only been sterilizing Romani women. They promise them that they will set them free if they consent to be sterilized and go without a fight. But after the women are sterilized, they never let them go. They never give them their freedom. I can't figure out why the doctors make these promises. They don't have to make promises to us at all. They have absolute power; they can do whatever they want with us. Sometimes I think they just like to give people hope and then take it away. It gives them some sort of sick pleasure to see these poor women fall into depression when they realize they've been lied to."

"That's really terrible," Bernie said.

"Yes, it is." Moriah was quiet for a moment, then she added, "You know, I often wonder how there are so many sadistic people. I mean, there really are so many of them. It's like all of Germany is filled with sadists. Do you know what I mean? I guess what I am saying is that if there weren't so many sadists, all of this could never have happened. The Nazi party had to find a lot of people who enjoyed inflicting pain on others. People who are willing to do the terrible things that they do here."

"But not all Germans are sadists, and not all Germans are Nazis," Bernie said. "I spent a summer working in Germany before this all began. I worked for a lovely German family."

"So, how did this happen? Why didn't the good ones stand up to the Nazis?"

"I think they were afraid. No one ever believed it would get this bad. The people who are in control are sadists who have a strong need for power. In my opinion, these people were small and probably never had any form of power or respect before they became Nazis. I saw that happen with a girl I knew. She was always an outcast, and now she's in the party." Bernie thought of Dagna, and then she thought of Elica.

"One of the women in my block who works in the office told us that she heard some of the guards say that Ravensbrück is where the

Nazi party sends its female guards to be trained. They must prove they can be cruel and heartless before being e given positions as guards."

"I believe it. The women here are even worse than any of the men. Maybe they are trying to be promoted to SS officers? Do you think that's it?" Moriah asked.

"No, I've heard that Hitler won't let women into the SS. They just actually *want* these jobs. Can you imagine anyone wanting these jobs?"

"I wouldn't want it. But I guess they must make a good salary."

"I'm sure they do, especially for women. But it wouldn't matter to me how much I got paid. I could never do this job. I would never do it," Bernie said firmly.

Moriah shook her head. "Me neither."

"It's hard to believe that Dr. Oberheuser is a trained doctor. But I have heard she is. So, I don't understand how she can do these things. I had a cousin who was a doctor, and he told me that he had to take an oath to do no harm. If she ever took the same oath, it seems she's forgotten it. Or maybe they aren't required to take that oath in Germany," Bernie said, shaking her head.

"I'm sure they are. From what I've read and heard, before Hitler, Germany was always at the top of all the countries in science, art, and everything really. It's so hard to believe that this is what it has come to."

"Yes, it's hard to believe. But it's true. We are living in hell because of it every day," Bernie said.

They were both quiet for several moments. "It is so cold out here," Bernie said. "I wish we had coats."

"Yes, me too."

"You know what? I think we have to focus on good things, and you were lucky that Oberheuser decided not to use you in her experiments."

"I wonder why she decided not to. No one ever told me, and I dare not ask. But you're right. I suppose I am lucky. However, I wish they had not put me on road work. I am not strong enough for it."

"I know," Bernie said. "You are so tiny. Don't worry. I'll help you as much as I can."

"I appreciate anything you can do to help me. And I am happy we're friends," Moriah said.

CHAPTER THIRTY-SEVEN

Bernie kept her promise to Moriah. Although she was exhausted, she did her own work, and then she did as much of Moriah's work as she could possibly do. They ate together each day, and Moriah tried to give Bernie half of her bread to thank her for the help.

"I don't need as much as you do. I am small, and I don't work nearly as hard."

"I'm all right. Eat your food. You need your strength," Bernie said.

There weren't many male guards, but as it was, one of them became attracted to Moriah. His name was *Unterscharführer* Maynard Graf, and he lorded over the kitchen workers as if he were the king of the kitchen, the giver of life, and the taker of it as well. And perhaps he was. After all, he had control of the food, and the inmates would starve to death without enough food. Many of them did. Often, he would walk by when Bernie and Moriah were eating their meager meal and hand Moriah a bit of extra bread. If he saw her in line, when the girl was ladling the single serving of soup into her bowl, he'd stop what he was doing and walk over to ensure that Moriah was given an extra piece of potato. And when these small blessings were bestowed upon Moriah, she always shared every bit of extra food with Bernie.

As winter pressed on, Bernie began to feel like the blood was freezing in her veins. Many of the women Bernie knew who had worked with her on the roads died. As she worked, she saw their bodies, which were left to rot in the snow. Moriah was so small and skinny and shivered so hard that Bernie was afraid her friend might drop dead, too. But then, one evening, as Moriah and Bernie were eating their soup, the *Unterscharführer* came out from the kitchen and walked over to Moriah. He was tall and handsome and wore a warm wool coat that Bernie wished she had. He smiled at Moriah. Bernie saw her try to return the smile, but her teeth were chattering. Then he said, "How would you like to come to work for me in the kitchen? It's warm there, and I might give you a little extra food."

Moriah looked at Bernie, who nodded her head. "Go," she said.

"What about you?"

"I'll be all right."

"Are you sure?"

"Of course. It will be easier on me if you are not working on the roads. I won't have to help you. You know that it slows me down sometimes," Bernie said. And it was true. But that wasn't the reason she wanted Moriah to leave the roads and go to work in the kitchen. She wanted Moriah to survive, and working inside would give her a much better chance.

Moriah looked at the Nazi. Her face showed that she was puzzled by his offer. But Bernie was certain that she knew what he wanted from Moriah. She hated to sanction something like this. She had always hated to see men take sexual advantage of women. However, if she didn't encourage Moriah to go, it wouldn't be long before Moriah would die from the cold.

"Yes," Moriah said. "I would love to work in the kitchen. What should I do? Tell me what to do?" Moriah said.

"Finish your soup. Then come to my office. I'll be waiting there for you."

Moriah nodded. "Yes, *Unterscharführer*."

"Hurry up," the guard said, then he walked away.

"Does he want what I think he wants?" Moriah said.

"He wants sex," Bernie said. "I'm almost positive about it."

"Oh. I don't know if I can do it. I've never had sex. I'm not that kind of girl. I'm a good girl. A virgin."

"Moriah, it's cold, it's very cold, and you're so small and weak. I wish I could do it for you. But I can't. He wants you. I can't believe I am going to say this, but you must do it. You must close your eyes and just let him do what he wants with you." Just saying this made Bernie feel sick to her stomach. And even though she wished she could protect Moriah, Bernie knew this would be best for Moriah in the long run.

When they finished their soup, Moriah stood up, and as bravely as she could, she said, "I'm going to his office."

Bernie could see that Moriah's knees were shaking. She couldn't tell if it was from the cold or from fear.

"I'll wait up for you. Come to my block after it's over if you can," Bernie said. "Don't put yourself at risk. If it's too late, just go to your own block, and we'll talk tomorrow."

"I probably won't be able to come to your block. I'll see you at roll call in the morning."

Bernie took Moriah's hand and squeezed it. "I'm sorry," Bernie said.

"For what?"

"For not being able to help you. For standing by and allowing something like this to happen. I am so sorry."

"It's not your fault," Moriah said. "But are you sure I should do it?"

"I am sure," Bernie said.

CHAPTER THIRTY-EIGHT

Bernie slept fitfully that night. She would fall asleep and then wake up abruptly, with thoughts of Moriah on her mind. *I hope Moriah is all right. What a terrible way to lose her virginity. But if she stayed working outside, she would most certainly die from the cold. I have to believe this is a blessing, even though it feels like a curse.*

In the early hours, just before dawn, Bernie stood shivering in the roll call line outside. Her eyes searched frantically for Moriah. But Moriah didn't come. Sick with worry, her mind racing, she went to get in line for her food. As she waited in the long line, Bernie shivered. *What if that Unterscharführer is some kind of sexual sadist, and he killed her? It would be my fault because I sent her to him. If something terrible happened to her, I would never forgive myself.* Bernie was so busy chastising herself that she didn't notice it when Moriah approached her from behind.

"Good morning," Moriah said softly.

"Oh, am I glad to see you!" Bernie sighed with relief. "Are you alright?"

"Actually, yes, I'm fine. I forgot that the kitchen help doesn't go to roll call. I know I promised to meet you there. And I was so afraid that you would be worried," Moriah said.

"I was. I was very worried."

"I have good news."

"Tell me."

"The *Unterscharführer* wasn't a bad man at all. In fact, he has allowed me to bring you to work in the kitchen with me. You won't have to be outside and work on the road anymore."

"Really?"

"Yes, he really wasn't all that bad to me. I mean, I would not have chosen to do this if I could have said no. But it wasn't as bad as it could have been. He didn't hurt me."

"Thank God," Bernie said. "All night long, I felt so guilty. I mean, I sent you to him. And if anything would have happened to you... Oh, Moriah. I am just so glad you're all right."

"Don't feel guilty. You were right. I had to accept his offer. It was our only chance of survival. It's too cold to be working outside, and the work on the road is much too heavy for me. Anyway, I must get back to the kitchen. Tomorrow morning, right after roll call, come and report to the kitchen. Maynard will be waiting there. After tomorrow, he said he would arrange it so that you can come directly to the kitchen instead of standing outside on roll call. Kitchen work starts much earlier than the other jobs. But even so, it's better. It's not cold in the kitchen."

"Did I hear you call that guard by his first name?"

"He told me to call him Maynard," Moriah said.

"I would be careful that no one else hears you call him that."

"I know. He told me that, too."

CHAPTER THIRTY-NINE

Bernie reported to the kitchen immediately following roll call the next day. A large black cauldron of hot water with a few cut-up potatoes and carrots was simmering in the corner. This was the soup that was served to the prisoners each day. It was mostly water. And quite often, insects fell into the pot. No one cared. They were so hungry that they ate the soup, anyway. Even Bernie, who had once been a fussy eater, had learned to eat the soup, including the insects. *Starvation changes you, that's for sure.* Bernie thought. And although the soup wasn't very nourishing, the pot of boiling water did give off some heat. And in the frigid months of winter, it was very welcomed.

Moriah was standing at a long wooden table. She and several other girls were busy kneading dough for bread. This bread would be served to the guards and officers. The prisoners were given the bread that had gone stale. When Bernie entered, she looked up from her work, and their eyes met. Moriah smiled.

Bernie smiled back.

As Bernie settled into her job, she was able to watch the *Unter-*

scharführer. It seemed that he was obsessed with Moriah. He was constantly pulling her away from her work and taking her into his office. The other women who were working in the kitchen noticed it, but no one said a word. Bernie felt ashamed for Moriah. Everyone knew what the *Unterscharführer* was doing to Moriah. And Bernie thought that even though they seemed to be looking down on Moriah, they would do the same if they were in her position.

When Sunday came, Bernie and Moriah had to work because, although the other prisoners were off on Sunday, the kitchen help was required to work. Everyone still had to eat. However, they finished early, and Bernie went to speak to Moriah. She found her sitting outside again. "It's too cold to sit out here. Let's go into your block where we can talk."

"I don't want to. The other girls are being mean to me. They don't like what's happening with Maynard and me. I don't like it either. But I am just trying to survive."

"I know," Bernie said. "Listen, why don't you come to my block, and we can sit inside there?"

"Because everyone knows about what is going on. Everyone. No matter where they work. No matter what block they are in. They all know. Gossip spreads in this place like the disease that spreads in here."

"I know. But who cares what they say? Let's get out of the cold, and then we can talk. Come on. No one will say a bad word to you if you are with me," Bernie said.

"All right," Moriah finally agreed.

The ground was covered with dirty gray snow and sheets of slippery ice. They walked slowly and silently. When they arrived at the block where Bernie slept, they sat down on the floor in the corner. Several of the other prisoners glared at them both. Rumors about Moriah and the kitchen boss had spread through the camp, and many of the girls hated Moriah for what she was doing. Others were jealous because they heard Moriah was given extra food and a better job because of the *Unterscharführer*. And there was talk about the fact that Moriah had helped Bernie to get transferred off the roads and into the kitchen. They didn't say anything when Bernie could hear because Bernie had become known as strong and fearless, and they were afraid of Bernie's anger. But behind her back, Moriah became known as the Jew pig whore.

"I lied to you," Moriah said quietly so no one else could hear her as they sat shivering on the cold ground. "I should never have lied to you. I don't know why I did. I'm sorry."

"About what?"

"Remember when I told you I was a virgin?" She didn't wait for an answer. "Well, it wasn't true."

"You never have to lie to me," Bernie said.

Moriah shook her head. Then she shrugged her shoulders and said, "I was ashamed. I'm even more ashamed now. You know they call me the Jew pig whore."

Bernie didn't look into Moriah's eyes. "Don't pay them any attention. They don't deserve it. If they were in your position, they would do the same thing. And I want you to know that you can tell me anything. No matter what it is. I won't hold it against you."

There were several moments of silence. Then Moriah said, "There was a boy. I was young. He was a few years older. Well, more than a few years. He was almost ten years older than me. But he was so charming, and he was certainly handsome. Oh, he was so handsome. He wasn't Jewish. My girlfriends and I secretly went into the city one day. That's how I met him. He worked in the city." She smiled sadly. "If my parents had ever found out, my father would have beaten me. I wasn't allowed to go anywhere out of our little village. But we went anyway. We lied to our parents. Told them all kinds of tales. They were so busy with our younger siblings that they didn't realize what we were up to."

"And you fell in love?"

"I did. But he didn't. I guess a relationship formed on lies, ends with more lies."

"I'm not sure what you mean," Bernie admitted.

"What I mean is that I lied to my parents, and this boy who I became infatuated with lied to me. Well, he was quite good at lying. Quite convincing. He promised me that we would run away together. I believed him. I believed him because I wanted it to be true."

"Sometimes we believe what we want to believe, even though in our hearts we know better."

"Yes, that's what happened. I let him, well, you know."

"You mean have sex with you?"

"Yes. And... I got pregnant. When I told him I was pregnant, he got angry. Called me stupid. Told me that I should have done something to prevent this from happening. But what could I do?"

"It wasn't your fault. It takes two people to make a baby."

"After that, he wanted nothing to do with me. He wouldn't even speak to me. He told me to go home and never come back. But I couldn't just leave. I followed him home one day because I wanted to talk to him. That's when I saw him open the door to a house in town. A young woman came to greet him. She carried a young child in her arms. I should have followed him earlier, before I trusted him. But I wanted so much to believe the dream he had spun. Anyway, he kissed the woman and tickled the baby. I felt awful, so betrayed and rejected and so alone. I had no one on my side. So, I had to tell my parents because I was starting to show. My father was furious. He beat me so badly that I fell down on the floor and lost the baby." She started to cry. Bernie moved over and put her arm around Moriah.

"It's all right."

"I almost died. The beating was that bad, and the miscarriage was even worse. There was so much blood. I will never forget how I felt. I saw the blood and felt like my actions had murdered my baby. I was sick from all of it. My father didn't even come to the hospital. I lay there for over two weeks, but he never came. My mother and sister did even though I'd brought shame upon them," she sighed.

"It's all right," Bernie said. "It's over now."

"Yes, it is, and somehow, I survived it. Even so, that wasn't the worst of it. My parents were ashamed of me. My father called me a *kurva*, a whore in Yiddish. He told me that I should go and live in a whorehouse so that if anyone ever finds out about my tainted life, it wouldn't hurt my younger sister's chance of finding a good husband."

"What did you do?"

"Nothing. I stayed there. I couldn't leave. I had nowhere to go. My father didn't speak to me. He only allowed my mother and sister to talk to me when it was absolutely necessary. And then... well... and then the Germans began bombing Poland. My sister was scared. She forgot about my father's demands. We huddled together during the bombings. You want to know my most shameful secret?"

"Only if you want to tell me," Bernie said.

"I was glad for the bombings. I was glad that at least my sister and I were close again. I wasn't as lonely as I had been. I didn't feel as shunned. And I would rather have died than spend the rest of my life living with my family but being alone. If the Nazis had not invaded, I would have spent my life living with them, but as long as my father lived, they would never have spoken to me. My father said that he would never try to make a match between me and any of the local boys. He said no Jewish boy should get stuck with a girl like me. I was damaged and dirty."

"Oh, Moriah," Bernie said. "That's terrible. There is nothing wrong with you. Nothing at all."

"I am an idiot. I should never have fallen for that fellow."

"It happens. We all make mistakes when it comes to love."

"Did you?"

"Me?" Bernie asked.

"Yes, you."

"There are things you don't know about me."

"Of course, there are. That's why I'm asking," Moriah said.

"I'm a lesbian," Bernie admitted. She still had her arm around Moriah. Bernie could feel Moriah tense up as if she was afraid of catching a disease. "It's all right. I know you like boys, and that's all right. I don't expect anything from you. I would never expect anything from you."

"I was just a little shocked to hear that, I guess. I didn't realize it."

"Yes, well, it's true."

Bernie told Moriah about Elica. She explained that she had adored Elica when they were children. But Elica liked boys. "I used to dream about Elica when we were young. But I always knew it was just a dream. She was going to grow up and marry a boy. Eventually, and I admit it was difficult, I learned to love her as a dear friend. Then I went to Italy by myself, and something wonderful happened. I met the love of my life. Another girl, her name is Viola. She lives in Italy."

Moriah relaxed. "I don't think I've ever met a lesbian before."

"You'd be surprised. You probably did, and you just didn't know it. Most of us learn to hide it early."

"Yes, I can imagine. I'm sure that people make life hard for you. So, what happened to your friend?"

"Elica or Viola?"

"Both."

"Well... there's quite a story there," Bernie said.

"We have plenty of time."

"That's true," Bernie said, nodding her head. Then she told Moriah all about Elica and Daniel and all about Theo. She explained how Elica had left him with her, and for his safety, she'd taken him to Italy to an orphanage where she left him with Viola. "I won't tell you the exact location of the orphanage or the church that runs the orphanage just in case the Nazis find out about Theo and start questioning you. It's better for you if you don't know anything."

"I don't need to know that, anyway."

"But there is something that I would like to talk to you about."

"Go on..." Moriah said.

"If I don't survive."

"Don't say that. It's bad luck. Poo poo poo," Moriah spit on the ground.

"Listen to me. Please. I have to tell you this," Bernie said. Then she took Moriah's hands and looked directly into her eyes. "Are you listening?" She asked in a firm and serious voice.

"Yes, Bernie. Of course, I am."

"When this war is over... If I don't survive, you must search for either Anna Levinstein or Elica Frey. You must tell them to look in the box, the blood sister's secret tin box." Bernie handed Moriah a small piece of dirty paper. On it was written an address. "That's the last place I know of where Elica lived. Anna's home was taken over by a German family. So, her home address would not do you any good." Moriah took the paper and tucked it into her uniform pocket. Then Bernie continued, "Of course, there is a possibility that they might both be dead. But who knows, they could survive and live somewhere in Vienna or even somewhere else. If you find either of them, tell them that you knew me here at Ravensbrück. Tell them I said that instructions on how to find Theo are in the blood sisters' tin box. They will know where to find it. And, if by chance, when you are looking for them, you run into a girl named Dagna Hofer, do not trust her. Do not tell her anything. We knew her when we were children. She wanted to be a part of our group. But you must be careful of her because she is a terrible person and a danger to Anna and to Theo. Now Moriah, please, you must not forget a word of this conversation. Please, Moriah."

"The blood sister's tin box? The two friends. The girl called Dagna Hofer, who I must be careful of. I will remember all of it. I promise you."

"Yes, don't forget. Please don't forget any of this." Bernie's voice was frantic.

"I won't forget a word of what you've said. I promise. But, Bernie, what if I don't survive?"

"You will. You must."

"I could say the same thing about you."

"I know. And I agree with you. I will do everything I can to survive this place. But, just in case, I wanted to tell you about Theo."

"What if I can't find either Elica or Anna?"

"Then we will have done our best, and Theo's future will be in God's hands."

CHAPTER FORTY

On a cold afternoon in mid-February, Bernie was peeling potatoes. Prisoners received the peelings for their soup, while the potatoes were used to prepare a meal for the guards. She'd gotten used to the idea that only spoiled potatoes were given to the prisoners. As she poured a large bowl of peelings into the soup pot, she saw Moriah walk out of the office of the *Unterschar-führer,* clutching her arms around her chest. Even though Bernie was halfway across the room, she could see that Moriah's eye was all red, half closed, and badly bruised. Her lips were still bleeding, and blood ran down her chin and across the front of her uniform. Risking a beating herself for leaving her station, Bernie dropped the bowl she was holding and rushed over to Moriah.

"What happened?" Bernie said, gently touching Moriah's eyes. "Are you alright?"

"He hurt me," Moriah said. She shook Bernie's hand off of her and put her head down.

"Are you alright?" Bernie repeated.

"It doesn't matter if I'm all right or not. I have to work here, anyway. I have to take whatever he gives me and put up with him. I can't say a word. I dare not complain." She began to cry. "And I can't go back to my block and lie down even though I feel sick and this pain in my shoulder is terrible. They use us like cattle until they've taken everything we have away from us. Then they throw us away when we're dead."

"Let me help you. I'll help you with your work today. I'll do what I can to make things a bit easier for you."

One of the female guards saw Bernie and Moriah talking. She walked over and hit them across the shoulders with a wooden club she carried. Moriah let out a scream.

"What's this? What have we here?" The guard said, "I look over and see you two are standing around talking like your guests at a party. Get to work before I beat the hell out of both of you."

CHAPTER FORTY-ONE

S lowly, ever so slowly, the winter passed. The snow melted, and the spring rains arrived. With them came the hope of a new life. There was new grass and new green leaves on the trees. Bernie tried to raise Moriah's spirits. But *Unterscharführer* had beaten her several more times since that first time, and she was fighting depression. Nothing seemed to matter. And then, to make things even worse, they faced the relentless heat of summer.

Working in the kitchen was not as desirable in the summer as it had been in the winter. With the ovens going all day and the cauldrons of soup boiling, it was always blisteringly hot. Bernie had lost so much weight that she hardly recognized her own body. She'd always been slender with long, lean muscles. But now she was little more than skin and bones.

But even though *Unterscharführer* Maynard Graf beat Moriah relentlessly, he was still obsessed with her. Every morning, as soon as Moriah and Bernie arrived in the kitchen for work, he called Moriah into his office. She didn't resist him. She had no fight left in her. And that lack of fight was scaring Bernie. There was no anger, no hatred, no fight. Her eyes had become blank. She never laughed anymore. And Bernie finally asked her if she was all right. Moriah just shook her head. "I am as all right as I can be," she admitted. "He's good to me sometimes, you know. I am very confused. I hate him, and yet, I also care for him. Sometimes I even think I love him. But I am also terrified of him. I think of nothing else but him. I don't know what I feel. Sometimes I just wish I was dead."

"Don't wish that. Don't ever wish that. I pray every day that we will survive. You must pray for that, too, if we can ever hope to get out of here."

"I wonder if I would miss him?"

"Miss him? He has almost killed you. You would be blessed to get away from him. You can't trust him," Bernie said. She wanted to shake Moriah until she could shake sense back into her.

"I know that. He doesn't promise me anything. Sometimes he is so warm and loving that I want to ask him to help us escape. But then I remember what he can do to me, and I dare not. He has a way of always reminding me that there is a line that I dare not cross with him. And I don't. However, I want to tell you something."

"Of course, tell me."

"There is something I feel very guilty about."

"What is it?"

"He gives me chocolates. I wanted to bring some for you. I feel so bad that I am eating chocolate and can't share it with you. But he won't let me. He makes me eat them while he watches."

Bernie smiled and touched Moriah's hand. "It's all right."

"Sometimes, I hate myself for caring for him. I know he is one of them, and I don't mean anything to him. But the constant sex is confusing to me. I am so lonely, and this intimacy makes me feel things I don't want to feel. Things I know I shouldn't feel. And even worse, I've missed my period. I'm afraid that I am pregnant."

"Did you tell him?"

"No. I would never tell him. I am afraid of what he might do. I think he might kill me."

"You're right. Never tell him. Never. I don't know what he would do. And we can't trust him not to do something terrible. Let me see if I can find out if there is a doctor here who can help you."

"Get rid of it? Or have it?" Moriah asked.

"You must get rid of it. You wouldn't want to bring a child into this place, would you? Look at the children who are here in this camp. They suffer terribly. Would you want your child to suffer like they do?"

Moriah shook her head. "No. No, I wouldn't. But I have always wanted a child."

"Not here. Not now, and not in this place," Bernie said.

"No, not here. You're right." Moriah looked around. "Not in this place."

Bernie began her search of the camp for a prisoner who was a doctor. But she didn't find one. However, after a week of asking everyone if they knew of a doctor who was imprisoned, a young woman sent Bernie to speak to a woman who was known amongst the others as 'Esther, the midwife.' In her previous life, before the Nazis had invaded the city of Lodz in Poland, she had been an orthodox Jewish midwife and doula working primarily for other orthodox Jewish women. When Bernie met Esther, she found her to be kind but firm and yet very understanding as she explained Moriah's situation.

"I know that asking you to do something like this is probably against everything you believe in," Bernie said. "But my friend is in trouble. If the Nazi who fathered the child finds out she's pregnant, he might kill her. And if he doesn't, the child will be born here in this terrible place."

Esther nodded. "My beliefs are not so firm as they once were. Ravensbrück changed that for me. I must admit that there was a time when I would have refused to do something so heinous. But now, well..." she sighed. Then she straightened the scarf she wore on her head and said, "We'll have to do it on a Sunday."

"My friend and I work in the kitchen, so we'll have to find a way to get Sunday off."

"Yes, you will. Don't you girls switch Sundays so you can take a day off or something like that?"

"Sometimes we do. Don't worry. I'll figure it all out," Bernie said. Then she looked into Esther's eyes and said, "But I must ask you, will she be all right?"

"I hope so. Of course, I can't guarantee anything, but I'll do my best. Getting rid of pregnancy is dangerous. But since I have been here, I have helped women in this way before. I'll do what I can for your friend. There is only one problem."

"What is it?" Bernie asked.

"She will have to tell the guard that he must not touch her for a couple of weeks after the procedure."

"How can she do that? She doesn't want to tell him anything about this."

"But she must find a way. He can't do anything with her sexually for at least a couple of weeks."

Bernie put her head in her hands. "What am I ever going to do?"

"Talk to her. Tell her what I said. Let her know her options before we make plans. Then, once she decides, let me know what you want to do."

"And how will I pay you?"

"How can you pay me? What do you have?"

Bernie laughed bitterly. "Have? I have nothing. But I'll steal a loaf of bread for you from the kitchen."

"Well, right now, a loaf of bread is worth more than a diamond. Yes?"

"Yes," Bernie admitted.

Esther smiled. "Go now, talk to your friend. See what she wants to do."

"All right," Bernie said. "All right."

CHAPTER FORTY-TWO

Bernie discussed the situation with Moriah. She told her everything that Esther had said.

"I don't know what to do. If he wants me, I can't say no. I tried once, and he beat me so badly that I couldn't move my arm the next day. But if I dare to tell him that I've aborted his baby, he might kill me."

"And if you tell him you're pregnant, he might kill you, too."

"That's true."

"So, how can you keep him from entering you while you heal?"

"Oh, Bernie, that sounds so dirty. So obscene," Moriah said, looking away.

"Yes, of course it does. But that doesn't matter. What matters is your life. We need to figure this out. I must ask you, have you ever done anything to him with your mouth?"

"Bernie!"

"Answer me."

"No, never."

"You must do this. This is what you must do while you are heal-ing. You must pretend that you are trying something new for the fun of trying something new. He must never suspect that you are doing this for any other reason."

"I don't think I can. It makes me sick to think of it."

"Then don't think of it. It's what you must do. You must make it seem like it's a game that you are playing for his pleasure."

"Oh, Bernie. I could vomit."

"Don't vomit. You want to live. I want you to live. This is what must be done," she said firmly.

Moriah looked away from Bernie. They were sitting in her block, and in the heat, the hideous smell from the latrines was even more pungent. Mixed with the thought of what she must do, it made her gag. "I don't know. I don't think I can do this. Maybe I will just have to tell him the truth. Maybe he'll be happy to know I am pregnant."

Bernie shook Moriah's shoulders. "Are you crazy? You can't trust him. Do you think he cares about you? You are just another prisoner to him. You are like a toy to him. He won't put his job at risk for you. He'll shoot you without thinking twice and find another girl to take your place."

"Are you sure?" Moriah asked. "Are you absolutely positive? I would love to have a child."

"I'm not sure of anything. But we can't take that risk."

"Isn't there something else I can do?" Moriah asked.

"I don't know. I just don't know. This is all I can come up with. And we must do it soon. The longer we wait, the more danger we will put you in."

"I'm not ready. I need to think about it. I need a little time," Moriah said.

Bernie nodded, then she got up from the hard ground and left Moriah's block, heading back to her own.

Two weeks passed. Bernie was starting to panic. But Moriah refused to discuss the situation. All she said was that she hadn't made a decision yet. Then one day after work, as Moriah and Bernie were eating their soup made with potato peels, Moriah started to cry. "Maynard told me today that he's been promoted. He's leaving the kitchen."

"*Unterscharführer* Graf is leaving the kitchen?"

"Yes."

"Who is coming? Is he moving you with him?"

"No. He's not taking me anywhere. I don't know who will be in charge of the kitchen once he's gone."

"When is he leaving?" Bernie asked.

"I don't know. All I know is that he told me about his promotion today. All he said was that he was leaving Ravensbrück. When I asked him what was going to happen to me, he said I would have to fend for myself. He said I have been relying on his kindness for too long. I begged him to let me stay in the kitchen. I told him that I would die if I went back outside to work on the roads. It's too hard for me. He said he would see what he could do. But I know he is done with me."

"Believe it or not, this is great news, Moriah. Now Esther can help you."

"But I feel so lost. So alone and abandoned. What if he sends me to another job? What if it's worse than this? I could become one of the doctor's rabbits. She could take off my limbs..."

"Listen to me. Let's just hope that you don't get sent to another position. And as far as Maynard is concerned, he wasn't your boyfriend. He was just a Nazi guard who was taking advantage of his power. You must put him out of your mind."

Moriah fished two half-melted chocolates out of her uniform pocket and handed them to Bernie. "I put these in my pocket when he wasn't looking. I brought them for you."

Bernie took them. "Are you sure you want to give them away?"

"Very sure. In fact, no matter how long I live, I will never eat chocolate again."

CHAPTER FORTY-THREE

The following morning, when Bernie and Moriah arrived at work in the kitchen, *Unterscharführer* Graf was gone. There was no trace of him. However, there was also no mention of transferring Moriah to another job. A new female guard had taken Graf's place. She was standing in the middle of the kitchen with the prisoners arrived. She was a heavy-set woman with frizzy blonde hair that she wore in a bun at the nape of her neck and a no-nonsense attitude. She introduced herself and said, "I am the new boss of the kitchen. And I expect this work to be done with no talking and no nonsense. Now do your jobs, and you won't have any trouble. But I will tell you right now that I won't stand for any loitering around. Get to work."

The work was the same.

Bernie could tell that Moriah was depressed. She wished she could talk to Moriah. While the *Unterscharführer* was in command of the kitchen, Moriah had spent most of her time in his office. But now she had to work and work hard. There was very little time for speaking, and the new guard demanded that the girls remain silent.

That evening, after they finished in the kitchen, Bernie asked Moriah if she should arrange for the midwife to take care of things on Sunday. Moriah nodded in agreement.

CHAPTER FORTY-FOUR

Esther, the midwife, was knowledgeable. Everyone who knew her said she was good at her job. Bernie went to see her and told her that Moriah was ready. Esther explained that she thought it would be best to do the procedure on a Saturday night. "If I do it on Saturday night, she'll have all of Sunday to recover before she needs to return to work."

Bernie wondered if Esther felt bad about all of this being a sin. But she didn't ask. She was glad Esther had agreed to help Moriah. And whatever her reasons were, Bernie didn't need to know them.

Bernie went back to tell Moriah what Esther had said.

"On a Saturday night? Right after the sabbath?" Moriah said.

"You told me you were not religious." Bernie was annoyed again.

"I'm not. But do you think God will understand?"

"Yes, I do. I think so," Bernie blurted out, her slightly harsh tone. Then added in a softer voice, "yes. I think God will understand."

Moriah nodded. "All right, then Saturday night, we'll do it."

"And you will have Sunday to rest. Esther will sneak over to our block after the final roll call on Saturday. Once we are locked in for the night, she'll do what she must do. Then she'll stay here with you for the rest of the night, just in case you need her."

"What if she gets caught? They'll kill her if she gets caught."

"Yes, I know. She knows it too. But you aren't the first girl she's helped out of a bad situation."

Moriah nodded. She was quiet for a few minutes. Then she said, "It wasn't all bad."

"What?" Bernie asked.

"Him. Maynard. He and I. It wasn't all bad."

"He was a Nazi. It was bad."

"I know, and I know you're right. But, Bernie, I have been so lonely," she said, then she sighed. "And he brought me chocolates. And sometimes, he was kind to me."

Bernie wanted to slap Moriah across the face. She wanted to slap some sense into her. But she didn't. She just said, "Moriah, he was raping you. Forcing himself on you. You would never have slept with him if he had not done that. Now, would you?"

"No, probably not. But there are no men here. At least, almost none. And before Maynard, I found that I really missed the attention of a man. Even when it was bad. It was better than nothing. It was better than this terrible loneliness."

"I suppose," Bernie said. She didn't look into Moriah's eyes. She didn't want to admit that she was hurt. After all, Bernie was lonely too. And because they had become close friends, she found that she had begun to have feelings for Moriah. However, she knew she could never tell her. Moriah would never feel the same. This is my curse. She thought. *I will always carry love in my heart that no one wants. And it hurts deeply to know that Moriah would prefer the arms of a sadistic Nazi to mine.* There was no point in discussing any of this. To change the subject, Bernie said, "Do you want to play cards? I have a deck of cards."

"No, I don't feel like it," Moriah answered.

There was silence for a few moments. Then Moriah whispered, "I think I want to have the baby."

Bernie reached over and gently turned Moriah's chin so that Moriah was looking up into her eyes. She stared into Moriah's eyes, holding her gaze for a moment. Then she said softly and as gently as possible. "I know how you feel. We've already discussed this. But I will tell you again. You can't have a baby here. These bastards kill children. They murder infants. If you both survived the birth by some miracle, the child would be in terrible danger all the time."

"I think it might help if I told them who the father is. They might be kinder to my child?"

"Moriah, I've said this before, and I will say it again. I think they would be worse. They would hurt your baby. Kill it, probably. You're Jewish. There are laws against a Jew and a non-jew having a child. You know this."

"I do, I do know it. And you've told me a hundred times. But it's hard to kill my child. I wish there were some way out. Sometimes I think I should have told him I was pregnant before he left."

"You've gone mad. No, you should not have told him. He would probably have killed you himself. After all, he broke the law. Oh, Moriah, I know you want a baby. I understand why you would. A child can be a blessing. But not in here. Now, I know you are lonely, but you can't do this to yourself or the child. If you had a child here in this place and they hurt your child, it would be the most horrible thing that could ever happen. You would never forgive yourself. This is your only option."

"I can't talk about it anymore. We discuss this and say the same things over and over, and I still can't decide what to do. I know you're right. But I just can't bring myself to do it. I'm sorry. I'm tired. I'm going to my block. I want to go to sleep. In fact, I wish I could just go to sleep and never wake up. I can't stand my life. I can't live like this anymore. I wish I could just die." Moriah got up and left Bernie sitting on the floor.

All night long, Bernie was worried that Moriah would kill herself. *After all, she is faced with a terrible choice. She can't think straight. And I don't blame her. But she is acting irrationally. She knows her child is the offspring of a Nazi, but it's not only his. It's also hers, and she's Jewish. I can understand how she feels. But as ugly as this is, she must do it. She has no other choice. If she doesn't, the guards will kill them both. They will know that the father is one of them because there are no other men around, and they will want to protect their Nazi coworker. At least, that's what I think. Poor Moriah. I just hope she doesn't decide that her only choice is to kill herself because she can't do this.*

Bernie lay there for hours, unable to sleep. She knew she needed the rest. The new kitchen boss was sure to work her hard the following day, but it didn't matter. She couldn't sleep. She considered trying to leave her block and making her way over to Moriah to make sure she was all right. But there were guards right outside. She could hear them talking and laughing. *They must be drinking.* They often drank during the night. And she knew that if they caught her, there would be hell to pay. Depending upon the mood of the guards, she could easily be forced to pay with her life. The thought of being beaten to death made her rethink her plan. She was tired. The girl she'd been, the courageous girl that was always willing to fight for what was right, was exhausted. The courage had been beaten out of her.

What was left behind was a cautious, careful woman whose back and legs ached and who was just trying to stay alive long enough to get back to those she cared about. Besides, Bernie knew that no matter what she did, she couldn't control Moriah. If Moriah was determined to do something to herself, she would do it. If not tonight, then tomorrow. If Moriah decided she didn't want to live, it was just a matter of time before she ended her life. The thought left Bernie feeling sad and frightened. She wished she knew the right words to say, words that would encourage Moriah to go on. But, in reality, Bernie asked herself, *what is there to live for?*

CHAPTER FORTY-FIVE

Unterscharführer Graf walked into the Gestapo headquarters. He looked around and smiled. "Good morning. My name is *Unterscharführer* Maynard Graf," he said. "I am the new supervisor here." He sauntered around the office, asking each one of the Gestapo agents his name.

When he came to Ulf, Ulf looked at his new superior officer. Then he said, "My name is Wolfgang Fischer."

Graf looked Ulf up and down. Graf was tall with sharp features. His eyes were intense. Ulf managed a half smile as he wondered if he was going to be a difficult boss.

Just then, a woman opened the door and walked up to the window. She wore a scarf over her hair. *Typical German hausfrau.* Ulf thought as he observed her.

"I need to speak to someone," she said. "I have information that I would like to give you in exchange for a little food, maybe? Please have mercy. I have two children to feed. They're always hungry."

"I'll give you some bread if the information is worth it," Graf said.

"It is," the woman said. "I promise you, it is."

"What do you want to tell us?" one of the other officers asked as the woman was led inside.

She sat down. "There is a Jewish family hiding in my neighbor's attic," she said

Ulf lit a cigarette as he listened. His hands were shaking as he thought about Anna and her family. *I took a hell of a risk. I could have been killed trying to be a hero. What was I thinking?*

"You'd better not be lying. If we find out that you are wrong and there are no Jews there, you'll choke on that bread. You can mark my words on that," Graf said. He was smiling. His voice was soft and gentle, but his eyes and words were terrifying.

"I swear to you, they are in the attic next door. They are hiding. I have seen a child peeking out the attic window." The woman was trembling.

"Give me the address," Graf said. Then he turned to one of the agents. "Take her name and address, too. Just in case we find out that she tried to fool us, and we have to pay her a visit." He winked at the woman. Ulf could see that her lips were trembling.

After the woman left, Graf turned to Ulf. "I've heard you have been taking a lot of time off work. With me in charge, this will not be acceptable. Now, you will go with me and make the arrest."

Ulf nodded, but he was nervous. He'd always gone on arrests with his partners, but never with a superior officer. And after what had happened with Anna and her family, he knew he must appear casual and confident to not arouse any suspicion.

"Let's go," Graf said, grabbing the address from the table. "Let's see what you're made of."

Ulf followed Graf out the door, and into the waiting black automobile parked alongside the building. Then Graf turned on the siren. As they drove towards the house where the housewife had sent them, Ulf noticed, as he always did, that people on the street looked at them with fear in their eyes.

They knocked on the door. But as expected, no one answered. Graf asked Ulf to help him, and together they kicked the door in.

Once inside, they headed right for the attic. Graf climbed the stairs, with Ulf right behind him. When they got to the attic door, Graf kicked it in. Inside, a little boy was crying in his mother's arms. A young man in his early thirties was standing in front of them as if he believed he could somehow protect them by sacrificing himself.

"Jews!" Graf said, then he turned to Ulf. "Shoot the child."

"No, please. Please, I beg you. Not that. Anything but that," the woman said as she held the little boy tightly.

"Shoot him. Show me how loyal you are to the party. Shoot the child."

Ulf's hands were shaking. He pulled out his gun.

The child's father threw himself in front of his son. "I beg you to kill me, not my boy."

The room began to spin. Ulf felt like he might faint.

"Shoot him, then kill the boy. Are you a coward?" Graf said.

Ulf didn't know if he could do it. He was afraid he might faint. It was hot in the attic. So hot that sweat ran down his face.

"You're taking too long!" Graf screamed into his face. "Kill the man. Then kill the child." Ulf aimed his gun at the man. Graf screamed again, "Kill him. Kill him now. Do it now!"

Ulf shot the pistol and blood spurted all over the child's face. The child began to scream in a high-pitched voice.

"Don't stop now. Kill the child. Kill him. Coward. Coward. Do it."

The high-pitched screaming, Graf's yelling in Ulf's face, the heat, the smell of sweat, and unwashed bodies. All of these things made Ulf feel sick. He almost vomited.

"Are you too weak to be an Aryan? Are you unworthy of your position?"

Ulf fired the gun and killed the little boy. His mother let out a scream. Then she began to pull out her hair as she wept and fell upon her son. None of this affected Graf in the least. He tore the mother away from her child and raped her next to the dead bodies of her husband and son. At first, she screamed and wept. But then she fell silent.

"Rape her," Graf said when he had finished. "You've never had a Jew, have you?"

"But it's illegal," Ulf said. He was sick to death from all of this.

"No one needs to know. When you've finished with her, we'll kill her."

The woman didn't even whimper. Ulf took down his pants. He looked down at the woman, and for a moment, he saw Anna's face. He didn't know what it was that made him excited. Perhaps it was the power he held over her as she stood above her. But he surprised himself. He liked the feeling of being in control, liked it enough that his manhood got hard. Her eyes were closed. She was resigned to her fate. He didn't care. He raped her. When he was finished, he sighed with relief. Then he shot her, and he and Graf went downstairs to look for the family hiding these Jews. They were gone. They'd run away while Graf and Ulf were torturing their victims.

"Don't worry. We'll find them," Graf said. Then he took two bottles of beer off the shelf and handed one to Ulf. "To power," he said. They both drank. "I worked in a concentration camp. We had absolute power. We could do anything we wanted with the Jewish women. I tell you, that was something. Can you imagine it? Can you imagine doing anything you want with a woman, and there are no consequences?"

Ulf thought of Anna, and he felt himself getting hard.

CHAPTER FORTY-SIX

Bernie sighed with relief the following morning when she saw Moriah in the kitchen. Their eyes met, and Bernie gave Moriah a half smile, which Moriah did not return. *She is going to be all right.* Bernie told herself. *I believe she will be all right if she made it through last night. She will survive this.* That night, as they walked back to their respective blocks, Moriah turned to Bernie, and in a flat, emotionless voice, she said, "I'm going to do it. Will you please help me make all the arrangements?"

"Of course," Bernie said. The following day, Bernie arranged for them both to have this Sunday off from work. She paid two other women to cover for them with stolen potato peelings. Then she and Moriah made a plan. They would both go to Moriah's block that Saturday night right after roll call. It would be difficult to slip by the guards, but Bernie had become quite good at hiding in the shadows. Then, as soon as things grew quiet, Esther would make her way to Moriah's block. Esther said she would have done this without payment. However, Bernie brought half of a loaf of bread she'd stolen and hidden under the bed. She planned to give it to Esther in exchange for her help.

On Saturday night, Bernie made her way to Moriah's block with the bread under her uniform. When she arrived, she hid it under Moriah's bed, then together, they waited for Esther. Time was ticking. Soon the lights would be out. Esther was still not there. "What if she doesn't come?" Moriah asked.

Bernie shrugged. "I don't know." Then she looked at the worried expression on Moriah's face and said, "Don't worry. She'll be here."

Ten minutes later, Moriah asked, "What if she got caught leaving her block? What if they are punishing her right now, and it's my fault?"

"Don't think about that. She'll be here," Bernie said. But she wasn't sure she believed it. She was more apt to believe that Esther had changed her mind or, worse, she had been caught. If that were the case, everyone would hear about it in the morning at roll call. The guards might even punish all of them for Esther's actions and take away their privilege of having Sunday off. *Esther might already be dead. They could have killed her. Or they might be torturing her, trying to force her to tell them where she was going. Would she tell them that Moriah was pregnant?* Bernie's mind began to race. She was overcome with worry and fear. Sweat beaded on her brow. Her head began to ache. And just when she thought she couldn't bear it anymore, she saw a woman's form slip through the window of the block. It was dark, and she couldn't be sure it was Esther. Bernie stood up and walked over to the woman.

"Bernie," the woman whispered.

"Yes," Bernie said, her body almost limp with relief. "Esther. Thank God you're here."

"I'm here. I almost got caught. I was rushing to get here and didn't see the guard until he was a few feet in front of me. Then I had to hide behind the side of the building and wait until he walked away. He stood there smoking until, finally, another guard came, and the two of them left together. I was very close to getting caught. I am a little shaken up. That's why it took me so long to get here. I'm sorry."

"It's all right. I'm glad you're safe, and I'm glad you came."

"Where is Moriah?"

"Follow me. She's over here." Bernie led Esther to Moriah.

Moriah lay on the ground, her head buried in her arm.

"Are you asleep?" Bernie asked.

"No. How could I sleep?" Moriah said. "I'm terrified."

"I know. I'm here with you." Bernie took Moriah's hand and held it tightly.

"The first thing I need to do is examine you to determine how long you have been pregnant. If you have been pregnant for too long, we might not be able to do this," Esther said. "Now turn over."

Moriah did as she was told.

"I wish I had a light. I couldn't get my hands on a candle," Esther said, shaking her head.

"Does anyone have a candle?" Bernie asked.

No one on the block answered her.

"Turn this way," Esther instructed. "I can see a little better over here because of the moonlight that's streaming in."

Moriah did as she was told. Then she reached for Bernie's hand and squeezed it while Esther examined her.

"I'm here with you," Bernie assured Moriah. "I'm right here."

Moriah started to cry.

Then someone walked over to Esther, carrying a candle. "Here. Use it sparingly. It's the only one I have."

"It's a *mitzvah* you've done, letting us use it," Esther said. "Thank you."

The woman handed her a couple of matches. "These are all I have."

"I understand. I will only use one," Esther promised.

She lit the candle and then examined Moriah by candlelight. After a few minutes, she stopped. "Moriah," Esther said firmly in a whisper, "you're not pregnant."

"What? Are you sure?"

"I'm quite sure. I've been a midwife since I was seventeen, and I've seen plenty of pregnancies. You're not pregnant."

"But my period stopped."

"Yes, I understand, and that can happen. It has happened to a lot of girls here. Your menstruation stops due to the lack of food and being overworked. But the good news is, you're not pregnant."

"That is good news," Bernie said, squeezing Moriah's hand. "That's wonderful."

"Will my period ever return? Will I get it back if this ever ends? If I survive this. I mean, if it ever ends, I want a child someday. Will I be able to have children?"

"I can't tell you what will happen in the future because I don't know. Until I got to this place, I had never seen women so starved and abused. I hope this thing will end someday. I pray for it constantly. And I pray that we won't all be dead before it ends. I hope that by some miracle, we will survive this terrible abuse, and you will be able to have children. But, right now, just be glad that you are not pregnant."

"Thank you," Bernie said. Then she went to get the bread that she had hidden for Esther. It was gone. "Where is my bread?" She asked in an angry whisper. But no one answered. "What have we all become? Thieves? Liars? I am ashamed to know you," Bernie said. Still, no one spoke up.

"Esther, I am so sorry. Someone stole the bread that I had hidden for you."

"Yes, we have all become thieves, haven't we?" Esther said sadly. "That's what starvation will do to you. No matter." She let out a long sigh. "It would have been nice to have a little extra, but if you don't have it, you don't have it." She picked up the small bag of tools she had brought and stood up.

"I shouldn't talk about the others. After all, I am a thief too. I stole that bread from the kitchen. And now, someone has stolen it from me," Bernie said. She turned to Esther. "I'll find a way to get you another one. I promise you. I'll get it as soon as I can."

"If you can, it would be very nice. If not, I understand. It would have been helpful to have a bit of extra food. My mother is here with me, and she is so weak. A bit of extra food might help her. But the truth is, I didn't do anything for your friend. So, you really don't owe me anything."

"But I do owe you. You put yourself at risk coming here during the night. I owe you for that. And I promise I will get you more bread. I'll steal it from the kitchen as soon as I see an opportunity." Then Bernie said to the rest of the women, "Yes, starvation has made us all thieves. Even me. But I'll tell you this. No matter how bad things get, I will never steal from another prisoner. I'll steal from the Nazis, but I will never steal from you. When we start to steal from each other, we lose any sense of who we are and what we stand for."

CHAPTER FORTY-SEVEN

A few days later, the new female guard was taking inventory of the kitchen when she noticed that half of a loaf of bread was missing. She called the group to attend and warned them that the thief would be caught and would pay dearly. Then she chastised them by not allowing them to eat that night. They were told that they would be shot if they were caught putting a single morsel of food into their mouths. After that, the guard began to watch the food supply even more closely. Bernie knew she had brought this punishment to the group, and she felt terrible. But there was little she could do. It was not like Bernie to break a promise, and she had made a promise to Esther to somehow get her the loaf of bread. So, since she was unable to steal more bread, she began to save half of her ration each day to give Esther. However, after two days, Bernie began to grow weak.

"That's enough for you to give her," Moriah said. "I've saved a little too. We'll give this to her, and that will be the end of this. You need to eat. You are looking pale. I don't like it."

"I haven't been feeling well," Bernie admitted.

"I hope you aren't coming down with something."

"It wouldn't surprise me with all the diseases going around in here," Bernie said.

"You can't get sick, Bernie. You know there is no mercy here for anyone who is sick."

"I know, Moriah. I know. I'll be all right," Bernie forced a smile. But she wasn't sure that she would. She'd never felt so ill and so tired.

"I'll give Esther the bread that we have. But, from now on, you had better eat your ration."

"I will," Bernie said. But she felt chilled all over. But at the same time, her face was flushed, and her forehead was hot. She knew she was running a fever. And for the last three days, she'd been coughing up blood. She hadn't told Moriah about it because she knew it would send Moriah into a panic, and right now, she didn't have the strength to deal with it. "I just need to rest," Bernie told Moriah. She was hoping she would feel better in the morning. However, when morning came, she felt worse, her joints ached, and she was too tired to move. In fact, she couldn't force herself to get up. Her limbs would not cooperate. When she didn't show up to walk with Moriah to the kitchen that morning, Moriah came to Bernie's block. She found her lying still on what served as a bed. It was just dirty straw filled with lice that lay over hard wooden planks.

"Bernie," Moriah said, and she ran to Bernie's side. "You're very sick."

"I can't go to work today," Bernie admitted. "I tried, but I can't move."

"You have to go," Moriah said. "If they find out you're sick, they'll send you to the hospital. No one ever comes out of that hospital. Everyone they send there dies. They'll kill you, Bernie."

"I know. I know it, but I can't get up."

"Oh, dear God. What am I going to do? Work will begin soon, and I'll miss the roll call. But I can't leave you here. They'll find you. And then..." Moriah began to cry.

"I'm dying, Moriah," Bernie said sadly. "I am going to die here."

"No, you can't die. You can't leave me in this place alone. I can't live here without you. I'll never make it. Please don't leave me. I'll do anything. I'll even be your girlfriend if that's what you want. You won't be lonely anymore. I am not that way, but I'll try for you. Just please don't die. Please don't leave me here alone."

Bernie laughed a little. "I appreciate your offer. I really do. But that's not quite what I would want from a girlfriend, anyway. I had a lover who loved me, and I am grateful to have had the time Viola and I spent together. But now..." She hesitated, then continued. "Moriah, now it's my time to go."

"No. No, you can't."

"I'm sorry. Please, you must remember your promise to me. When this is all over, you must go and find Elica or Anna if you can and tell them about the box. When they find the box, they will find all the information they need about Theo."

"What about your girlfriend? What about her? Should I go and tell her what happened?"

"Viola. My sweet Viola. I don't want her to know what I went through or how I died. Don't search for her. My story will only make her sad. When I don't come back, she'll go on. She'll find someone new. She's young. We only had a few weeks together in total. If I don't return, she'll forget, and I only want the best for her."

"Bernie, you can't do this. Please. You must get up. Just get up. You're strong. We have to go to work," she said, her voice filled with desperation.

"I'm sorry," Bernie said. She closed her eyes. Her breath was raspy. There was blood on her lips. Moriah began to cry. Bernie took Moriah's hand and squeezed it. "Thank you for being my friend," she said. Then the raspy breath stopped. She was gone.

CHAPTER FORTY-EIGHT

The forest was thick with trees and shrubs that scratched and cut Anna's flesh. So far, the food and water Ulf had brought were sustaining the Levinsteins, but it was diminishing quickly. Though the family was in peril, Anna cherished being outside in the sunshine and fresh air after being in the attic. They continued to walk. They had no idea where they were going. All they knew was that they couldn't risk meeting Ulf again. He'd been wonderful and kind, but it would be disastrous if he had a change of heart. So, Anna and her father walked together because they could walk faster than her mother and Anselm, who followed a little behind. They had been walking for days now, hoping to find water. They hadn't found it yet, and Anna had no idea where they were. All she knew was that they were deep within the woods, closely surrounded by trees. Although they could not see the animals, the sounds of the forest told them that dangerous animals lurked everywhere.

Anselm never complained, but Anna could see by how his face was drawn that all of this walking was hard on him. He constantly coughed, and she saw him spit blood a couple of times. There was nothing she could do, nothing her parents could do. She prayed for him each night and often as she walked along during the day as well. Although it was apparent that Anselm needed a doctor, he was unable to receive medical help. And so there was nothing Anna could do for him. Her brother's life, and the future of her entire family, were in God's hands.

During the height of the day, it was hot, so hot that the sweat soaked through Anna's undergarments and dress. "We need to find a pond, a stream, a river, water of any kind," Anna's father said. He carefully rationed the water they had. "We are all thirsty, especially in this heat, but we must drink as little as possible until we can find a place to refill these containers Ulf brought us." He said this, holding up two glass bottles Ulf had brought, one empty and the other only half full.

The night was more comfortable. When the sun began to go down, the air grew cooler, and it would have been so much better, except that with the dusk came swarms of biting insects. They bit and stung, leaving large red itchy welts on Anna's flesh. But once the sun set and darkness fell upon the forest, the wolves howled and owls hooted, and the Levinstein family huddled together in fear. "I don't know which is more terrifying," her mother said, "the Nazis or the wild creatures in this forest."

"The Nazis, by far," Anna's father said.

CHAPTER FORTY-NINE

After days of walking, not knowing where they were headed. Knowing only that they must keep moving, Anna's father finally spotted a pond. The sun beat down on Anna's head as she knelt at the pond and drank. Once she'd drunk to her fill, she submerged her face in the cool water, and then she wet her entire head. The water felt cold but wonderfully cleansing. With wet hair, she lay down on the ground on her back and breathed deeply. Anselm and her parents were busy filling the water bottles and drinking as much as they could. Once they'd finished, Anna's father suggested that she and her mother take a bath while he and Anselm waited on the other side of the pond. "Once you two have finished, Anselm and I will bathe," her father said.

Anna removed her dress but not her undergarments and was careful as she got into the water. She didn't know how deep it was. But it was a shallow pond, and she waded in up to her waist. Because they had been in hiding. It had been some time since her body had been submerged in water. And even though she had no soap, it felt wonderful. Her mother followed her into the pond. And for a long time, the two women didn't say a word. They just stood in the water, enjoying the sensation of washing the sweat off their bodies.

"Come on, girls," Anna's father called out after a half hour had passed, "give us a turn."

"All right. We'll get out right now, Michael," Anna's mother said to her father.

When they got out of the pond, Anna looked down at her stomach and let out a scream. Then she began jumping and shaking. "Help, papa. Help!" she was screaming in terror. A fat leech had attached itself to her belly. Hearing her scream, her father came running. "What is it?" he said, not looking at her.

"A leech. Look, it's on my stomach. Please hurry and get it off."

"Stand still so I can get it," her father commanded.

Anna's mother looked down at her own body. She grunted in disgust when she saw that she had leeches on her legs. She began picking them off.

"Shhh, it's all right," Anna's father said.

But Anna's whole body trembled with disgust and outrage.

Her father quickly plucked the leach from Anna's stomach. But when he looked down, there were two more thick black leeches on her calves. "Hurry, papa. Please hurry and get them off me."

"I'm going to get all of them. Don't be afraid."

Anna was jumping and shaking.

"Hold still," her father commanded.

She did. And he plucked the filthy things from her legs. Anna shivered as she saw thick black worms filled with her blood fall to the ground. Once the leeches were gone from her body, Anna slipped her dress back on. Her face was red with embarrassment. "I'm so ashamed, papa."

He smiled. "It's all right. I'm your father, Anna. I wasn't looking. I promise."

She tried to smile back at him. Her father had never seen her in her underclothes before, and she felt embarrassed. But he didn't seem to notice. It was as if he'd already forgotten the incident. He was busy helping Anselm to wash without getting into the pond. Anna watched her father and her brother for a moment. They bathed as best they could but did not submerge their bodies in the water because of the leeches.

Nothing is ever completely good here in the forest. There is always a tradeoff. If we are enjoying the drop in heat, then we are victims of insects. Why must it be filled with leeches if we are blessed to find a pond? Anna wondered.

They were almost out of food. Anna's mother refused to eat. Anna knew her mother must be hungry, yet she would not accept her share. "Give it to the children, Michael," she would say to her husband.

"But Lilian," her father would argue, "you must eat too."

She wouldn't listen. She would only shake her head and wrap her arms around her chest. No one could make Frau Levinstein eat while her children went without. Her mother had not been changed by their circumstances, but her father had. He had once been a wealthy, powerful man who owned a factory. People had obeyed him, and others had taken his advice. If she were to admit it to herself, her father was arrogant in those days. He listened to no one. Anna still remembered that evening when she'd brought her friend and potential suitor, Daniel, home to have dinner with her family. How her father had disliked Daniel. That was because, although Daniel came from a family that was even more wealthy than her own, he was a champion for the poor working man. And even a bit of a communist. He had openly argued with her father. And after he left that evening, her father forbade her to see him again. She had refused to follow her father's orders. Daniel was her first love interest, and although she knew that since her father didn't like him, they would never be able to get married, she continued to see him in secret. That was until Daniel and Elica, Anna's best friend, fell in love.

Ahhh, well, that was a long time ago. And since then, so much has happened. I was hurt by the betrayal at first. But I never loved Daniel, not really. I liked him a lot. But now, Daniel and Elica are married and have a son. And Daniel has been taken away by the Gestapo. It makes me shiver to think about it. Elica has gone to look for him. But I don't trust Dagna. She hates Jews, and she might turn in Elica to the police. And they could do anything to a gentile girl who married a Jew. She broke their law. So, where does that leave their little boy? What will become of him? I wonder if Bernie was able to get him all the way to Italy. I hope she didn't return to the house and get arrested for hiding us. Anna let out a sigh. *And my papa? He's a broken man. His years of being a powerful businessman did nothing to help him to get ready for what we are facing now. I know he has been through a lot in his life. I know he and my mother came to Vienna when they escaped from Russia during a pogrom. But that was a lifetime ago. They were both very young. My papa was strong then. My mother was too. Now he is overweight and so much older and slower. If he ever knew how to hunt or fish, he has forgotten. Without the food Ulf was supposed to bring, I am afraid we will all die of starvation.* Anna wanted to sit down on a tree stump and weep. *I am so tired and hungry. At least we have the water from the pond to drink, or we would die of thirst. I know it's wrong to think this way, but sometimes I feel it would be easier to just give up. To just lay down and go to sleep.*

But there was no time to lie down and give up. Herr Levinstein insisted that they keep walking. "We'll look for another pond. One without leeches," he said.

They began walking again, putting more distance between themselves and the spot where they had agreed to meet Ulf at the end of the month.

"Papa!" A loud cry broke through the sound of the birds chirping and the branches breaking under their feet. It was Anselm. "Papa. I fell. I think I twisted my ankle. And I cut my leg on a sharp tree branch. I'm bleeding badly. Come, please and help us. Mama can't lift me up, and I can't get up."

Anna and her father ran towards Anselm. They found him on the ground. His leg was bleeding profusely. Anna's father knelt and looked at the wound. "It's deep," he said, shaking his head.

No one said a word, but they all knew what this meant for

Anselm. He had been born with a blood disease, and a deep cut like this left untreated could cause him terrible problems. Even death.

Their father helped Anselm to his feet, but his ankle was twisted, and he couldn't walk.

"Well, this is as good a place as any for us to hide. If I were to guess, I would say we are deep in the forest, somewhere east of Vienna. But I am not sure. It doesn't matter, anyway. We will camp here, and then I will go off and do my best to look for water, where I will try to do some fishing. Will you come with me, Anna?"

"Of course, papa."

"Meanwhile, while we are gone, perhaps you can set up our blankets and make sure to cover whatever food and water we have, Lilian? There could be bears here. I don't know how close we are to the mountains. I can't tell. But just to be safe, make sure the food is covered."

"I will take care of everything," Lilian said. "Of course, I will do whatever needs to be done, Michael."

Anselm looked away from his family. Anna saw him staring out into the forest. She knew he felt responsible for causing the family to stop in the middle of the forest without water nearby. Standing up, she brushed off her skirt. Then she walked over to her brother, and in a reassuring voice, she said, "We're far enough away from our original place that if Ulf comes looking for us, he won't find us. And don't worry, Papa and I will do our best to find water."

Anselm swallowed. His Adam's apple bobbed up and down. Something about the sight of it made Anna want to cry. *He's so sickly. Every doctor has always warned us that he might not live long enough to grow up. But what's kind of ironic is that his sickness might not be the reason we lose him. My whole family is in peril. It looks like we are all probably going to die.*

Anselm's eyes looked old on his young face. He nodded. "This is all my fault. I am pretty sure that Papa wanted to try to get to the Carpathian Mountains. At least that's what I heard him say to mama. And now, we can't because I can't walk."

"And how would that help us? How would getting to the mountains make any difference in our lives? Anselm, we are in trouble. We can't find food. Without food..." She shook her head as her voice trailed off.

"I know. I thought the same thing, but I would never say that to papa," Anselm whispered. "I think perhaps we should have stayed where we were and taken our chances that Ulf would not turn on us. After all, he did rescue us in the first place."

"I know. And you're right. It's true. He went out of his way to help us. I made a big mistake. I asked him too many questions. I made him very angry with me. I should have kept my mouth shut. I don't know what came over me."

Their father stood up and walked over to where Anna and Anselm were sitting. "Come, Anna. Let's go and see if we can find water," he said.

"Yes, papa," she said, then turned to her brother and touched his shoulder. "Rest now, Anselm. I'll see you when I get back."

CHAPTER FIFTY

They began to walk in silence. The forest was thick, and so far, they had not found any trace of water.

Then, without warning, Anna's father stopped in his tracks. He plopped down on a large rock. Anna studied him. Then she asked. "What is it, papa? Do you feel all right?"

"I was just thinking as we were walking."

"Yes?"

"We must be careful not to get lost from your mother and your brother. The more we walk, the more I feel we are getting lost. I think I can get back to them now, but if we keep going, I am not sure." Then he scratched his head. "I'm beginning to think we should have stayed by the pond with the leeches. We could have stayed hidden by the forest, but at least we would be near water. We couldn't submerge in it, but we would have drinking water and use it to wash our faces and hands."

"I was thinking that too," Anna agreed. Then she sat down on a tree stump not far away from her father. "But there has to be water somewhere near here."

"Perhaps, but I am afraid to stray too far from your mother and brother. And your brother can't walk now that he's hurt himself. If we wander looking for water and can't find our way back, your mother and brother will be alone in the woods." He put his head in his hands and let out a long-frustrated sigh. Then in a slow voice, he said, "When your mother and I left Russia and made our way to Austria, I thought if we could just get there, if we could just find our way to Austria, we would never have to face hardships like this again. I believed that the terrible pogroms would be a thing of the past, and although we might not be loved because we were Jews, I didn't think we would face persecution again. Of course, when we left Russia, I was a young man in my late teens. I was strong and healthy. And Austria was such a civilized country compared to Russia. We came here and built a life, your mother and me. I worked hard. I built a business from the sweat of my brow. I stayed at the factory for long hours while your mother took care of you and Anselm all by herself. That was how it was for us in the beginning. But then, I was smart and made some good business decisions. That was when I began to make money — plenty of money. For many years, our lives were good, Anna. I was kind and generous and gave to charities for those less fortunate. I know your friend Daniel thought I was selfish because I didn't give in to the workers' demands. But I paid a fair wage, and I didn't expect the workers to work the long hours I'd had to work when I was an employee. I did the best I could, Anna. I didn't want to lose what I'd built. Maybe I wasn't as good to the workers as I could have been. But I was afraid I wouldn't be as successful if I gave them too much, and I was grateful to have the life we had. But now... look what has become of us? Just look at us, Anna."

"Papa, you're upsetting yourself. None of this stuff matters now. We're alive. We're together." Anna was frightened. She'd never seen her father so vulnerable. He looked like he might cry. She hoped he wouldn't. *Papa has always been the strong one in their family. If he crumbles, who will we look to for strength?*

"I think we should turn around and go back to your mother and brother. I believe we have enough water left for a few days. After that, I don't know what we will do. But I still think it's best if we all stay together."

"I think perhaps I should go alone to search for water," she said. "You go back and stay with Mama and Anselm. I'll do my best to find water. I won't get lost."

"Absolutely not. I forbid this, Anna. You will stay with the rest of us."

"Papa, let me do this. Please."

He looked at her and shook his head. Then, in a small voice, he said, "I am scared for you. You're my little girl."

She noticed his hands were shaking. It unnerved her.

"I know, but I am not a little girl anymore. I will find water, and then I will find my way back to all of you. Now you go back to Mama and Anselm."

"Are you sure you can do this, Anna? I am scared for you. I hate to let you do this..."

"I know. But I must."

He nodded. "All right. All right. Please, be careful."

"I will."

She watched him walk slowly away, back towards the camp where they'd left her mother and brother. *He looks so old and so help-less.* She thought, and that made her feel sick to her stomach. She forced the feelings of pity for her father out of her mind. Then, after taking a long deep breath, Anna stood up and began to walk in the other direction in search of water. The trees were close together, and the foliage was thick. It was dark, but it created a protective shield for her head from the sun, and she was grateful. As she made her way through the thick brush, she remembered that evening long ago when she'd brought Daniel home for dinner. How arrogant and in charge her father had been in those days. She'd hated him at the time. In fact, he'd been so demanding that she'd become angry and had secretly defied him by continuing to see Daniel when he had forbidden her to. But now that her father was a broken man, she wished that, somehow, he would regain that strength he'd lost. She missed the self-assured man that he had once been. He wasn't perfect then, but she always felt safe when he was around. Now, he could no longer be depended upon to be her strength. She had to rely on herself. A tear slipped down her cheek. She wiped it away with her hand. *Water? How am I ever going to find water? But I must. Because, without water, we will die. So, what should I do? Where should I look? Which way do I go? And I must be careful not to get lost, or I'll never find my way back.*

There was a rustle in the trees. Anna was frozen where she stood. *It could be a wild animal or a Nazi. It could be a Russian soldier or a partisan. It could be anyone or anything.* Her heart began to beat wildly. She could hear it in her ears. *Oh, please, God, don't let me faint. And please, protect me from whatever is hiding on the other side of these thick trees.*

Then she saw him. He was tall and wore a uniform with a swastika on the sleeve. His blonde hair was dusted with what looked like small pieces of tree bark. A ray of sunlight filtered through the trees, blocking her vision of his face, and most of all, she could not see his eyes. Then he turned and saw her standing there. He looked shocked as he stood perfectly still and stared at her. *A Nazi. I've been caught by a Nazi. He'll take me in now. My family will never know what happened to me.*

"Anna?" the blonde man said.

CHAPTER FIFTY-ONE

Anna squinted to try to see his face. He looked familiar, like someone she knew. But it wasn't Ulf. This man was smaller in stature than Ulf. *He knows my name. Who is this? Is this a dream, a mirage of some sort?* "Do I know you?" She asked in a small voice.

"Of course, you know me," he said. "Don't you remember me, Anna? It hasn't been that long since the last time we saw each other. Perhaps this will refresh your memory. When we were just children, I told you I would marry you someday." He laughed a little. "I never thought I would find you wandering in the woods. You are far away from our home in Austria. But then again, so am I."

Her heart was in her throat. "I'm confused."

"You were the first girl I kissed. It's me, Oliver."

"Ollie?" She recognized him. "Is that really you?"

"Yes, it's me."

"You have really grown up," she gasped.

"So have you. But you're still as pretty as I remember."

This is so strange. He knows I am Jewish, yet he acts like we are old friends meeting in town. When the reality is, we are prey and predator, meeting in the woods in a country far from our home. "What are you doing here?" she asked in a soft voice. She was hoping he didn't plan on arresting her.

"I am the counselor of the camp of the *Deutsche Jugend*. We are on a retreat a mile or so from here," he said.

"Oh," she gasped, "just like the Hitler Youth?"

"Yes," he smiled. Then he asked, "why are you here? Are you alone?"

"No, I'm with my family—" She stopped herself, realizing that she had said far too much. *What am I saying? What am I telling him? He may be an old friend, but he is a Nazi, and I am a Jew. I can't trust him.*

"Where is your family?" he asked.

"I lost them two days ago," she lied. "They are at least a two-day walk south of here."

"Anna," he said sincerely, "I know you are Jewish. So, I am assuming that you are hiding in the forest here from the Germans, aren't you?"

The sunlight shifted. She could see his eyes. They were soft and caring. *Could it be that he is still the same person I knew so long ago?* She was hopeful, but not completely trusting. "Yes. I am," she admitted. Then, in a small voice, she begged, "Please, Ollie, for old times' sake, don't take me in."

His jaw quivered. "I don't know what to do with you. I know what I am supposed to do. I mean, I know what I am expected to do if I find Jews hiding in the forest. But you? You're different. You're not like the other Jews. I mean, you're not a real Jew."

She tried not to look directly at him because she would have liked to spit in his face. But she knew better. He had a gun and had the power to kill her on the spot without any repercussions. It was obvious to her that he'd been seduced by the lies that the Nazis told about the Jews. Even though he'd known her and her family, he was still convinced by the nonsense the government was spewing. She would have liked to tell him that he sounded like an idiot. She wanted to tell him that Jews were just people, like her, like him even.

But she knew he wouldn't understand. Her feet wanted to bolt like a young colt surrounded by its enemies. *If I run, he might act without thinking and shoot me in the back. I must stay here and try to appease him. It's my only chance of survival.*

He shook his head as if he were trying to shake off cobwebs. "You said you are with your family, so why are you alone? Where are they?"

"Far away from here," she said quickly. "I have been walking for an entire day trying to find them, but I am lost."

"Lost... and they are far from here? How far?"

"I don't know, but very far."

"Did you say south? Was that what you said? Perhaps I can help. Jews should not be wandering these forests alone."

"South, yes, south," she said because she knew it was the wrong direction. "That way, I think," she said, pointing. Then she looked directly into his eyes and spoke softly, hoping to strike a chord of memory within him, "Ollie, you must know that if you take me to the authorities, there is a very good chance that the Germans will kill me. I was in hiding back in Austria. They broke into my hiding place and tried to arrest me. I escaped."

He looked at her blankly as if she were an animal that had gotten out of its pen rather than an old friend he'd once had a crush on.

She tried again. "Do you remember when you kissed me that day when we had that picnic with all of our friends in the park?"

His eyes grew a little glassy. "I have never forgotten it."

"You were always so handsome," she said, forcing a smile.

"Do you think so?"

"Of course. It's true."

There was a long silence. She held her breath. *Will he fall for such a stupid line, or will he know I am trying to soften him up, so he'll let me go?*

"Have you broken the law other than being Jewish?"

"No, Oliver. I am Jewish. That is all I have ever done that is wrong. If I weren't Jewish, we might be married."

"That's true," he said. "I know that it's true because you were always so special to me. That was, until I joined the party and understood why we Aryans must not mix blood with Jews."

She didn't know what to say, so she began to cry.

"Don't cry. If I bring you back, they won't kill you. They will only send you to a work camp until they can sort things out and figure out what to do with the Jews."

"Ollie, listen to me, please... for old times' sake, for the kiss we once shared. Please, please, will you pretend we didn't see each other here in the woods? Will you just let me go and never tell anyone that you saw me?" She could hear the pleading in her voice. She felt the hot tears running down her cheeks. Her entire life depended upon this man who she hardly knew anymore. A man who she could see had been so convinced by the doctrine that had been drilled into him that he was unable to think for himself anymore.

"I don't know what to do," Oliver said honestly, shaking his head. He turned away from her, and she could see that he was talking more to himself than to her. "I'm confused. I should arrest you," he said. "I should take you back to our camping grounds and turn you in. It's the right thing to do. It's what is expected of me."

"Ollie," she said softly as she walked over to him and put her hand on his upper arm. *I am desperate.* She thought. "We are old friends. I know you think that if you turn me in, they will send me to a work camp. But they won't, Ollie, they won't. They will hurt me. Maybe, probably, even kill me. Would you want that?" Anna was trembling. *My life lies in the hands of this fool of a man who I have not seen since we were in our early teens.* "Ollie," she said, rubbing his arm and whispering his name softly, hoping to stir warm memories. "You probably don't know this, but that time you kissed me in the park was my first kiss."

His eyes lit up. "Mine too," he said, turning to look into her eyes. She thought he might kiss her again, and she didn't care if he did, as long as he would let her go. For a long moment, he stared into her eyes. She thought he was lost in the memory. He leaned down, and then he kissed her. She didn't resist. She dared not resist. But she could feel her body trembling with fear. She had no idea what he was going to do next. Then he stood up straight and shook his head. Clearing his throat, he said, "Those days were so long ago. I am not the same boy I was then. I am a man now, Anna. I am an Aryan man. Kissing you like that is forbidden." He turned away from her.

"But those days were not long ago. They feel like they were just yesterday," she pleaded with him to feel something towards her. "Remember when you said you were going to marry me someday?" Anna was trembling with fear. *When do I run? When do I give up trying to convince him to let me go and start running? And even if I try to run as fast as I can, could I outrun him? He's young, healthy, and strong. I am weak and tired. And besides, I could never outrun the gun he's carrying. One shot and my life would be over. What would my family do? They would search and search, but never find me. Dear God, help me, please.*

"How could I forget?" He laughed a little. "It seems rather silly now, you being a Jew. But at that time, I actually did believe you would be my wife someday. But of course, now that's utterly impossible..."

"Ollie." She walked in front of him so he could see her face. She took his hand in her own and squeezed it gently. There was fear and confusion in his eyes. He tried to pull his hand away but didn't pull hard enough. It was more of a gesture than a real attempt. She massaged his hand in her own trembling one.

"Anna, I don't know what to do. I am an important man. I am the counselor of the *Deutsche Jugend* camp. I have a big job. A big responsibility. Now I know this sounds like something of little consequence to you. But it's not. I assure you it's not. I am responsible for shaping the minds of the Aryan youth. It is through me and my actions that they learn right from wrong. And... everyone knows it is wrong to protect Jews. Jews are the enemy," he said, but he didn't sound firm in his conviction.

"Let me go. Pretend you never saw me. No one will ever know. Please, Oliver. We've known each other since we were children. I am begging you. Please, just look the other way, and I will run. I will be gone as if I was never here. Let me go, Ollie."

He nodded. Then he swallowed, and Anna saw his Adam's apple bob up and down. He held her hand tight, and she could feel his hand trembling. "I can't turn you in. Anna. I know it's what I should do. I am going against everything I know is right, but..." he said, hanging his head, "but I can't do it. Run. Get out of here. Run."

"Thank you, Ollie. I'm going to go now. Please, just turn the other way. I'll be gone in a second. And, please, Ollie, forget you saw me."

He nodded, but he did not release her hand. Anna was trembling. She wasn't convinced he wouldn't shoot her once she started running. She worried he might return to his camp, think this over, and then change his mind and send the Nazis after her. She thought about the frightening stories that Bernie had once told her about the Nazis using dogs to track down someone who escaped them. *Does Oliver have access to these dogs?*

Oliver squeezed her hand one last time. Then he released it. There were tears in his eyes. "Goodbye, Anna," he said. Then he coughed a little to clear his throat, and in a soft voice, he said, "Please, don't let me catch you out here again because if I do, I am going to have to turn you in. Now go, run, please get out of here. Please get as far away from here as you can."

Anna's feet ached from all the walking she'd done, but fear took over, and she began to run. She knew that she was running for her life. At any moment, Oliver might change his mind. The cuts on her ankles burned. Still, she ran dashing as fast as she could through the openings in the trees. The sharp branches jutted out; they scratched and tore at her tender flesh. The broken branches were like little razors; they burned her like fire wherever they cut her. But she could make it. She would make it. She did not look behind her. Anna kept running, even after she put plenty of distance between herself and Oliver. By the time she stopped running, Anna had no idea how to get back to her family. She was completely lost. And by nightfall, she had to accept the fact that she was all alone in the woods.

CHAPTER FIFTY-TWO

Anna leaned against the trunk of a thick oak tree. She had no water, no food, and no blankets. *I am going to die here, alone.* Every muscle in her body ached. Her head throbbed from dehydration. She closed her eyes and let sleep take her. *If this is the end, then please, dear God, let it be painless and peaceful.*

It was just as the sun began to rise when Anna awoke. She was no longer sleeping under a tree. She had been slung over someone's shoulder, and now she was being carried upside down. *Am I dreaming?* Her heart was thumping with fear. *Who is carrying me? Is it Oliver? Is he going to arrest me? Has he found my family?* As the light of dawn penetrated through the trees, Anna could see that the man carrying her was not wearing the Nazi uniform Ollie had been wearing the day before. She wanted to speak, to ask this person who he was and where he was taking her. But her stomach was upset, and her head ached, and when she tried to speak, her voice was so faint that he didn't hear her.

They arrived at some sort of camp. There were colorful wagons and horses everywhere. There were women in full skirts and men with thick mustaches. She looked around her. *Is this a gypsy camp?* She thought, remembering when she was very young, and the gypsies had set up camp in the outskirts of Vienna, and she and Elica had gone to spy on them. The man gently put Anna down on the ground. A middle-aged woman walked over to Anna. She had dark sunburned skin that looked like tanned leather with deep crow's feet around her eyes. "What's this?" she said as she looked at Anna. "Where did you find her?" she asked the man who had brought Anna to the camp.

"I was hunting, mother. I saw her lying against a tree. She was all alone, and I knew she was in danger, so I brought her back with me."

"I see that you brought her back. Oh, Vano, you were always one to bring the stray animals you found back to camp, even though I told you not to. Well, now you've brought this one, haven't you?" The woman said, then she went on speaking, not waiting for an answer from him. "Just look at her. She's so skinny, she looks half dead."

"Where am I?" Anna asked.

"You're awake?" the woman said.

"Please don't hurt me," Anna said. She was trembling. *I think they're gypsies.*

"We're not going to hurt you. But who are you?"

Should I tell them the truth? Anna wondered. *If they find out I am Jewish, they could kill me on the spot.* "I am... I am..." Anna had never been a good liar. She stumbled, not knowing what to say.

"She's Jewish," Vano said, "I can tell. It's all right. I know you are. And we aren't going to hurt you."

"Yes, I am," Anna admitted.

Vano nodded. "You're in a Romany camp. I am Vano. This is my mother, Lavina. I found you half dead in the forest," he said.

"My family is somewhere out in the forest. I don't know how to find them. I went out looking for water, and then I got lost," Anna said.

"It's easy to get lost if you're not familiar with these forests,"

Vano said in a matter-of-fact tone. "We, the Romany, have been traveling through here for centuries. We know this land."

"So, this is a gypsy camp?"

"Yes. We have been called that."

"Are the Germans searching for your people, too?"

"Of course they are," Vano said. "They're searching for everyone who isn't German. They're like a virus, a plague."

Another young man came walking over to where they stood. He smiled at Anna. He had an open and honest-looking smile. He joined the conversation, "I couldn't help but overhear the two of you. Nazis are like a hungry nest of hornets. They swarm angrily; they don't even know what they are angry about. I find them to be very stupid and easily outsmarted. You see, we are smarter than they are. There are several groups of our people all through these forests. We leave messages for each other that only other Romany can understand. So, when the Germans come to search for us, they are very sorry that they did because we know how to hide, and we know how to create an ambush and when to strike. Sometimes it's almost funny. They think they are hunting us, but it's us who are hunting them." He smiled. "By the way, I'm Damien."

"Excuse my brother," Vano said. "There is nothing funny about the Nazis. He just enjoys playing tricks. Don't you, Dami?"

"I suppose you could say that." Damien smiled. "By the way, pretty lady, what is your name?"

"I'm Anna," she said, then she added, "I am terrified of the Nazis. I am Jewish, and they hate the Jews. From what we heard, they are murdering Jews. In the city, before I came to this forest, I was hiding with my parents and my brother. Then we escaped and were left here in the forest. We were wandering but couldn't find water. Then my brother got injured, so I went to find water on my own. I got lost, and that's when you found me." She turned to Vano. "But I can't stay here. I must go back and try to find my family."

"What city were you in?" Damien asked.

"Vienna, Austria."

"How did you ever get so far away from home?" Damien said.

"It's a long story."

"So, I have time to listen," Damien said. Anna caught Vano, giving Damien a look of disdain. They had said they were brothers, but they were so different. Damien was tall, slender, and open to friendship, while Vano, who was just as tall, was more muscular, thicker built, dark, and brooding. Damien ignored his brother. He went on speaking directly to Anna, "Please, go on and tell me your story. How did you get here?" he said as he sat back on his haunches. "Perhaps I can help you find your family once I know the details."

Vano began to chop wood to make a fire, but he was not far away, and Anna knew he was listening.

She spent over an hour telling Damien about Ulf and Oliver and all that had happened.

Damien nodded. "We know about the German camp for young people. It's located a few miles from here. So, your friend Oliver is the camp counselor?" he asked.

"I don't know if I would call him a friend anymore. Although he did let me go. And I was very fortunate that he did. But, yes, Oliver told me he was the counselor of the *Deutsche Jugend* camp."

"I know where the Nazi children's camp is. How far is your family from there?"

"I'm not sure. But closer than we are now," Anna said.

"All right. Why don't we get you something to eat? Tomorrow I will go out and find your parents and your brother."

"Can I go with you?"

"No, it's best you stay here. But don't worry, I'll find them," Damien promised.

Just then, a pretty dark-haired girl came out of one of the wagons and walked over to where they were sitting. "Vano, I've been looking for you all day," she said.

"I'm sorry, Sabina. I was hunting when I found this girl in the forest. I am hoping we can help her find her family," Vano said. Then he added, "So, what do you need?"

"Firewood," Sabina said.

"I'm chopping it now. I'll put a pile by the side of your vardo," he said.

"Thank you, Vano. Please put it on the right side of my wagon."

"I will," he said.

Anna thought she could see in Sabina's eyes that she was in love with Vano.

Then Damien smiled at Sabina and said, "Sabina, this is Anna. Anna, this is Sabina."

"I can tell by looking at you that you're not Romany," Sabina said.

"Of course, she's not Romany." Damien smiled, then without malice, he added, "She's a Jew. Running from the Nazis like all the rest of us."

"A Jew? Are you?" Sabina asked.

"Yes, I am Jewish," Anna answered.

Sabina turned away from Damien and looked directly at Vano. "Oh, Vano, I don't think it's a good thing that you brought her here. She could cause us trouble. If the Nazis are looking for her, it could bring them right to our camp. We have little children here with us. We must think of our own well-being as well. It's not a good idea to put all the people here at such risk."

"They know we're here," Damien said. "They've visited our camp before. If they wanted to arrest us, they would have done so already."

"We can't make them angry at us. It's dangerous," Sabina said.

"You're right. We don't want to make them angry. But I'll be damned if I let them dictate everything I do. And as far as the children are concerned, I do think of their well-being. That's why I get up at the crack of dawn or go out late at night to hunt or fish every day so that the children are fed. But I will not allow a helpless girl like this one to wander through the forest alone and lost. She can't find water or feed herself. If I send her away from our camp, either the Nazis will get her, or she'll starve to death. Either way, she'll be dead in a few days," Vano said as he chopped another block of wood.

"That's not our problem," Sabina said. "We have our own problems."

"Sabina, you should know Vano better than that. He's not going to send this girl away. But I'll tell you what I will do," Damien said.

Anna stood listening. She was frightened of the outcome of this conversation.

Vano wiped his brow as he watched his brother.

"Tomorrow, I will go and find her family. Once I have found them, I will bring her to them. That is the only right thing to do, Sabina," Damien said.

Vano did not speak. He just watched Damien, who was acting like he had the power to solve any problem.

"Yes, that's a good idea. But do you even know where to look for them?" Sabina asked.

"I have an idea. But it doesn't matter where they are, I'll find them. I know these woods. My brother and I played here when we were children. We know every hiding place in these woods. After all, our people have been traveling here for years, even before I was born. If her family is here in this forest, I'll find them," Damien said.

"I would be forever grateful to you," Anna said. "I am desperate to find my parents and my brother. I need to be reunited with them. Even if we starve, at least we will be together."

"Good, I'll go tomorrow morning." Damien smiled, then he turned to Anna. "Come with me. I am going to have my mother give you something to eat. Then perhaps you would like to get some rest. It's safe for you to rest here in our camp."

"Thank you," Anna sighed. She was filled with appreciation. As they walked through the gypsy camp, she felt tears threaten to fall from her eyes. "You are so kind to help me. And I am so grateful to your brother, too. If he hadn't found me, I would have died out there in the forest. I would like to thank him, but he's hard to talk to."

"Yes, you're right. He is rather hard to talk to. But I'll tell him that you said thank you."

"I appreciate it."

"Now follow me. You'll feel better once you've had something to eat."

Anna walked beside Damien through the gypsy camp. She couldn't help but notice that everyone looked up as they walked by.

CHAPTER FIFTY-THREE

"My mother's wagon is right over here," Damien said.

He led Anna over to a newly painted wagon. It was well kept up, and Anna assumed that Vano and Damien took care of it for their mother.

"Mother," — Damien put his arm around his mother's shoulder — "Can you please give this young woman something to eat? Vano found her in the forest. She was separated from her family." He pointed at Anna.

The older woman shook her head. "I already met her. Vano introduced us. Your brother, Vano, is always bringing home strays."

"Did he tell you that her name is Anna? I am going to help her to find her family. But meanwhile, she's starving. So, a little food, a little water, yes, mama?"

"I don't know if the stew is done yet."

Damien walked over to a large cauldron and dipped a heavy black ladle in, then he brought it to his mouth and blew on the contents before tasting the rich, hearty stew. "It's ready, and as always, it's delicious," he said. Then he turned to Anna. "My mother is the best cook in our group. And she is as pretty as any of the young girls."

"Oh Dami, how you exaggerate," his mother said, blushing, but it was clear that she was flattered. Then she turned to Anna. "Vano went hunting early this morning, so we will all have a nice meal today." Afterward, she ladled a large spoon of piping hot stew into a bowl she set in front of Anna. She also poured Anna a glass of water.

"Go ahead and eat. I have some things to take care of right now. My mother will give you anything you need. And then early tomorrow morning, I'll go out into the forest and find your family," Damien said, smiling.

Anna nodded. "Thank you." She sat down on the ground to eat.

Once Damien had gone, his mother sat down beside Anna. "I'm Lavina," she said.

"I'm Anna."

"Anna," Lavina said, "I can see that you are not one of us. You are a stranger to our way of life."

"Yes, I am."

"I know. I can tell. If I had to wager, I would guess you are a city girl. We are travelers."

"I am a city girl. I came from Vienna. But I appreciate everything you are doing for me."

"I believe that you do," she said. Then she was quiet for a moment before she continued, "My sons are good boys. They have kind hearts like their father; he should rest in peace. And the fact that they are handsome is not lost on me. Now, I can see when my Damien looks at you that he is smitten. However, he is betrothed to a girl from another camp. And we both know you could never live this lifestyle. You are unaccustomed to it. So, please keep that in mind, and as soon as he finds your parents, please return to your family.

"You coming here is not a good thing for us. My boys are both fascinated by what is forbidden, and they are also fascinated by that which is strange or different. You fit that description, and that will only cause trouble for all of us. So, tomorrow when Dami finds your family, I am asking you to please sever your friendship with him. It will only cause heartache and trouble for both of you and probably for Vano, too. If I am right, my boys are in competition to see which of them can get your attention. They are always competing. They have been this way since they were babies. Now, I don't know if you met Sabina, but she is betrothed to my Vano. She is a good girl. She's been like a daughter to me. I know that Vano has never been in love with her, but they are very close. It will be good if they will marry. I don't want you to get in the way of that. Do you understand what I am trying to say?"

"I'm not sure," Anna said, "but I am not looking to cause any trouble here. As soon as I find my family, I will go." She was eating too fast. She knew it, but she was famished, and the hot stew with meat and vegetables was irresistible.

"I am trying to tell you that I want you to leave my sons alone. Don't make any plans to contact either of them again after you leave here. Let them both be comfortable in their world. If there aren't any options, my Dami will marry the girl he is betrothed to, and Vano will marry Sabina. Once they are married, they will both learn to be happy. These girls are travelers like us. They know our ways of life."

"Once I find my family, I promise to go and leave you alone. I am grateful for all you have done for me," Anna said.

"Good. Thank you. Now, enjoy your food."

Anna finished the bowl of stew and gulped the water. But five minutes later, she was sick with stomach pains. She ran into the bushes and vomited. She had to tell Lavina that she had gotten sick because she didn't want anyone else to become ill from the stew. But when she told her, Lavina said, "You ate too fast. You haven't eaten such a large meal in a long time, have you?"

"No, not in years."

"Next time you eat, eat slowly, even if it's difficult."

Anna looked at Lavina and wondered why she had waited until Anna got sick to tell her this. *Why didn't she tell me before I started eating? She seems nice, but I don't feel like I can trust her.*

CHAPTER FIFTY-FOUR

Damien returned to his mother's wagon and stayed with Anna for the rest of the day. They sat outside under the shade of a large weeping willow tree.

"I'm so worried about my family," Anna admitted. "I am afraid that Oliver changed his mind about arresting me and went searching for me. I have no idea what he might do if he found them."

"I know you're worried. And I don't blame you. But Vano and I will go in the morning, and we'll find them."

"What if you can't?" she said, more to herself than to him.

"Don't worry. We will."

They sat silently for a few minutes. Then Damien smiled and said, "When we were just children, people always said that Vano was like the moon and I was like the sun. Together, we can accomplish anything."

"Why is he the moon and you the sun?" she asked.

"Because he's dark and mysterious. He doesn't talk much, but he's a deep thinker. And me, well I'm like the sun. I'm open and bright."

She smiled. "You wouldn't say humble, now would you?"

"I don't know what you mean?" he said, then laughed. "No, I'm not humble. I know I am a good man. I work hard to be the kind of person that I am. But, I guess you might say my brother is humble. He never brags about his accomplishments. In fact, he hardly ever speaks. And when he does, it's mostly to me."

"You two are very close?" Anna smiled.

"We're twins."

"Really?" Anna was surprised.

"Yes, we aren't identical, as you can see, but we are twins."

She smiled and said, "I was a nanny for two twins one summer. They were wonderful boys. We became such good friends."

"Two boys. They must've been a handful. Do you ever talk to them anymore?"

"No, I had to leave them abruptly." Anna frowned.

"What happened?" he asked.

And she told him about Ulf and the boys.

CHAPTER FIFTY-FIVE

"Daniel is dead," Dagna said smugly as she lit a cigarette. "I laughed when I saw him die."

Elica gasped.

"Poor little Elica. You're so accustomed to getting your way. Well, not this time. You left me in an apartment I rented to help raise your bastard son so that you could be with Daniel. You left me without a word for a Jew. I had to find a way to pay the rent without your salary. It wasn't easy, Elica. But you didn't care." Dagna paused for a moment as she stared Elica up and down. "No, you don't care about anyone but yourself. Well, just look at you now. That Jew husband of yours is gone. He can't protect you anymore. And now the only thing you ever really had going for you, your beautiful face, is ruined too. Where is your Jew child?"

"I told you, he's dead," Elica lied. Her voice was choked up. She could hardly breathe, but she knew she must convince Dagna that there was no point in searching for Theo. The reality of Dagna's words was sinking in, and she asked in a small voice, hoping she'd heard wrong, "What do you mean Daniel is dead?"

"He was killed here at the police station when he was arrested. I told you; I saw it all." She put her cigarette out in the ashtray, then she shrugged and added, "And now, your precious husband is nothing but another dead Jew."

"Dear God..." Elica said, and she put her hands, which were covered with dried blood, over her eyes. "My poor Daniel."

"You are such a fool, Elica. You had everything: beauty, men, so many men. After all, you were born a pure Aryan. But you weren't satisfied with that. You had to get entangled with a Jew. Do you know what I would have given to have been you? I wanted so much to be like you. Now, I look at you and could spit on you for how ugly you are."

"I don't know you, Dagna. I feel like I never really knew you. How could you turn into a monster like this? We were friends."

"You sure know how to treat a friend, don't you, Elica? You left me with a lease that I worked two jobs back-to-back to pay for. And all because I wanted to be your friend," Dagna said, then she turned away and walked up the stairs, leaving Elica alone in the dark, damp cell. Dagna's footsteps echoed loudly in the chamber until the door slammed shut with a resounding bang.

Elica lay down on the cold concrete floor and wept. She thought of Daniel, of his eyes, his smile, his gentle touch. She remembered how he'd lift Theo high in the air until Theo giggled with delight. *I really loved him. I never thought I'd ever know love like this.* Elica sighed. *When I first met Daniel's parents, they rejected me. Because of his parents' disapproval, Daniel tried to stay away from me. But that changed once he learned that he had a son. And who was it that told him about his son? Who was it that helped me, even though I had been a terrible friend to her? It was Anna. I hurt and betrayed Anna when we were young. But when things got tough, it was Anna who came to my aid. She was the reason that Daniel found it in his heart to marry me. And how did I thank her? I turned on her again. And now I have to live with myself, with this disfigured face and the knowledge that it was me who turned in my best friend, Anna, and her family to the Gestapo. I didn't want to. But I had no other choice. It was the only bargaining power I had. I hoped the Germans would give me Daniel in exchange for Anna and her family. I am a monster too. I am no better than Dagna. If it weren't for Theo, my poor child who still needs me, I would find a way to make these Nazis kill me. Well, at least I know I can trust Bernie. She is a good friend, not like me. She will take good care of Theo. Even so, I must find a way to get out of here and get back to him somehow. I am a terrible friend and a horrible person. But I tried. I really tried to be a good mother. I wanted to be a good wife and mother, but everything went badly.*

Elica began to weep, long heart-wrenching sobs.

Suddenly it dawned on Elica, and her entire body began to shake. She felt chilled and nauseated. Her head ached. The cut on her cheek burned like a brand. For a moment, she thought about the mark of Cain. Elica stuffed her fist into her mouth and bit down hard. She wanted to feel the pain, the pain she felt she deserved. *I turned in Anna and her family to the Gestapo.* She could hardly breathe. *The Gestapo would have had to go to Bernie's house to arrest the Levinsteins. If they went right away, Bernie would be on her way to Italy with Theo. They would arrest her mother. But once Bernie returned home, the Germans would arrest Bernie, too, for hiding Jews. That's a crime, a serious crime. And... oh dear God, what have I done... what if she was delayed and she hadn't left yet? Then the Nazis would have Theo, too. What was I thinking? I am so stupid. The Nazis would take him, too. And who knows what they would do to a child? They are demons. All of them are demons.*

She began to retch. *My baby, my little boy, my Theo. No, please, Dear God, not my child. What would I do if they killed Theo... Oh God, it's too hard to even think about. To even imagine. Please, God, let it not be true...*

CHAPTER FIFTY-SIX

Vano and Damien's mother insisted that Anna stay the night in her vardo. Anna was not fooled by Lavina's kindness. She knew that Lavina only made that offer because it allowed her to keep watch over Anna. But Anna didn't care. Although she liked Vano and Damien, she wasn't interested in a romantic tryst. All she truly wanted was to return to her family. With so much on her mind, Anna didn't think she would be able to rest. But as soon as she lay her head down, she was fast asleep.

When she woke up, it was early in the morning, just after sunrise. The sound of birds singing and the smell of food cooking filled the wagon. She looked around her. There was no one else with her. Anna got up and walked outside, where she found Lavina sitting on a tree stump and making ersatz coffee in a pot over an open fire. In another pot, she was cooking some sort of grainy cereal.

"My boys went to find your family," Lavina said. Her voice wasn't cruel, but it wasn't tender either.

"You don't like me," Anna said.

"It's not that I do or don't like you. It's that I am older. I can see things more clearly."

"I don't understand."

"You're coming to our camp will mean trouble for us. I can see that clearly." Lavina stirred the pot of cereal.

"As soon as I find my family, I will leave here and never bother you again."

The older woman let out a short, bitter laugh. "So, you think?"

"I promise you."

Lavina didn't say another word. She just shook her head. A few long moments of silence passed, then Lavina said, "I read the cards about you this morning."

"The cards?"

"Yes, the tarot cards," Lavina said. "I read your fortune. And the cards told me that you are going to be trouble for us. I am sick to death about it. However, I know there is no avoiding it, so do you want a cup of coffee?"

Anna looked into Lavina's eyes. The woman wasn't resentful or angry. She seemed resigned. "I would love some coffee. And, please, I wish you would believe me. I don't want to cause you or your people any problems."

"Yes, yes. I know that you don't," Lavina said as she handed Anna a cup of the thick black liquid, which they called coffee, that she was stirring.

Anna took a sip. *It's bitter, but at least it's hot.*

Lavina didn't say anything else. They sat there outside Lavina's vardo for a little over an hour without speaking. Anna watched the boys' mother as she closed and opened her eyes, whispering softly to herself under her breath. And Anna decided that Lavina must be praying. She couldn't blame the woman. After all, both of her sons were in the forest, and the forest was filled with danger.

It was late morning when Sabina came over to visit with Lavina. She carried a basket filled with vegetables, potatoes, squash, and carrots. "Good morning, mother," Sabina said, "I've brought you some vegetables for your dinner tonight. Let me help you put up a stew."

"You're such a good girl, Sabina," Lavina said as she took the basket.

Next, Sabina went into Lavina's vardo and came out carrying a large black cauldron. "I'll be right back. I'm going to the river," she said to Lavina. Then she left the camp. When she returned, the pot was filled with water. She and Lavina cut the vegetables and emptied them into the pot. Sabina moved the coffee off the fire and put the cauldron with the vegetables and water where the coffee had been. Next, Sabina sat down and began to stir the mixture.

"I don't think we'll have meat tonight. That is, unless the boys decide to go hunting on their way back to camp," Lavina said.

"Where did they go?"

"They went looking for her family," Lavina pointed at Anna.

"Oh," Sabina said.

"I know you're worried. I am too. But my Vano is very smart, and he knows this forest. If they're here, he'll find them. And he'll watch out for his brother, too," Lavina said.

The sun was high in the sky. It was the heat of the day when Vano and Damien walked into the camp. Damien carried the bodies of two large rabbits, which he placed in front of the pot of boiling vegetables. Vano sat down.

"You went hunting, I see," Lavina said.

"I saw these rabbits, and I figured we could use the meat for dinner," Vano answered.

"He's lying," Damien said. "He insisted we hunt before we returned."

"Yes, of course, he did," Lavina said, then she turned to Vano. "You're such a good boy."

Vano didn't answer his mother. He didn't smile. His eyes searched for Anna.

"Did you find the girl's family?" Lavina asked.

Vano nodded. "Where is she? Damien and I need to speak to her."

"In the *vardo*."

Vano stood up. "Come on, Dami," he said, then they went inside

MY SISTER'S BETRAYAL

the wagon. Anna was sitting on the bed alone. When she saw him, her heart began to pound. "Did you find them?"

"Yes. I found them. But the news isn't good. Your parents are in the Nazi children's camp. They're tied up, so I assume they've been arrested," Vano said.

She gasped, "And my brother?"

"I am sorry. I found his body."

"He was injured. He twisted his ankle. He's dead?"

"Yes."

"From the cut? From infection?"

"I'm not sure. Both probably." Vano looked uncomfortable, helpless.

"I'm sorry, Anna," Damien said. He put his arm around her shoulder.

She began to sob.

Vano looked around awkwardly. Then, not knowing what to say, he left Anna and Damien in his mother's vardo and walked outside. Anna threw herself on the bed and cried. "Anselm is dead, and my parents have been arrested," she said.

"I know. I am so sorry," Damien said.

She looked up at him. "I will never see my brother again."

He nodded. "It's terrible. Let me get you some water."

She shook her head and looked away. "I need some time alone."

"I guess I'll go then," he said as he stood up. "I'll see you later."

After he left, Anna lay on the bed. Her mind was racing. She was filled with grief and fear all at the same time. And, because she'd made the mistake of telling Oliver that her family was with her, she also felt guilty. *Oliver must have had second thoughts. He knew they were somewhere near where we were. He must have hunted them down after he let me go.*

Anna didn't know how long she lay there. But the sun was beginning to set when Vano returned to the wagon. Anna looked up when he entered. "I'm sorry I walked out and just left you like that," he said. "I'm not very good when someone is crying. Especially a woman. I never know what to say or do." He cleared his throat. "But I took a walk and gave all of this some thought. And I think you should stay here with us. You can stay in my mother's wagon."

"Have you talked to your mother about this?" Anna asked.

"I told her that I think it's best."

"And what did she say?"

"She agreed that it was a good idea. She said she couldn't put you out all alone in the forest. Her conscience wouldn't let her."

Anna was stunned. *That doesn't sound like Lavina. She said she wanted me gone as soon as possible.* "Are you sure?"

"I'm sure. My mother and I talked, and she knows you are in need. She wants to help. It will be all right. We agree that you can't go back out into the forest all alone. You won't survive for long."

"And what about my parents? What can I do for them?"

He looked at her. "I can't try to rescue them. The Germans will take it out on our entire camp if I do. I would be putting all of these people in danger. I can't do that."

"But if we just leave my parents there, what will happen to them?"

He shrugged, his brow was deeply lined, and his eyes looked tired. "I honestly can't tell you."

"I can't stay here. I have to go back there and beg Oliver to release them. It's the best I can do."

"You can't. If you go back there, your friend will be forced to arrest you too. Even if he doesn't want to, he will be surrounded by the others, and he'll have to. If he doesn't, they'll turn on him. That's how they are. They don't even have any sympathy for their own."

"I can't imagine Oliver not helping me if I beg him."

"He can't and he won't. Besides, Anna, he has turned on you. He must have gone off and hunted your family down. This man, who you call an old friend, is dangerous. He has an important job with the Nazis. In fact, they may very well be hunting for you now. You can't go there. They will not take pity on you. The Nazis take pity on no one. Believe me, I know. I've seen some of the terrible things they've done in these forests. They are not human. They are monsters."

"But my parents?"

"Anna, you can't help them. Don't you see? You can't help them; you can only hurt yourself and also hurt all of us."

"But I thought I heard someone say that the Germans know you have a camp here. Don't you think they will come here looking for me?"

"Perhaps. But we can hide you. We know how to do that."

Anna put her hands on her temples and pressed hard. "I don't know what to do. I can't just forget about my family."

"You have no other choice. I can't break them out of that youth camp. I wish I could. I would do it for you. But there are too many of them there, and they all have guns. They have been training these young men to shoot and now are just itching to try what they've learned. Don't you see, Anna? There is nothing we can do," Vano said.

Just then, Lavina walked into the vardo. From the look on her face, Anna was sure she'd been listening.

"Mother," Vano said gently, "please, speak to her."

"Anna, it's all right. You must stay with us."

"But I promised you that I would leave..." Anna said.

"The cards told me you were going to stay with us. And even though I wish you could go on your way. I can't put you out all alone in the forest," Lavina said.

Sabina knocked on the open door. "It's me," she said. Then she entered, with Damien following close behind her. "Let's all go outside. I want to talk to you," Sabina said.

Damien, Lavina, and Vano followed Sabina outside the wagon. They walked a few feet away, just out of earshot, in case Anna was inside listening. Then Sabina said, "Damien told me what is happening. I think we should send her away. We can't put all of our people at risk for one girl who is a stranger to us. She's not even one of our own."

227

"We can't put her out all alone in the forest," Damien said. "Look at her. She will be dead in a few days. How can you agree to this? You are a compassionate person."

"Because I love all of you, my family, more than I love strangers," Sabina said. "Yes, I pity her, but not enough to endanger my own people. We could all be arrested because of her."

There was a long silence.

"Then I will leave and go with her," Vano said.

"And I will go too," Damien said.

Lavina glared at them. For a few moments, she didn't speak. Then in a quiet voice, she said, "No, you two boys must not go." Shaking her head, she added, "I know how you feel, Sabina. I understand that you don't want to endanger the rest of us. But we must do what is right."

"Perhaps we should speak to the Shero Rom," Sabina said. "Perhaps we should let him make the decision. After all, he is the head of our group."

"I've spoken to him already," Damien said. "He agrees that we cannot put her out."

"All right, so fate has won. Your friend will stay," Lavina said.

CHAPTER FIFTY-SEVEN

A month passed. A month during which Ulf was careful to collect as many blankets and as much dry food as he possibly could without causing suspicion. He was nervous as he drove back to the hidden campgrounds where he'd left Anna and her family. He had been unable to forget the question Anna had asked him about whether he had committed murder. And that was because he had. He had murdered not only on the battlefield but on that horrible day when he'd received orders to be a part of a firing squad and shoot what seemed like hundreds of innocent people and throw their bodies into a deep ravine. He'd lined them up, and then he'd shot them. He had not wanted to be a part of it, yet he knew he could not safely refuse. 'Kill or be killed' ran through his mind. *Eat or be eaten.* He remembered that quote from a book he read by Jack London before all of this began. When he'd read it, he never thought that it would become his personal motto. But it had, and he had learned to live by it.

Ulf had often wished he could leave his job and return to school. He would lie on his bed and daydream about returning to a time when he went to classes and talked about life. He hadn't realized what a joy it was to spend each day discussing deep life matters on a philosophical level rather than actually experiencing the blood and gore of it. However, he knew for certain that those days were over. But during the trials and tribulations of his career, when he felt he might go mad, he'd been fortunate to make a friend, Filip Brandt. Filip, like Ulf, had been a college boy turned military and, like Ulf, had shown such promise that he rose in the party to become SS. They met and discovered they had similar backgrounds when they worked for the Gestapo. Because of his friendship with Filip, Ulf found it easier to endure what was expected of him. Filip was also disheartened by the Third Reich. His experiences had not turned out the way he had hoped they would. And he shared this secret with Ulf. In fact, Filip trusted Ulf with all of his secrets, even with the fact that he had once had a Jewish girlfriend. And because Filip was candid about his illegal relationship with the pretty young Jewish girl who betrayed him, Ulf felt comfortable telling Filip about Anna. Filip was the only person who knew where Ulf was headed that day as he was getting ready to drive out to the clearing in the forest where he'd left the Levinsteins.

"Be careful, Ulf," Filip told him, as they had a quick breakfast together. "Even though we are SS Gestapo, we are never above suspicion. They are always watching us. And, quite frankly, I don't think any girl is worth the trouble you might get into."

"I know. I'll be careful," Ulf promised.

After taking a sip of hot coffee, Filip lit a cigarette. "I should quit," he said, smiling as he inhaled.

"You should," Ulf said, nodding.

"By the way, how did you ever get into the Gestapo, anyway?"

"My uncle. He was friends with Himmler. How about you?"

"My father knows Müller. He pulled some strings for me. You do realize that you and I are very fortunate to be SS and even more fortunate to be in the Gestapo. We are powerful, Ulf. We can do as we please with the criminals we arrest. We have no rules to follow. No girl is worth the risk of losing a position like this."

"I thought you didn't like the party and everything it stands for," Ulf said.

"I don't. But at least we have power. And during these very dangerous times, it's better to be a top dog than one who is on the bottom, no?"

"Yes, I suppose you're right." *Eat or be eaten,* Ulf thought, and shrugged. Then she shook his head. "Eh, I don't know what's the matter with me. Anna is different from any other girl I've ever dated. For some reason, she is on my mind all the time. I can't seem to get interested in anyone else. I don't know why."

"Is she that beautiful?"

"Not really," Ulf admitted. "She's pretty, but I've seen better. In fact, my ex-fiancée was prettier. But It's just that I have this strange feeling about her. It's like no matter what I do, she is never completely mine. Oh, she likes me. But she isn't madly in love with me. And I want her to be. Do you know what I mean?"

"Sort of," Filip said.

"Other women I've dated have fallen at my feet. But not Anna. She always seems to keep a part of herself away from me."

"Well, have you slept with her?"

"Not yet." He groaned. "I can't do anything with her parents around. I can't even trick her into it. They are too close by."

"That's what you need to do. Even if you must force her. Just do it. Once you do, you'll be able to put her aside. She's a Jew, and you know you are better off without her."

"I suppose so. But I don't think sleeping with her will end this obsession. It's more than that. She is the first girl I have ever known who I couldn't make fall madly in love with me. The others, including my ex-fiancée, were always begging for my affection and attention. Not Anna. Oh, I'll admit, she treats me kindly, but that's because she knows she and her family need me to survive. However, I never feel that she is in love with me."

"And her love is something you must have?"

"Yes! I think that if I could feel that she was like the others, desperately in love with me, I could get over her. But the more she holds herself at a distance, the stronger my need to own her grows. Does that make sense to you, Filip?"

"Of course it does. But I am worried about you, Ulf. I fear your obsession with this Jew will cost you your career or, even worse, your life."

"Cover for me, will you? I'll be back in a few days."

"Of course. You know I will. But you can't continue to do this. Eventually, you are going to have to explain where you are going."

"I know. I'll figure something out," Ulf said.

CHAPTER FIFTY-EIGHT

As Ulf was driving towards the clearing where he'd left Anna and her family, he thought about everything he and Filip had discussed. *I don't know if what I feel for Anna is love or not. I know that she doesn't love me, and that is driving me crazy. I must find a way to make her want me. Perhaps Filip is right. Perhaps if we slept together, she would become obsessed with me instead of the other way around.*

When Ulf arrived at the clearing, he was shocked to see that Anna and her family were gone. He searched the area to see if they had moved, but there was no trace of them. *Could I be in the wrong place?* He wondered, but he knew he was not because before he'd left, he'd carved a mark into one of the trees so he could find the area again. And the mark was there. But Anna was not. To be sure, Ulf ran his fingers over the carving in the tree trunk. *Yes, this is the mark I left.* He thought. Ulf walked around in circles for several minutes, thinking. It had been a day and night of driving, and he knew he must start heading back soon. But he was perplexed. *Where could they be? Perhaps there was a threat of some kind, and they went deeper into the forest.* Walking through the dense trees and bushes, he searched for anything that might be a sign but found nothing. He began to worry about himself and his family.

What if the Levinsteins had been found somehow and were arrested? Would Anna's family tell on me if they were tortured? They know my name. If they were tortured, they would probably tell the Gestapo that I helped them escape and that I murdered my partner? Would the Gestapo believe them and arrest me? Or would just think to themselves that the Levinsteins are Jews and Jews are liars? I don't know. I don't like that my safety and the safety of my loved ones lie in the hands of Jews. I am in danger. He was becoming frantic. *I have to find them even if I am late getting back to my job.*

Ulf walked through the woods, kicking branches out of the way with his heavy black jackboots. But he saw nothing. Not a trace of the Levinsteins. So he returned to his automobile and drove for over two hours further into the forest. He got out and walked around looking for any trace of the Levinsteins, but found nothing. Several times he drove for a few hours and then got out and walked around for a half mile or so. Each time, he returned to his car, feeling more desperate and defeated. After he had been driving for many hours, he was tired and almost ready to give up. He pulled the car over to the side of the road to get out to walk around one final time. This time he wanted to stop—more to stretch his legs—than to delude himself that he might find Anna. He ventured off the road and into the forest. Then the sound of birds chirping and crackling branches was broken by prepubescent male voices raised in song. Ulf recognized the familiar German tunes. They were melodies of the Nazi party. He'd sung them himself. *That sounds like it must be a camp or a meeting of the Deutsche Jugend in der Slowakei.* Ulf followed the singing until he came upon the camp. And as he entered the camp, he froze for a second when his eyes fell upon Anna's parents, Herr and Frau Levinstein. They were tied up and imprisoned in one of the dog cages. When Herr Levinstein saw Ulf, their eyes met. Ulf was certain he saw relief in the old man's gaze. Ulf gave a quick, reassuring nod. But he did not speak to either of Anna's parents. Instead, he walked over to the boys, who were standing like a choir and singing. He waited until they finished the song, then asked, "Who is in charge here, and where can I find him?"

The boys saw Ulf's uniform, and because of it, they were extremely respectful as they directed Ulf to the office of the camp counselor. Ulf followed their direction. When he arrived at the cabin, he knocked on the door.

"Yes, enter," a man's voice came from inside the cabin.

Ulf walked in and saw a handsome young man sitting behind a desk. "Heil Hitler." Ulf introduced himself with a fake name.

"Heil Hitler," Oliver returned the greeting. "I am Oliver Fredrich, counselor of the camp." Oliver could see by his uniform that he was a Gestapo.

"I was sent here to this forest to search for a family of Jews who escaped during an arrest." Ulf went on to explain.

"I think perhaps I have them. Come with me," Oliver said.

Ulf followed Oliver. Neither of them was aware of Anna's role in their lives. Oliver took Ulf to the cage where he had imprisoned Anna's parents. "There were two more of them, but the boy died, and the girl escaped."

"I see," Ulf said nervously. He heard what Oliver said, but all he really heard was that the girl had gotten away. That meant that Anna was still alive, and that she had escaped. He had given the Levinsteins that reassuring glance so they would not say anything that might give him away. "Well," Ulf said as officially as he could, "I'll take them back to headquarters."

"Good. I am glad to be rid of the responsibility of keeping an eye on them," Oliver admitted. "I have quite enough to do watching out for these boys who are under my charge."

"I can just imagine," Ulf said.

They both laughed.

"I'll be right back," Ulf said. "I have to bring my automobile closer. It's a bit of a ways from here."

"Of course," Oliver said

Ulf ran all the way back to where he'd left his car parked. Then he drove up the road, getting as close to the Youth camp as possible. He parked and walked the rest of the way.

When he returned to the camp, Ulf stole a glance at Anna's parents. He saw the looks of relief come over their faces. For a moment, just a moment, he felt pity for them. But then Oliver opened the cage and told them to get out and go with Ulf. They both had trouble standing up straight and walking. It made Ulf wonder how long they'd been in the cage. But he said nothing. He took them at gunpoint and led them to his automobile. Ulf did not untie their hands. He opened the back door of his car. Then, because they were moving slowly, he pushed them into the back seat of his automobile. Ulf turned to see Oliver standing there. Still watching him. Ulf raised his hand in a salute and said, "Heil Hitler."

"Heil Hitler," Oliver answered.

Ulf got into the front seat of the auto and began to drive away. A few minutes passed, and then Herr Levinstein said, "Thank God it was you who found us. Oy, Thank God you found us."

"Where is Anna?" Ulf asked.

"We don't know. We are worried sick about her," Frau Levinstein answered, "The last time we saw her, she was looking for a pond or a river. But she hadn't returned by the time we were arrested. I think she got lost."

"How did you get arrested? How did they find you?"

"I don't know," Herr Levinstein said. "One night, that man that you met, the head of that youth group, he came with two others while we were asleep and arrested us. Poor Anselm died from an infection the day before we were taken."

"I see," Ulf said. *As if I really care about Anselm. I don't care about anything but Anna.* "Where did you last see Anna?"

"Not too far from where you left us. But she never came back," Herr Levinstein said.

They drove for about a half hour. Ulf was lost in thought. He knew what he must do.

"You both must be hungry," Ulf said.

"We are," Anna's father admitted. "They hardly fed us. I was so glad to see you. I don't know how you found us, but I am certainly glad you did."

Ulf steered the car around a large tree as he pulled off the road. Then he drove for a few moments until he found a spot where the car could not be seen from the road. "Here, we can stop right here," he said. "No one can see us if they drive by. So, you can stretch your legs. Then we'll sit down and eat. Once we've finished, the two of you can set up camp here. We are far enough away from the youth group that you should be safe. Meanwhile, I will continue to search for Anna."

The Levinsteins did as Ulf suggested. They walked and stretched for a few moments. Then they sat beside Ulf, who was already sitting on the ground, and he untied their hands. He laid the loaf of bread down on the ground. It didn't matter that the bread was dirty. They were starving and began to devour the bread. Ulf took a small bite of bread, then he stood up. "I'll unload the rest of the supplies I brought," he said.

"Thank you," Anna's father said. "My wife and I are very grateful to you."

"Yes, we are," Anna's mother said.

Ulf nodded. Then he walked around for a few minutes unloading food, water, and blankets from his automobile. He glanced back at Anna's parents. They were old, and their suffering and starvation had made them feeble. He forced himself not to feel sorry for them. His stomach turned. Bile rose in his throat, but he swallowed hard to keep it from coming up any further. *They are so pathetic.* He thought, and then in a small apologetic voice, he said, "I'm sorry." His hand trembled as he pulled out his gun. "But, you see," he explained, trying hard to make them understand, "as long as the two of you are alive, my family is in danger. I don't like having to do this. I don't enjoy it at all."

Anna's mother stood up. "Run," she said to her husband. But he still hadn't comprehended what was happening.

"Don't try to run. I am an excellent shot," Ulf said in a matter-of-fact tone.

"What would Anna say?" Anna's mother asked. "What would she say if she knew you were holding her parents at gunpoint?"

"I know Anna would be shocked and angry. But it doesn't matter. When I couldn't find the two of you, I was distraught. I knew that if you were tortured into telling the authorities who had rescued you, I would not only be a dead man, but my little brothers and parents would also be dead. Can't you see? I have no choice. I must kill you."

"No, please. We would never say anything to anyone." It was as if Anna's father was awakening from a dream. He'd trusted Ulf, and now Ulf was about to kill them. "Listen to me," he said, but his voice was unsteady. "I give you my word that my wife and I would never tell on you, no matter what they do to us. No matter how much they would torture us." Herr Levinstein begged, "Anna is alone out there in the forest. We must find her. We can help you; we can find her together."

Ulf considered Anna's father's words, and there was silence for a moment. He just stood there with his gun pointed at Frau Levinstein. *Herr Levinstein will not run if he sees that I am ready to shoot his wife if he so much as moves. Damn, I wish I could believe Herr Levinstein, but I can't take the chance. If these old Jews are gone, they cannot cause me any problems. When I helped them escape, I never thought they would be captured again. I thought they were too savvy. But they are not savvy at all. They are old and feeble, and it's just a matter of time before they are picked up again. Then they can endanger my family. And I will be forced to worry about what they say or do. Besides that, Anna will never have sex with me if they are around. Better to get rid of them now.*

"I'm sorry," Ulf said sincerely, "but at least Anna will never know it was me who killed her parents. Because I know she could not forgive that. But if she doesn't know, well..." Before the Levinsteins had a chance to say another word, Ulf pulled the trigger once and shot Herr Levinstein in the back of the head.

Frau Levinstein let out an anguished cry as she scrambled to her husband's side. "No!" She took him into her arms and held him, rocking him back and forth as if she could somehow transfer life back into him.

But it was only a few moments before another gunshot rang into the stillness of the day as Ulf's bullet entered the back of Anna's mother's head.

Ulf looked at the scene. It was hideous. A bloody picnic. He shivered. *At least it's over.* He thought. *Now, I must hurry and return to work before they wonder where I have gone to. However, this is not over. I must find Anna before she dies in the forest. And as long as she doesn't know how her parents died, she will trust me.* Then he got into the car and drove away.

CHAPTER FIFTY-NINE

Anna woke one night covered in sweat. She had had a dream that her parents and brother were beside her. It was Rosh Hashanah, the Jewish New year. They were all still living in the house where she grew up. Hitler's army of thugs had not yet marched into Austria, and the home was filled with laughter and happiness. In her dream, she was in the kitchen baking with her mother. Anselm was sitting on the sofa reading, and her father was outside enjoying the cool autumn weather. The dream was pleasant until she walked outside and saw the German army marching down the street. Then she awoke with a start. Her body was trembling, and she was cold and shivering. *If only the Germans had never come to Austria.* She thought. Her body and mind were tired, but she couldn't fall back asleep. So, she lay in bed watching the sunrise.

Anna was grateful to be staying in the gypsy camp. The lifestyle was different from what she was used to, but she'd come to love the outdoors and felt safe, even though she desperately missed her family. She had become good friends with Vano and Damien, although her feelings for Vano were stronger and not exclusively friendship. She found him quieter and less interested in her than

Damien was. She looked into Damien's eyes, and it was easy to see that he was falling in love with her. And she often wished that it was Vano who felt this way. The boys were both kind to her, but every time she asked them if she should go back to the *Deutsche Jugend* camp and try to speak to Oliver about releasing her family, they told her in no uncertain terms that she should not. She had to do as they said because she could never find her way back to the camp on her own.

Anna did what she could to help Lavina with her chores and tried her best to befriend Sabina. Although they were both courteous, she never felt entirely welcome by either woman. Sometimes, like the rest of the group, she would sleep outside under the stars at night. Gazing up at the vast dark sky lit by twinkling diamonds, she wondered how she had previously missed all of this beauty. Not in her wildest dreams would she have believed that she would be living in a Romany camp. She remembered when she was in her early teens, and she'd seen bands of gypsies travel through her town in Austria. She thought the gypsies were fascinating and mysterious people. The women with their colorful headscarves and skirts and the men with their horses and cure-alls. How excited she'd been when she saw them. But that day seemed so long ago. It was actually not her but Elica who had discovered that the gypsies had parked their caravan on the outskirts of town. She had told Anna about the caravans, and the two of them had been curious. They hungered to know more about these fascinating people. Anna remembered how she and Elica planned to sneak out one night and go to the gypsy camp and look around. To do this, Anna had to convince her parents to allow Elica to spend the night at Anna's home. Elica had spent the night before, so her parents did not suspect anything. And since it was during the summer, there was no school to worry about in the morning. That night, after Anna was sure her parents were asleep, she and Elica slipped out of the house. They ran through the beautiful, manicured lawns in Anna's neighborhood for several miles until they reached the edge of town. There, surrounded by the golden light of fireflies, they saw the caravan of gypsy wagons. Elica grabbed Anna's hand and squeezed it. They looked into each other's eyes. Then, still being careful to remain hidden in the trees, they moved closer. Anna gasped at the scene before them. She watched as graceful women in their colorful dresses danced by the light of a bonfire to the haunting music of violins. Local men who Anna recognized were gathered around, watching and throwing coins. The gypsy men with thick mustaches were watching as they stood in the other corner, talking with some of the local men. They had a few horses tied up to a tree, and they seemed to be selling or trading these horses. Other men were selling elixirs. And some were selling handmade pots and pans. An old Romany woman was sitting on the ground reading cards for a younger local woman. Anna and Elica watched them all from a distance. They wanted to go into the camp, but they were too afraid.

Finally, it was very late, and the sun was beginning to rise as Anna and Elica turned and ran all the way back to Anna's house. They sneaked back into Anna's bedroom and climbed into bed.

"Wouldn't it be exciting to travel with a band of gypsies?" Anna asked.

"I don't think so," Elica said. "They are poor and dirty."

"Maybe you're right," Anna said.

"We should get some sleep. My mother will be awake soon," Anna said.

"Yes, let's get some sleep. I'm tired," Elica admitted.

After Elica fell asleep, Anna imagined herself in one of the colorful gypsy skirts whirling around a campfire and having the attention and admiration of dozens of men. She fell asleep that morning with a smile on her face. Little did she know that her vision was a premonition.

CHAPTER SIXTY

Ulf was sweating as he drove through the night. He had done something terrible. It seemed he was always doing things that made him nervous. He thought about his friend Filip, who was covering for him, and decided it was best to return to the Gestapo headquarters at Prinz-Albrecht-Strasse as soon as possible. When he parked outside the building, it was late morning. He would have liked to go home and get a few hours of sleep before starting work. But he didn't. He went inside without sleeping at all. Filip was sipping a cup of hot coffee when he looked up and saw Ulf. "You look terrible."

"I drove through the night. I haven't slept in two days."

Filip shook his head, "You should go home and get some rest."

"I had to get back here. I didn't want to arouse suspicion."

"Have a cup of coffee," Filip said.

Ulf poured himself a cup of coffee.

"How did it go?"

"Are we alone?" Ulf asked, his hands trembling.

"Talk quietly. The others are in the room across the hall."

"She wasn't there."

"What do you mean?"

"I mean, she wasn't where she said she would be. I got there, and they were all gone. But if her parents were arrested by that foolish counselor at the youth camp, and Anna escaped like he said she did, why didn't she return to our meeting place? Maybe she was running away from me. Can you believe it? After I risked my job, my family, and my life to save them?" He whispered.

"No, I can't." Filip shook his head. "So, you drove all the way there and then all the way back without ever seeing her?"

"I didn't see her, but I found her parents."

He went on to explain how he'd taken Anna's parents out of the *Deutsche Jugend* camp and killed them. "It was sickening," Ulf admitted. "They were old and, well... there was a lot of blood."

"I see," Filip said, "But the girl? Where is the girl? Anna."

"I don't know where Anna is, but it's driving me insane. She ran away from me. How could she do that?"

Filip lit a cigarette. "Do you want one?"

"I don't smoke."

"Try it. It will calm your nerves."

Ulf took a cigarette. Filip lit it. Ulf inhaled and began coughing. His face turned red. He gave Filip a dirty look. "This is terrible," he said, still choking.

"Take it easy, don't inhale so deeply until you get used to it," Filip said.

Ulf nodded, but he put the cigarette out in the ashtray in front of Filip. "I can't believe she had the audacity to run away from me after what I did for her and her family. How could she not trust me?" he said.

"She's a Jew. You know as well as I do that Jews are devious and selfish. They are prideful too. But somehow, that's what makes the Jewish women attractive," Filip whispered. "If you know what I mean. They only think of themselves, and that makes you want to own them in a way. It makes you want to dominate their every thought, their every move."

"Yes, I do know what you mean. I can't get this one off my mind. I know she's a liar, and she turned on me when she got the chance. But that only makes me want her more. You see, I have always been considered quite the catch. I am not bad-looking, and my family has plenty of money..."

"You are quite the braggart." Filip let out a laugh.

"No, I'm not bragging. I am telling you this for a reason. No woman has ever turned me down. This one is the first. And I did more for her than I have ever done for any other."

"I wish I could say that no woman ever rejected me. But it's not true. I've been turned down plenty," Filip admitted.

"Yes, well, that's not the point. The point is, I must have her. Anna must fall at my feet. Until she does, I won't be able to get her out of my mind. I am obsessed with her."

"So, what do you plan to do?"

"Take a week off. I am going to say that one of my brothers is ill and I must return home. I have a good rapport with our boss. He will understand. At least, I hope so. Once I can get back to the east, I am going to search until I can find her."

"And what if a week isn't enough?"

"Then I'll ask for a transfer. I'll explain that I cannot rest until I find the Jews who killed my partner. Our boss will understand such loyalty."

"Hmmm. Interesting. Do you really think so?"

"I hope so," Ulf said.

"And once you find her, then what will you do with her?" Filip asked.

"I don't know what I will do with her yet, but she will not get away from me again. This I can assure you."

"Remember when I told you about that Jewish girl who I was seeing secretly for a while?"

"Of course, I remember," Ulf said. "How could I forget? It's what forged our friendship."

"Well, I've often thought about how delightful it would be if I could own her like a dog. She was so arrogant when she broke up with me. I would like to see her on her knees begging. Do you know what I mean?"

"Not exactly, tell me," Ulf leaned in closer.

"Well, I'd like to keep her in one of those rooms in the cellar here in this building, where we torture prisoners. Or better yet, I'd like to keep her in a special room in my home and use her whenever I felt like it. Use her in any way I choose. I've had several versions of that fantasy for a long time."

"Yes, I would like to do that to Anna. She could never escape from me then. I would be her master, and she would be my slave," Ulf said, smiling. "Yes, I like that idea. I like it very much."

"What are you two fellows talking about?" One of the other Gestapo agents asked as he walked into the room.

"Nothing really," Ulf said, shrugging.

"You have been off work for a couple of days. I heard you were sick. Are you feeling better?"

"Yes, I am doing better, thank you." Ulf smiled. "Much better indeed."

That night when Ulf returned to his apartment, he was consumed with thoughts of Anna. He wasn't the same man he'd been when he had first met Anna. He'd held the power of life and death over many. And although he knew it was wrong, and at first it had caused him to be sick, over time, he'd come to expect it... even to enjoy it. The idea that Filip had planted in his mind of owning Anna gave him pleasure. *What if I really could own her? After all, nothing is impossible for an Aryan man. What would it feel like to keep her in a room tied up and available to do whatever pleases me? I must find her. And once I have her, I can do whatever I want with her as long as I don't get caught. I just have to be careful because I could be accused of hiding her if I am found out. But in a way, it would be worth it. I could talk my way out of anything.*

He lay down on his bed and closed his eyes. He imagined Anna begging him to make love to her. A smile came over his face, and he began to feel aroused and touch himself. "You never loved me, Anna. You ran away from me. But once I capture you, I will see to it that you will need me for everything. And because you do, you will bow to me and satisfy my every desire. If you don't behave, I will starve you or beat you. I am sure you will quickly learn who the boss is." He let out a little laugh. *Yes, having absolute power over her will be worth whatever price I might have to pay.*

CHAPTER SIXTY-ONE

"Come with me. Lavina wants me to show you where to take a bath and where to wash your clothes in the river, " Sabina said to Anna.

"I don't have any other clothes. I only have what I am wearing," Anna said.

"Well, then, you could bathe and try to clean yourself up a bit. Take some soap with you."

"Where is the soap?"

"Never mind, I'll get you some."

"Can I assume we are going to the river?" Anna asked.

"Yes. Follow me."

Sabina led Anna to the river. She showed her to a secluded spot. "Take off your clothes and bathe here. You can wash your clothes here as well."

"Thank you, Sabina."

Sabina smiled.

Later that evening, the Shero Rom called a meeting. Everyone sat around him in a circle. "I am not going to use any names. However, someone broke our rules. They bathed and used soap to wash their clothes at the top of the river. Now all of you must remember never to bathe or wash clothes at the top of the river. Always do these things at the bottom of the river. Does anyone know why we do it this way?"

"Yes," a ten-year-old girl answered proudly. "Because we use the top of the river for drinking water, and we don't want the water we drink to get dirty, right?"

"That's right. In order to preserve the health of our group, we must all adhere to the rules." The Shero Rom said gently but firmly.

Anna knew she was the one who had broken the rule. But it was Sabina who had told her to bathe at the top of the river. She glanced over at Sabina and saw the wicked half-smile on Sabina's face. Anna glared at her. *That girl set me up. She did it on purpose. She knows Damien and Vano like me, and she is afraid I will never leave here. She showed me that spot and told me to bathe there. I could say something about it. I could tell everyone that it was she who sent me to the top of the river. But I won't say anything because I am an outsider, and many of the Romany are uncomfortable having me here as it is. I don't want to alienate them even more. However, from now on, whenever anyone suggests anything to me, I'll discuss it with Vano or Damien before I do it.*

Vano and Damien had been sitting on either side of Anna, and she was hoping they couldn't see the look on her face. But when the meeting ended and everyone stood up to leave, Damien said, "I'll walk you back to my mother's wagon."

Anna nodded. She kept her head down as they walked.

"Something is wrong," he said finally when they arrived at his mother's wagon.

"Yes, it is," she said as hot tears fell down her cheeks.

He bent down to see that she was crying. "Anna? What is it?"

"It was me. I took a bath in the wrong place in the river. I don't know your customs. Oh, Damien, I feel like everyone hates me here. And I miss my family. I feel so lost and so all alone."

"Shhh, don't cry. Please. You made a mistake. You won't do it again. Everyone makes mistakes. Yes? Even me." He laughed, trying to make her laugh, too. But she couldn't.

"I want to go home. I want to see my parents and my brother. It's not that I don't appreciate everything you and Vano have done for me. It's just that I miss my family."

He knelt down on the ground so that he would be closer to eye level with her. "Anna, for now, this is the best I can do for you. We'll try to find your family as soon as it's safe. I'll help you in any way I can."

"Sabina hates me. Your mother does too. I am staying with her in her wagon, and I feel like such an intruder. I know she wishes I would leave."

"My mother? Was she mean to you?"

"Not exactly, but I know she thinks I don't belong here."

"But you do. You belong here because I say you belong here," he said. "And why do you think Sabina hates you?"

"Because she came to me and tricked me into taking a bath at the top of the river."

"Oh, that little minx," he said, shaking his head. "Yes, well, that would be just like her. She wants my brother to marry her. But what she doesn't understand is that he would never marry her. He wouldn't marry her, no matter what. And I would never agree to marry a girl my mother has arranged for me to marry either, not even if I'd never met you. My mother has been trying to arrange a marriage for me for years, but she knows she doesn't have my consent."

"I feel like everyone hates me here except you and Vano," she said.

He stood up and shook the dirt off the knees of his pants. "Well," he said, smiling, "we'll have to change that now, won't we? It sounds like you need a friend."

"I don't know how to make friends here."

"Leave it to me," Damien said, winking at her.

CHAPTER SIXTY-TWO

That night, the moon was new, leaving the sky very dark and filled with stars. Anna looked up and could see some of the constellations she had been taught about in school. The memories of school made her smile. As she lay on the cool ground, she thought about Damien and Vano. She liked Damien very much. *He is kind and good-hearted. He is open and easy to talk to.* But when she thought of Vano, she felt butterflies in her stomach. There was something so attractive about Vano. He was always serious, and no one ever knew what he was thinking. That intrigued her. Damien was right. His brother was not a talker. He was quiet, and although she couldn't be sure, Anna thought Vano was a deep thinker. She remembered that it was Vano who had rescued her, and now she wished he would talk to her more.

CHAPTER SIXTY-THREE

The following morning, Damien was sitting outside the wagon with his mother when Anna awoke. She glanced over at him. He was sipping coffee when he saw her. His face broke out into a smile.

"There she is," he said. "Good morning!"

"Good morning," she said.

He took a cup and poured Anna a cup of coffee. Then he walked over to her and handed it to her.

"Thank you," she said, smiling as she sat up.

"Did you sleep well?" Lavina asked.

"Yes, thank you."

"Good, because today I am going to introduce you to some very good friends of mine," Damien said.

Anna smiled.

"Have something to eat, and we'll go."

"All right," Anna said. She stood up and walked over to where a large pot of hot cereal was simmering over an open fire. Lavina ladled some of the cereal into a bowl for Anna.

After Anna finished eating, she followed Damien to the open

field. There she saw several horses roped to the trees. "Have you ever ridden a horse?" he asked.

"Never," she said, "I'm afraid of horses."

He laughed. "Don't be afraid. There are a few rules you must follow, but otherwise, horses make great friends."

She laughed too. "These are the friends you wanted me to meet?"

"Well, yes, they are, but I also want you to meet Nuri. She takes care of the horses, and she should be here any minute."

A few minutes later, a young woman walked to where Anna and Damien stood. She smiled. "Damien!"

"Good to see you," he said. "I brought you a student."

"Oh?" And what is your name?

"Anna."

"So, Anna, you want to learn to ride?"

"Oh, I don't know," Anna said, "I'm a little afraid."

"Don't be. I'll teach you."

"Nuri is the best rider we have, even though she's a woman," he said. "Women don't usually ride as well as she does."

"Don't listen to him," Nuri said. "I love horses. I've loved them for as long as I can remember. Even my father doesn't trade my favorites. He knows how attached to them I am."

"So, you'll teach her to ride?" Damien asked.

"Of course, I'll teach Anna to ride. You go back to camp and leave us. When you return, you'll find Anna has become an expert rider."

"Oh, I doubt that," Anna said.

"Just trust me," Nuri winked.

CHAPTER SIXTY-FOUR

Anna stood far away from the horses. They were the largest animals she'd ever seen.

"All right, now, don't be afraid. Come here," Nuri said.

Anna walked over gingerly. Now go ahead and pet his face. Anna's hand was trembling as she petted the long nose of the auburn-colored horse. He stood quietly for a moment, but then he rubbed his face against Anna's face.

"He likes you." Nuri smiled. "By the way, let me introduce you to him. His name is Zino, and it means red. It's because of the color of his coat. Would you just look at that shade of red in the sun? He's a handsome devil. Isn't he?" Nuri said. Then, without waiting for an answer, she added, "Why don't you introduce yourself."

"To the horse?" Anna said. "Does he understand when I speak to him?"

"Of course. Just say 'Hello, Zino. It's nice to meet you. I'm Anna.'"

Anna let out a laugh. "If you say so," she said. Then she turned to the horse and said, "Hello, Zino, it's nice to meet you. I'm Anna."

The horse rubbed his face against Anna's cheek. She turned to Nuri and said, "You're right. I think he does understand."

"Of course he does. And he's very gentle. But always be careful not to stand behind the horses. It bothers them, and they might kick you. They are very strong and very powerful, and you could get hurt. Always stay in front where they can see you." Nuri rubbed Zino's face. "Good boy," she said. "It looks like Damien saddled him up for you. Lots of our horses refuse to wear a saddle, so we ride them bareback. But Zino is so good-natured he doesn't mind the saddle at all. But once you get used to it, you'll be riding bareback like the rest of us." She smiled, then she patted Anna on the shoulder. "So, are you ready to ride?"

"I don't know. I'm not sure I can do this. I'm kind of scared."

"I think you're quite ready." Nuri winked. "Damien talked to me about you yesterday. He told me about your family and how lonely you are feeling here in our camp. We both agreed that there is nothing like a horse to help a lonely girl feel accepted. Once you have a horse for a friend, you will know you have a real friend," Nuri said, then she walked Anna over to the saddle. "Come on, I'll give you a leg up."

Nuri was a small girl, but she was strong. She practically lifted Anna up into the saddle. Then she handed her the reins and showed her how to use them. "You pull this way if you want him to go left and this way if you want him to go right. And pull both reins, and he'll stop. A gentle kick will get him walking a little faster, and he'll trot."

"It's very high up here," Anna said, looking at Nuri, terrified.

Nuri laughed. "Don't be afraid. You're going to walk just a little today, so you can get used to being on a horse. Now, first of all, I must tell you a few things. Zino is an animal, but he has feelings too. And you must show respect for his feelings if you want him to respect yours."

"I'm not sure how to do that."

"Well, usually, he will do what you ask of him because he is a loving and kind creature. But sometimes, he will refuse you. When he firmly refuses to go in a particular direction, you must respect that. And why is that? It's because sometimes he sees things that you cannot."

"Like what?"

"For instance, you could be going straight into the path of a snake. He sees it, but you don't. He is telling you that he wants to go in a different direction. Listen to him, or he could get angry and refuse to have you on his back. That's when you get into trouble. If you insist on having your own way, he might throw you. So, pay attention to what he is trying to tell you."

"All right," Anna said.

"In short, you must not try to dominate him. You must respect him and his wisdom because every creature has wisdom, and they all have much to teach us. Do you understand?"

"Sort of," Anna admitted. "I have never thought of animals in this way, but I am learning."

"And while you are here with us, you will continue to learn so many new and wonderful things."

"I'm really glad we met," Anna said, sitting very still on Zino's back.

"So am I," Nuri answered.

"I've been feeling so alone here. Except for Damien and Vano, the others don't like me."

"Yes, well..." She hesitated. "By the others, do you mean Sabina?"

"Yes, and Lavina."

"That's because you pose a threat to what they want. But that doesn't really matter. In the long run, things will be exactly as they are meant to be, and even if Lavina wants one of her boys to marry Sabina, they will do as they please. They are strong-willed boys, and they will marry whoever they choose to marry," she said. "Now, let's learn to ride a horse. What do you say?"

"I say all right," Anna said tentatively.

At first, when Zino began to walk slowly, Anna was very tense. And for a half hour, Anna sat on Zino's back and rode him in a circle.

He was patient. And just as Nuri had promised, he was kind. He allowed her to relax, and soon, she became one with the rhythm of his gait.

CHAPTER SIXTY-FIVE

By the end of the week, Anna was no longer afraid of Zino. She loved getting up in the morning and meeting with Nuri for her riding lessons. Zino was a friend. She began to see what Nuri meant about him being more than just a creature. He had feelings and instincts, and she began to understand him. And as the days passed, she found she had also made a friend in Nuri. "You were right," Anna said as she dismounted the red horse and stood beside Nuri. "I feel at peace when I am riding. I feel a deep attachment to Zino. He's a wonderful horse."

"He is, isn't he? He's one of my favorites," Nuri admitted.

"I still miss my family, but when he trots, I feel the wind in my hair. I look down and see the flowers, or I look up and see the trees from a higher elevation, and something happens. I somehow don't feel as miserable."

"Told you, you'd like it," Nuri said.

"Well, before I met you, I didn't have any friends here except Damien and Vano. I've been living in Lavina's wagon. She's polite, but I always feel like deep down she hates me."

"Lavina? She doesn't hate you. She's afraid you're going to steal one of her sons. She adores her boys. And before you came, she expected one of them to marry Sabina. But the boys never wanted that. They both made it clear."

"Why would Lavina want them to marry anyone if she is afraid of losing them?"

"Because she can control Sabina. She has been like a mother to Sabina since Sabina was very young. Sabina's parents died when she was a child, and Lavina raised her. So, she will do whatever Lavina says. But Lavina knows she has no control over you."

"But I am not going to marry Damien."

"You don't like him?"

"I do. I do like him. He's a wonderful friend. But I am not ready to get married."

Nuri laughed out loud. Then she looked at Anna. "I wasn't talking about Damien. I was talking about Vano."

Anna looked away quickly. She felt her skin get hot, and she knew her cheeks were red.

"Can't you see the way he looks at you?" Nuri said.

"Vano? He doesn't even speak to me."

"He doesn't speak much, with words, but look at his eyes when he looks at you. He is always watching you."

"Vano? I have never thought he was interested in me."

"Well, my dear child. Think again. Next time you see him at the bonfire at night or at dinner, mark my words. Take a look at his eyes when he looks at you. You'll see his feelings. They are there. Plain as day."

"So, you think he wants to marry me?"

"I think Vano is falling in love with you and love leads to marriage. At least, that's the way it is in our culture. But... I also think that Damien is falling for you, too. You are going to have quite a dilemma on your hands."

"Hmmm, I don't know how I didn't see it. I guess I just haven't been paying attention. But if you say it is so, I believe you. You see, Nuri, I have been so concerned with my family and their wellbeing.

Besides that, I am always worried about the Nazis. I am afraid of what they will do to my family, and I am also afraid of them following me here. I don't want to put you or your people in danger. So, because of this, I haven't given much thought to romance."

"It's understandable. I can't imagine how you must feel."

"I feel afraid, always afraid. Even though I am comfortable here, it could all change in the blink of an eye."

Nuri nodded. They were quiet for several moments, then Nuri said, "I don't really know much about you or your past before you came to our camp. One day, perhaps you will tell me about your family and how you ended up here. I would like to hear your story. But for now, remember what I told you. Keep a watch on Vano and Damien. You'll see what I'm talking about. You'll see how they look at you. Eventually, I think one of them will declare his love. Of course, I could be wrong."

"What about you? I don't know anything about you," Anna said.

"Me, I have a sad story to tell. I was betrothed to a wonderful fellow, but he got sick and died last year. No one knew what he had died from. He got sick one day, and by the end of the week, he was gone. Our medicine woman tried everything she could to help him. I stayed by his side and begged him to get well. But he couldn't fight it, and he died anyway. It was hard on me. We had such plans for our future," she said. "So, for now, I am alone." Then she smiled a half smile. "But I have my horses."

That night, everyone at the Romany camp gathered around the campfire. The men played their violins, and the women danced. Anna sat with Damien on one side and Vano on the other.

"I love violin music," Nuri said as she sat beside Damien.

"I can play the violin," Anna offered.

"Really?"

"Yes, a long time ago, I was dating a boy who taught me to play." She closed her eyes for a moment and remembered Daniel teaching her. It seemed like a lifetime ago.

"I love music. Can you sing too?" Nuri asked.

"No, but I can play piano," Anna said.

"We don't have a piano, but you must play the violin for us," Nuri said, and without another word, she stood up and walked over to a handsome young man who had been playing his violin. She waited patiently until he finished his song, and then she whispered something in his ear. He handed her his instrument. Nuri motioned for Anna to come to her. Anna did as Nuri asked. "Play for us?" she said, handing Anna the violin.

"Sure, I would be happy to," Anna said, taking the instrument. She was glad for the distraction. Besides that, music had always been an outlet for her emotions, and right now, she needed that. So, as everyone stood watching and waiting, Anna ran her fingers along the smooth wood of the violin.

"Anna's going to play for us," Nuri said, loud enough for everyone to hear. The circle grew very quiet. The only sound was the crackling of the fire. And then Anna placed the instrument beneath her chin and closed her eyes. Then she began to play.

The sad, haunting timbre of the violin told her story. She was a Jew, misunderstood and hated by the Nazis. The loneliness she felt came through with every note. Tears ran down her face, which was illuminated by the firelight.

When Anna finished, she was trembling all over. She opened her eyes and put the violin down. Then everyone began cheering. Anna bent her head. "Thank you," she said. Finally, for the first time, she felt accepted.

CHAPTER SIXTY-SIX

Anna handed the violin back to Nuri, who handed it back to its owner. "I'm Luke," the owner of the instrument said, "and you must be Anna?"

"I am," she said, smiling.

"You play beautifully," he said.

"Thank you. That's very kind of you to say. But I haven't played in a long time. It's been years."

"You're a born musician. I am too. Do you sing?"

"No, actually, I don't have much of a voice."

"I love to sing. When I sing, I feel like I can let go of anything that is in my heart, be it joy or pain. I feel like all of my emotions bubble up through my lungs and spill forth with my breath. Once I've finished a song, I am empty and ready to fill again."

"I think that all music is a way to express emotions."

Luke put his violin under his chin and began to play a sweet, haunting tune. Then he stopped, and in a rich tenor voice, he sang a song in Romany. Everyone stopped to listen. Anna was captivated. She could hardly catch her breath. No one said a word until Luke had finished. "That was a love song. An old Romani love song," he said.

Just then, Vano walked over and put himself between Anna and Luke. "Thank you for allowing Anna to use your violin," he said to Luke. Then he turned to Anna. "It's getting late. You should get some rest."

Anna nodded to Vano. It was late, but she felt she could detect some jealousy. *Nuri is right.* She thought. Then she turned to Luke and said, "Thank you for the song. And for allowing me to play your violin."

"Perhaps we will see each other again?" Luke said, but before Anna could answer, Vano led her away.

CHAPTER SIXTY-SEVEN

"Move into my wagon," Nuri said to Anna, "you'll be more comfortable there. Lavina sees you as a threat to her boys and her way of life. You will be happier with me. And besides, I could use the company."

"Are you sure?"

"I wouldn't have suggested it if I weren't."

"I'll ask Damien and Vano if it's all right with them," Anna said. "I don't want to offend them in any way. They have both been so kind to me."

"You don't have to ask them. I already did. They both agreed that you would be more comfortable with me."

"Then it's settled. I'll move in."

After Anna moved in with Nuri, things were better for her. Anna had a friend, someone she could talk to and someone she felt she could trust. Nuri gave Anna a pair of pants to wear when she was riding. And this made her more comfortable on horseback. Each morning, Damien met Anna in the field with two horses. Then they spent several hours riding together. Sometimes he brought food, and they stopped to picnic. He told her jokes and stories that made her laugh. Often she would see Vano watching them as they rode away, but he was so quiet and reserved that he never tried to come along. The more time she spent with Damien, the more she could see what Nuri was talking about. He cared deeply for her. This meant a lot to Anna, who had no one left but Damien, Vano, and Nuri. Sometimes she wondered what it would be like to be married to Damien. Her life would be far different from what she had ever dreamed it would be, but she would be loved, and what was more important than that? *Damien is gentle and kind, but he is light and joyful. He doesn't understand my moments of darkness when depression falls upon me like a black rain, reminding me that I might never see my family again.* She felt she had to hide these terrible feelings from Nuri and Damien, who she didn't think would understand them. But she felt that somehow Vano would be able to relate.

CHAPTER SIXTY-EIGHT

A month passed before Elica was released from custody and allowed to return home. However, the deep scar on her cheek left her wounded in a way from which she could never recover. When she got out of jail, she covered her face with a scarf and walked all the way back to the home she'd shared with Daniel and his parents. She realized the lock had been changed when she tried to open the door with her key. She knocked. A woman answered the door, who appeared to be in her early thirties. Elica was so shocked to see another family living in Daniel's parents' home that, for a second, she allowed the scarf to drop from her cheek. The woman could not hide the horror in her eyes when she looked at Elica's scar, and Elica looked down at the ground, embarrassed. The young woman quickly recovered from the shock. She tried not to stare at the scar as she smiled at Elica.

"Come in," the woman said.

Elica walked inside. Everything was the same. The rugs on the floor, the sofa, the coffee table. Memories flooded Elica's mind, and she felt hot tears begin to form in the back of her eyes.

"May I ask who you are and what you want?" the young woman

questioned. She was a slender beauty who reminded Elica of her former self. "Please, won't you sit down?" she said, perplexed about who Elica was and why she had come. Elica studied her, and she saw the kindness in her blue eyes. But how could she possibly be a good and kind person while she had stolen this house from Daniel's family? In fact, here was proof she was living in Daniel's parents' home. Elica glanced around the room. The photographs of Daniel's parents' wedding, which had once sat on the coffee table, had been replaced by another photo of a handsome young officer in a German uniform. His arm was around the young woman who stood beside Elica.

Elica sat down on the sofa. Immediately, her thoughts went to Daniel. Once, long ago. So, very long ago. She and Daniel had made love on this very sofa when Daniel's parents were away. Elica felt the bile rise in her throat. Her fingers went to the scar on her cheek. She touched it and winced. It no longer hurt physically, but the emotional scar was as strong as the day the Nazi cut her.

"This was my home," Elica said in a small voice. She did not tell the woman her name, nor did she ask the woman's name. Instead, she touched the fabric of the sofa and looked down. "I lived here with my husband and his family." She was careful not to mention Theo. In order to keep him safe, she knew she must never speak of him again. "My husband was Jewish. The Nazis took him away. They killed him, and they cut up my face. You see the scar? It's a star of David. They did that to me because I was married to a Jew. And then they stole our home and gave it to you."

"I'm sorry," the pretty woman said. There was sincerity in her voice. "I don't know what to say. All I can tell you is that my husband was awarded this home for his loyal service to the Reich. We have two young daughters who are in school right now and a little boy who is asleep. This is our home now."

Elica nodded. She wasn't going to fight or argue, even though she had no money and nowhere else to go. "I see," she said, then she added, "do you have the photographs that were on this coffee table and also the ones on the mantle of the fireplace? If you would be so kind, I would like to have them, and then I will go."

"I never saw any photos. When we arrived here, there were no photos at all," the woman said, "I can't help you. I wish I could, but I can't."

"The ones on the mantle were of myself and my husband. Are you sure you didn't see them? They are all that I would have left of him. I have nothing else."

The young woman had tears in her eyes. "I truly am sorry. If I had seen any pictures, I would give them to you. But I never saw any," she said. Then she began to cry softly, "I would give you your house, but I can't. We need it. My family needs it. Please understand."

"I do," Elica said. Then she stood up. "Thank you for your time. I'm going to leave now."

The woman nodded.

Elica walked out and gently closed the door behind her. Then she fell to her knees on the side of the building and wept.

CHAPTER SIXTY-NINE

Elica's mother had just returned from work when Elica knocked on the door. She opened it and gasped when she saw her daughter. It had been a long time since Elica had seen her mother, and she knew her mother was horrified by the scar on her face. Elica looked down at the ground, "Can I come in, please, *mutti*?"

"Yes, of course. Come in," Frau Frey said, "Sit down." Then she added in a small voice, "What happened to you?"

"Daniel and his parents were arrested. I think they're all dead," Elica said, her voice shaking, "I went looking for Daniel at the police station. The police did this to me. They kept me in custody for a month. They beat me and starved me. It was horrible, mother. Horrible."

"*Mein Gott!*" she said, putting her fist in her mouth. *My God!* "What happened to the baby?"

"He died," Elica lied.

"So, you are alone, all alone?"

"Yes, I am."

"I don't know if you have heard that the Levinsteins are gone? No one knows what happened to them," Elica's mother said. "One day, they were in their house; the next day, they were gone."

"Yes, I know. I heard from Dagna."

"You saw her? Where is she?"

"She turned on me, mother. She's responsible for this disfigurement," Elica touched her face.

Frau Frey shook her head. "I have some bad news, Elica. It's about your father."

"Where's father? What's happened, *mutti*?"

"Oh, Elica. I hate to have to tell you this with everything you have been through. But I must tell you. Your father was killed two weeks ago in an accident at the factory," her mother moaned. "When it happened, I needed to see you. I didn't care about anything but having you by my side. I no longer cared what you had done. You were my only family; all I had left. So, I went over to Daniel's house where you were living. I had to find you. I knocked on the door, and another woman answered. Another family was living there. I didn't know where to find you. I couldn't understand what had happened, but now I do."

"Oh, *mutti*. *Vater* is dead, and I never had a chance to say goodbye." Elica looked away. "We never got along, really. But I wish I had seen him at least one last time." She felt a flood of emotions come over her. Elica's mother went over and put her arm around Elica's shoulder. "Yes, I know he had his faults. But I will miss him too."

"Can I stay here, mother? I have nowhere else to go."

"Yes, of course you can stay."

CHAPTER SEVENTY

Nuri was right. Zino, the auburn horse, was a friend and a companion. The more Anna rode him, the more he was able to predict her every move. When she was sitting on his back, they were as one being. And within a month, they were galloping through the open fields. Many mornings she and Damien raced through the fields on horseback, challenging each other to see who could ride faster, and often, Anna won. Slowly, she learned to laugh again. It wasn't that she ever forgot her family, but she now had another family. Nuri and Damien and always in the background, Vano. Nuri was like the sister she had never had. And if she had learned anything from living amongst the Romany, it was that although their clothes and customs were different, they were the same inside. And Anna began to wonder if all people weren't the same inside.

One morning, Anna woke up to find that Vano was not in the camp. Several hours passed, but he did not return. Anna began worrying, but Nuri said he often did things like this. "He probably went for a long walk to think things over. Or he could have gone hunting."

"Doesn't he always go with Damien?"

"Most of the time, but not always. Vano's a deep thinker. Since he was a child, he would often go off by himself. He has deep feelings, and sometimes he needs to be alone to sort them out in his own mind. He'll be all right."

"What if the Nazis find him?"

"They won't. He knows this forest. Our caravan has been coming here for many generations. Vano used to wander this forest alone when he was just a little boy. He'll be all right."

"But I am afraid I might have a Nazi chasing me." Anna hoped Ulf and Oliver had forgotten about her, but she couldn't be sure.

"I know. Vano told me everything. He said you knew the counselor of the Nazi children's camp from before the war."

"I did. We were friends. It's hard to believe, but it's true."

"Yes, well, this war changed a lot of people. But don't worry, Vano will be fine."

Vano didn't return at all that day. And Anna could not sleep all night. But when she awoke in the morning, he was sitting in front of a fire, eating breakfast with a big smile on his face.

"I was worried about you," she said, a little angry.

"I'm all right," he said, not looking directly at her, but she could see a half smile on his face, and she wondered if he was happy to hear she'd been worried about him. Then he gave her a small pile of clothing. "I got these things for you. I've noticed that you needed them."

"Thank you. Thank you so much," Anna said. She did not question Vano about how he came by these dresses and undergarments. She didn't want to know where he'd acquired such things. She was just glad to have clean clothes.

CHAPTER SEVENTY-ONE

Vano and Damien went out to hunt at least four times a week. They left early in the morning and usually returned by early afternoon. The boys shared whatever game they caught—squirrels, rabbits, and hedgehogs—with Anna, Nuri, Sabina, and Lavina.

At first, Anna found it difficult to help prepare the animals that Damien and Vano hunted. She tried to hide it from Lavina and Sabina when she gagged. And to make matters worse, she found it hard to eat the meat. But as the weeks passed, she got used to the open fire and the smell of fresh meat roasting. After a while, Anna no longer cooked with Lavina and Sabina. Instead, she and Nuri made their own fire, and Vano and Damien made sure they had meat to cook whenever they went out to hunt. Nuri and Anna took long walks, searching for wild mushrooms. Nuri explained which ones were safe to eat and which were poisonous. And as time went on, Anna adjusted to her new life.

Depending on the weather, but whenever possible, Nuri and Anna slept outside with blankets under the star-filled sky. From where they slept, Anna could look across the campsite and see Vano, who always slept outside, even in the rain. Often, she would catch him looking at her, and before she could look away, he would smile. Anna would look away quickly, but then she would turn back and see that he was still staring at her and smiling. And she had to smile, too.

CHAPTER SEVENTY-TWO

Each night Anna played the violin along with the other musicians in camp. There was a cello, a mandolin player, and several other violinists. The girls danced. Vano and Damien watched Anna as she played. One night, after everyone had gone to their wagons or to their blankets under the stars, Vano went to the area outside of Nuri's vardo, where he found Nuri and Anna asleep. He stood there watching Anna for several minutes until she stirred awake. When she saw him, at first, she was frightened. She jumped, but she relaxed once she was fully awake and realized it was Vano. "What are you doing here?" she whispered so as not to awaken Nuri.

"I wanted to talk to you," he said.

Anna nodded. "All right, give me a minute," she said, then got up and put on her shoes. "Let's go for a walk, so we don't wake Nuri."

They walked under the light of a full moon until they were well into the forest and far enough from camp to speak without disturbing anyone. Then Vano sat down on a broken tree branch large enough to hold them both. He motioned for Anna to sit beside him. She did.

"I am not a man who has an easy time talking about his feelings," Vano said, his voice choked. "Even now, as I hear myself speaking, I feel like I sound ridiculous. Laughable even."

"You don't. I promise you that you don't," she said, "please, go on."

"I am trying," he said, managing a smile. "I don't know how this happened. I tried to fight it. I tried very hard because I know how my brother feels about you. But when I saw you and Damien looking into each other's eyes. It almost killed me. I don't know how to say this, but... I mean... well... I mean..."

Anna looked down at the ground. She thought of Damien. She knew he cared for her, and she cared for him, too. But her heart belonged to Vano.

The moon shone like liquid silver, and the breeze sent a shiver up Anna's spine as she walked with Vano. He was such a quiet man, but his eyes spoke to her, and as she looked into them, she could feel his emotions. She walked up close to him, her heart beating faster with anticipation. They stood looking at each other for a long time. Then, without warning, Anna leaned in and kissed him. It was electric, and as their lips touched, she felt a wave of warmth wash over her. She was amazed at her own boldness as they pulled away, both of them breathless. They smiled at each other. Then Vano took her into his strong arms, and she felt the power of him surge through her like lightning. But as they leaned in to kiss again, they heard a rustle in the bushes. Anna felt fear strike her heart as she pulled away. She looked into his eyes. "Don't worry. I'll protect you," he said. And then, there was another rustle in the bushes, and they realized they weren't alone.

CHAPTER SEVENTY-THREE

After Dagna saw Elica with the deep wound on her face, everything changed. Dagna no longer worshiped or admired Elica. That was because Elica was no longer beautiful. However, Dagna was still bewitched by the memory of the beautiful, carefree girl who Elica had been. And slowly, Dagna began to turn herself into the old Elica. She went to a hairdresser and had her hair bleached blonde. Then she styled it in the same way Elica had worn hers in their youth. She was working and earning a decent living. So, she was able to purchase a few dresses that were the same styles and colors as the ones Elica had worn. Dagna had memorized the hand gestures that Elica had used. Things like rubbing her thumb over her collarbone to bring attention to her decolletage when she was speaking. And Dagna began to imitate them.

Each day she left to go to work, Dagna spoke to herself in the mirror.

"Good morning, beautiful. You are as pretty, if not prettier than Elica ever was," she would say. And some days, she would even call herself Elica instead of Dagna. Then she would carefully put on the lipstick she had once stolen for Elica and smile at herself before leaving the house. Elica's disfigurement gave Dagna a strange form of confidence. When Dagna looked in the mirror, she did not see herself. Instead, she saw a young and pretty Elica. In Dagna's mind, the two of them were now one.

Dagna found out that Elica had been released by the police. And she heard that Elica was staying with her mother. But she never went to see her. Instead, she left their friendship in the past and requested a transfer. Dagna wanted to start a new life. With a new job somewhere, she could be anyone she wanted to be, and she wanted to be Elica.

Before Dagna started working at the police station, she went to school for secretarial training. When Elica left her to pay the rent on her own, she needed a better job than working on an assembly line in a factory. It wasn't easy because she had to go to school at night after a long day of factory work. But she was determined, and when she was determined, her mind was strong. She would leave the factory exhausted each day, then rush home and eat something quickly. After that, she took a bus to school, where she attended night classes and found that she excelled at secretarial work. Dagna quickly became a good typist. She was fast and accurate, and although shorthand was a little more difficult, she learned it. The classes ended after dark, and she had to make her way back to the dingy apartment where she lived. And each night, as she rode the bus, terrified by the looks of the derelict men, she cursed Elica.

Elica left me when Daniel came back into her life. Elica did not care at all about how I would survive once she was gone. Our salaries together had just been enough for us to pay the rent and buy some food. Elica knew that if she left me alone to pay the bills in the apartment, I did not earn enough to survive. But Elica was selfish. When Daniel returned to her and said he wanted her back, that he wanted to take care of her and their son, Elica didn't care at all about what would happen to me. She just walked out of the apartment, taking Theo and her things, leaving me desperate to find a way to pay the rent.

After Elica left her without much thought, hatred for Elica began to grow within Dagna. Not only did she hate Elica, but she had also always hated Jews, and Daniel was Jewish. Dagna's hatred for Daniel grew beyond measure. She swore to herself that she would see him dead someday. She would find a way to destroy him. But in the meantime, she had to find a place where she could afford to live. So, she went to the landlady and asked if she had any smaller flats to rent. She explained that Elica had moved out, and now she could no longer afford to pay the full rent. The landlord just so happened to have a small studio apartment in the basement of the building next door. If Dagna thought that the apartment she shared with Elica had been terrible, it was only because she had not yet seen this one. It was small, cramped, and looked more like a closet than an apartment. There was one tiny window that hardly let in any light, so it was always dark. The bed was hard, and the sheets and blanket were dirty.

Dagna took the apartment because she knew it was all she could afford, and every day, as she tried to clean up the place, she cursed Elica and spit when she thought of her. Looking around her, Dagna knew she must find a way to get out of this apartment. She could not go home; her mother had moved in with some man. Dagna was on her own, and so that was when she signed up for the secretarial classes. Once she had mastered secretarial skills, she went to the police station to find work. They tested her skills and found her to be an excellent typist and very fast at taking shorthand. That was when she was hired. Within a month, she was able to move to a nicer flat in a better neighborhood. But she still hated Elica and waited like a spider on a web for her opportunity to get revenge. And then she finally got her chance. It all began when Daniel and his family were arrested. Daniel's father, an outspoken man, had been shot before the family arrived at the police station. His mother, who would not stop crying and screaming, was killed soon after. And Daniel was murdered when he arrived at the police station. Dagna was glad that Daniel, the arrogant Jew who didn't deserve the life he'd been given, had witnessed the death of his parents. In fact, she wished that Anna had suffered the same fate. But nothing fulfilled her hatred and anger as much as seeing Elica's beautiful face ruined. In fact, it was she, Dagna, who had suggested that the guard carve the Star of David into Elica's cheek. And she watched him as he did it. Not once did she feel sympathy of any kind as she listened to Elica scream and watched the floor grow slippery with her blood. No, she didn't feel sick to her stomach, nor did she feel pity. She felt that she had finally gotten her revenge. And the hold Elica had once had over her no longer existed. As the knife pierced Elica's delicate flesh, Dagna smiled because it was severing any ties she'd once had to Elica. It made her even angrier when she thought of how much she had done to win Elica's friendship and all the years that she had bent over backward just to be a part of Elica's life. She'd prayed and dreamed and hoped that someday she would be like Elica, beautiful, desired, and accepted. She took pleasure in Elica's pain.

Dagna was finally free. She no longer hated or pitied Elica. She had no feelings for her at all. And that was when she decided she would become Elica. The old Elica, the one who men fell to their knees for. Dagna knew Elica's every move. And she copied it to the letter. She copied Elica's facial expressions, her quiet smile, and the way she lifted her eyebrows. She worked on her voice until it was soft like Elica's and her laughter until it sounded so much like Elica's she couldn't tell the difference. She imitated Elica's little half smile, which Elica had reserved for men she wanted to seduce. Dagna practiced these things until she mastered them. She went on a strict diet to lose the excess weight that kept her from wearing the kind of form-fitting dresses Elica had worn. Dagna looked in the mirror every chance she got and smiled. Now she was as pretty as Elica had once been; if not, she was close enough to be happy with the results.

It took a few months for a transfer to be available, but Dagna waited. Then she received a letter saying that she was to go for an interview at a place called Sobibor, where a job was available in the office for keeping records. Sobibor was located in Poland, but she didn't mind going east. Hitler was trying hard to encourage more

German women to go east. It was true that she wasn't exactly German. She was Austrian, but so was the Führer. And she considered herself to be German. The idea of the adventure made her feel excited and giddy. At night, she practiced the voice inflections that Elica had used when she flirted with men. None of this was difficult for Dagna to remember. She had always wanted to be like Elica. But while Elica was in her life, and while she was still the most beautiful girl that Dagna had ever known, Dagna could not become Elica. It felt too contrived. However, since the real Elica was no longer the great beauty she once was, it felt right. And Dagna was ready to try her new image out on people who had never met her.

CHAPTER SEVENTY-FOUR

Dagna had been waiting for a half hour to be interviewed for the new job she hoped to acquire. When her name was called, she stood up and smoothed her skirt. Then she walked into the office of her interviewer. *How would the old Elica, the still beautiful Elica, have behaved in this situation?*

"Heil Hitler," Dagna said, then she smiled fetchingly.

"Heil Hitler," the man behind the desk answered. He looked over, hesitating for a moment on the swell of her breasts and the curve of her hips. "You may sit."

Dagna sat down. She crossed her legs at the ankle and flipped her bleached blonde hair off her shoulder.

"I'm *Ortsgruppenleiter* Armbrect. You are Dagna Hoffer?" he said, looking through the papers she'd filled out.

"Yes," Dagna said, her voice soft and breathy the way Elica's was when she wanted to get a man's attention.

"So, Fräulein Hoffer? It is Fräulein, isn't it?"

"Yes, I am not married."

"All right then, Fräulein Hofer. So, why do you want to work at Sobibor?"

"I want to help the fatherland in any way that I can. I know that I am only a secretary, but a good secretary can be a big help to her boss."

"I see," he said, tapping a pencil on his desk. He was still studying her as if she were a painting. "I am assuming you can type fast and accurately and take shorthand."

Dagna sat up straight. "Yes. I can type sixty words a minute and take shorthand just as fast."

"Hmmm. I will have the girls out front give you a typing test. However, if you can actually do what you say you can, well... we can always use a good secretary. However, before you start working, I will be sending you for training. May I assume that this would be satisfactory?"

"Yes, of course."

"There is a little facility up in Northern Germany where we like to send our female guards to train. Now, I know you are applying for a secretarial position, but there is a position open for a guard. And working as a guard pays much better. Are you interested?"

"Oh, yes."

"Good, I knew you would be. The camp where we train is called Ravensbrück. I am going to send you there to see what you are made of."

CHAPTER SEVENTY-FIVE

Her blonde hair, illuminated by the sun, waved around her head like a golden crown as she stepped from the train. The black skirt she wore accented her slender hips and long legs, and her tight white sweater curved over her large breasts. A baggage handler almost fell over his own feet, trying to help her as he took her suitcase.

Two German officers stood at the train station.

"Wow, did you see that gorgeous woman?" one of the men said to the other.

"How could I miss her? You don't see girls like that every day."

"That's for sure. I think I know her," the first one said.

"Really? From where?"

"She lived in my neighborhood when I was growing up in Vienna."

"I don't believe you. Go over and say hello."

"All right, I will."

The two German officers walked over to the woman, who was standing with her back to them.

"Elica, do you remember me? It's Rolf," one of the men said as he tapped her on the shoulder. "What are you doing here in Poland?"

The woman whipped around to face the men. She saw Rolf, and a half smile of recognition came over her face. "Oh yes, I remember you, Rolf. You called me ugly once. Do you remember? We were in the park with our friends. Of course, we were just children, but I never forgot it." She let out a laugh, but it wasn't a genuine laugh. It was a cruel and vindictive sound.

He shook his head. She looked like Elica, but not exactly like Elica, at least not when they were standing this close. She wasn't as pretty as he remembered, but that could have been the result of growing up during a war. Still, there was something about her face that was no longer soft or gentle. Her eyes were hard, and her lips were thin and pressed together. "I never called you ugly," he said. "I would never have done that."

"Oh yes, you did, and for years, the memory of it haunted me. You hurt me that day, Rolf, and the funny thing is you didn't even know it. You called me ugly. You probably don't even remember. But I do. In fact, I could never forget it. Oh yes, and by the way, my name isn't Elica. It's Dagna. Dagna Hofer."

CHAPTER SEVENTY-SIX

U lf was consumed by anger. He felt that Anna had betrayed him. And this made him want to punish her. *I have the power. She is Jewish, and she has no legal rights. But to punish her, I have to find her. And I don't know how I am ever going to do that.* He was so livid with himself for rescuing her and her family that sometimes he could not sleep. And as much as he agonized over Anna, he still had no idea where she could have gone. But he was certain she couldn't have gotten very far alone and on foot. However, if she was picked up by soldiers or a group of partisans in the forest, then that was a different story. And it was quite possible. There were all sorts of people wandering around in the forest these days. She could have encountered anyone. Perhaps she was dead. *If Anna did not find anyone to help her and she was in the forest alone, she would never be able to find food, so she would already have starved to death?*

One night after work, he went over to Filip's house to talk to him. He knocked on the door. Filip opened it wearing his undershirt and undershorts. "Come in, my friend," he said.

Ulf walked inside. He was surprised to find the house a complete mess. There were issues of *Das Reich*, the newspaper Dr. Goebbels produced, all over the floor. Ashtrays filled with ashes and cigarette butts overflowed on the tables.

"Sit down, please," Filip said.

The house smelled of sauerkraut and garlic. Ulf sat down in a heavy chair.

"Would you like a shot?" Filip asked, pulling out a bottle from under his chair.

"Sure," Ulf said.

Filip stood up and got two glasses off the shelf. He held them up to the light to check and see if they were clean. Then, satisfied, he poured a shot of schnaps into each one and sat across from Ulf. "So, to what do I owe the honor of this visit?" he asked.

"I need to talk, Filip. I can't get that damn Jew out of my mind," Ulf said, shaking his head. His nails were bitten to the quick. His cuticles had dried blood on them. "I risked everything for her. My job, my friends, my security, everything. I even killed an Aryan man, a worthwhile human being. I did all this for her. And this is how she thanks me? She runs away from me?"

"You forgot one important fact. She's a Jew, Wolfgang. She's a Jew," Filip said, using Ulf's full name to let Ulf know how serious he was about this.

"I know, and I also know, just like a Jew, she has bewitched me."

Filip nodded. "I'm not surprised. Jews consort with the devil. I am sure you know that."

"I do, but I couldn't help myself."

"Of course not. That's the spell. She did that to you."

"Yes, she did," Ulf said.

Filip lit a cigarette.

Ulf was quiet for a moment, then he said. "You know that I killed her parents. But even that didn't break the spell."

"There's only one way to break it. At least that's what I think."

"How?"

"By owning her completely. Once you possess her for a while, you will be able to forget her." Filip said, taking a long drag of his cigarette.

"Do you really think so?"

"I do, and the best part about it is that she's a Jew. If you get caught, they'll kill her, but you'll only get a slap on the hand. No one cares what we do with Jews."

"That's true," Ulf said, nodding. "That's very true. So, how do I do it?"

"Do you have a cellar in your house?" Filip asked.

"Yes. But I never go down there," Ulf admitted. "I've never even seen it."

"Perhaps we should go down there and set it up. Once we find her, you'll need a place to keep her locked up. You want to own her, don't you? Isn't that what you said?"

"I don't know. This seems crazy."

"Of course it does. It is crazy. However, you can get away with it because she's a Jew. There are no police protecting Jews. You can do whatever you want with them. You can either let her go or kill her when you're finished with her. Either way, there will be no consequences. She wouldn't dare try to turn you in. She's a Jew. She'd be in more trouble than you. That's for sure," he laughed.

Ulf laughed too, but it was more of a nervous laugh than anything else. He wanted Anna. He wanted her badly. *If I captured her, I could make her love me.* He thought. *I could keep her captive long enough for her to know I am not a terrible man. I would give her food and anything else she might need. She would see the good in me.*

"So? What do you say?"

"How do I do it?" Ulf asked.

"You must set up a small area. A prison of sorts, where you can keep Anna once you find her. A place that she will never be able to escape from. I think you should use your cellar. I think it will be perfect. Because, like I said, just finding her and turning her in won't be satisfying for you. The only way you will feel gratified is if she is at your mercy."

Ulf sat back in his chair. "You're right. I don't want to turn her in. That would be counterproductive. I want her to fall in love with me."

"She might never love you. But she will belong to you. And you will have the power to do anything you choose to do to her."

Ulf nodded. He liked the idea. A smile came over his face. Then he said, "So, will you help me?"

"Of course, I would be happy to help you set up the prison for her. But I cannot help you find her. You must tell your superior that you cannot rest until you find the Jews who tricked your Gestapo partner. Tell him that you believe these Jews have escaped into the forests. Ask for time to search for them. You are well-liked. You will get permission," Filip said, then he gave Ulf a wink and a smile.

CHAPTER SEVENTY-SEVEN

Building a small prison in Ulf's cellar became a project for Ulf and Fillip. Ulf didn't want to imprison Anna in a torturous prison. He just wanted to keep her so she couldn't run away from him again. Filip had other ideas. He was obsessed with the prospect of building a fortress, a place Anna would never be able to escape from. He brought over a large cage, which he said he had purchased for a dog he had several years ago.

"You can keep her in here when you leave the house. I would keep this in the cellar," Fillip said.

"Keep Anna in a cage?" Ulf said.

"You can't let her wander around the cellar. She's a Jew, and they are born criminals. You could lock her up, and she'd find a way out. She'll escape again."

"That's true. She might."

"Of course she will. You must lock her up every time you leave."

"The cellar is dark and dirty," Ulf said, looking around him. "Look at the spiders. She will be terrified here. I'd rather keep her in my bedroom."

"You really care for this Jew girl, don't you?"

"I do," Ulf said.

"But you must never forget that she's a Jew, and you just can't trust Jews. You should realize that. After everything you did for her, she ran away from you. She's like a bad dog. You have no choice. You must keep her in a cage," Filip said.

"I suppose you're right. But I have no idea how I am going to find her. The woods are so vast. And I am going to be wandering through acres and acres of trees and brush, looking for a girl who is hiding from me," Ulf said.

"It's too bad you don't know anyone you could use to lure her if you find out where she is."

"Lure her?"

"Well, yes," Filip said. "She would never come to you. But perhaps she would come to one of her friends. Do you know any of her friends?"

"I worked with Dagna Hofer at the Police station, but she hates Jews. And although she knew Anna before the war, they were never really friends. In fact, she was working for a family a few streets away from my parents' house that same summer that Anna was working for my parents as a nanny for my twin brothers, Klaus and Gynther. We didn't know Anna was Jewish, but Dagna came to my parents' home and told them."

"She told your parents Anna was a Jew?"

"Yes. And it was illegal for Jews to work for Aryans."

"They fired her?"

"Right away," Ulf said.

"And your brothers? How old were they?"

"Ten at the time, I think," Ulf said.

"How did they react?"

"They were devastated. They loved Anna, and she loved them too."

And it was at that very moment that Wolfgang Fischer knew

exactly what he was going to do. *Of course, I will use my brothers as bait. I will find her, and I will use them to lure her. Anna will come to them easily, effortlessly. And they need never know what I have in store...*

AUTHORS NOTE

I always enjoy hearing from my readers, and your thoughts about my work are very important to me. If you enjoyed my novel, please consider telling your friends and posting a short review on Amazon. Word of mouth is an author's best friend.

Also, it would be my honor to have you join my mailing list. As my gift to you for joining, you will receive 3 **free** short stories and my USA Today award-winning novella complimentary in your email! To sign up, just go to my website at www.RobertaKagan.com

I send blessings to each and every one of you,

Roberta

Email: roberta@robertakagan.com

ABOUT THE AUTHOR

I wanted to take a moment to introduce myself. My name is Roberta, and I am an author of Historical Fiction, mainly based on World War 2 and the Holocaust. While I never discount the horrors of the Holocaust and the Nazis, my novels are constantly inspired by love, kindness, and the small special moments that make life worth living.

I always knew I wanted to reach people through art when I was younger. I just always thought I would be an actress. That dream died in my late 20's, after many attempts and failures. For the next several years, I tried so many different professions. I worked as a hairstylist and a wedding coordinator, amongst many other jobs. But I was never satisfied. Finally, in my 50's, I worked for a hospital on the PBX board. Every day I would drive to work, I would dread clocking in. I would count the hours until I clocked out. And, the next day, I would do it all over again. I couldn't see a way out, but I prayed, and I prayed, and then I prayed some more. Until one morning at 4 am, I woke up with a voice in my head, and you might know that voice as Detrick. He told me to write his story, and together we sat at the computer; we wrote the novel that is now known as All My Love, Detrick. I now have over 30 books published, and I have had the honor of being a USA Today Best-Selling Author. I have met such incredible people in this industry, and I am so blessed to be meeting you.

I tell this story a lot. And a lot of people think I am crazy, but it is true. I always found solace in books growing up but didn't start writing until I was in my late 50s. I try to tell this story to as many people as possible to inspire them. No matter where you are in your life, remember there is always a flicker of light no matter how dark it seems.

I send you many blessings, and I hope you enjoy my novels. They are all written with love.

Roberta

MORE BOOKS BY ROBERTA KAGAN
AVAILABLE ON AMAZON

The Blood Sisters Series

The Pact

My Sister's Betrayal

When Forever Ends

The Auschwitz Twins Series

The Children's Dream

Mengele's Apprentice

The Auschwitz Twins

Jews, The Third Reich, and a Web of Secrets

My Son's Secret

The Stolen Child

A Web of Secrets

A Jewish Family Saga

Not In America

They Never Saw It Coming

When The Dust Settled

The Syndrome That Saved Us

A Holocaust Story Series

The Smallest Crack

The Darkest Canyon

Millions Of Pebbles

Sarah and Solomon

All My Love, Detrick Series

All My Love, Detrick

You Are My Sunshine

The Promised Land

To Be An Israeli

Forever My Homeland

Michal's Destiny Series

Michal's Destiny

A Family Shattered

Watch Over My Child

Another Breath, Another Sunrise

Eidel's Story Series

And . . . Who Is The Real Mother?

Secrets Revealed

New Life, New Land

Another Generation

The Wrath of Eden Series

The Wrath Of Eden

The Angels Song

Stand Alone Novels

One Last Hope

A Flicker Of Light

The Heart Of A Gypsy

Made in the USA
Monee, IL
15 January 2024

51828921R00178